ELDRYAN ELDERS

THE LAST LUMENIAN SERIES

BOOK V

S.G. BLAISE

info@thelastlumenian.com.

First paperback edition December 2024

Book design by Tim Barber from Dissect Designs
Map Illustrated by Clif Chandler
Edited by Julie Tibbott and Andy Meisenheimer

Publisher: Lilac Grove Entertainment LLC

Paperback ISBN: 979-8-9885265-1
E-Book ISBN: 979-8-9885265-6-8

www.sgblaise.com

To receive exclusive content, sign up for the S.G. Blaise newsletter at sgblaisenews.com

DEDICATION

To Alex: whose support has been multifaceted and much appreciated.

To Gabe: yes, we are back with Lilla in this book.

To my mom: yes, there are eleven POVs. No, I am sure there must be that many.

To all of you, Dear Readers, who have been following Lilla's journey—I hope you'll enjoy this book as well.

MAP of CATHAL

CHAPTER 1

LILLA

Groaning, I blink my eyes open. The ground shakes under my numb body. I am lying on my back, staring up at the sky.

With effort, I scramble to my hands and knees. My vision contracts to a pinpoint. A concussion hammers my head with near unbearable pain. Nausea and dizziness threaten to overwhelm my body.

Explosions mix with shouts of anger and agony, creating a chaotic cacophony.

Blood flows to my neck from the various cuts on my face, then to my back under my black shirt, stinging all the wounds. My vision blurs. I swipe a long strand of dark violet hair out of my eyes, trying to figure out how I got here.

There is no time for that! Moira yells in my mind. *We are in the midst of a battle! Get up, now!*

I push to my feet. Swaying, I take in the battlefield.

Fights rage around me like a churning maelstrom. The army of the Archgod of Chaos and Destruction surrounds black-clad Teryn warriors.

How are we going to win? I ask Moira. *We are outnumbered a hundred to one.*

Even now, more humongous dark fiends and rotting dark servants from all over the Seven Galaxies advance from among the thick, vine covered, and orange-brown trees of the Cathal jungle.

Don't give up! Moira snarls, her voice strained and tired. *You are the Sybil and the true Teryn! We never give up!*

Thank you for the reminder, I snap back, as if I could forget. *I wasn't planning to give up.*

I gather multiple threads of Fla'mma, T'erra and A'qua magic from my pulsing bright white magical orb. The familiar hot-and-cold-and-hot-again feeling envelops me as I layer them on my glowing right arm.

Around me, sounds of laser shots blend into nightmarish snarls and howls. The air smells of blood, rot, smoke, and disturbed soil of the jungle floor.

The worn Teryn warriors, many in their beastly battle forms, combat the nightmarish army, who has seemingly constant reinforcements.

The ground shakes again under my feet.

A thirty-foot-tall shadow passes over me, blocking out the orange sun for a few seconds.

We are running out of time, Moira yells.

I know.

Lifting a thick thread of Fla'mma from my arm, I shape it into an infernal spray and burn the pressing feline dark fiends. They shriek and draw back.

I curse under my breath, wishing I could use my Lume magic, but I have to preserve it.

A rustling sound comes from a nearby thicket.

I whirl toward another group of dark fiends that look a lot like A'ice wolves.

Without waiting, I wrap them in A'qua threads, freezing them the second the ribbons touch their rotting furs. They drop to the muddy ground among the twisted roots and vines, growling but staying put.

Black dots dance in my vision. I am dangerously close to overusing my magic. A consequence I never had to deal with before, nor do I dare to risk, as I still don't know what overusing my Lumenian magic entails.

Do something! Moira yells.

Like what?! Maybe instead of complaining, you could offer some solutions?

Moira lets out a frustrated roar.

Not helping.

A group of dark fiends approach me from the left, stepping over their injured brethren. One of them, an insectoid, lunges at me.

I kick out. My foot hits its chitinous chest, propelling it backward. Then I grab the last magical ribbon I gathered, T'erra, and shove it into the ground—a magical fighting technique favored by my mage friend, Ragnald.

The ground opens up under the insectoid fiend's feet, swallowing it up to its waist. It scrambles with four of its jointed arms but stays stuck.

More dark servants reach toward me with their emaciated arms but stay in place as if they are waiting. Then they part for an Acerbus-disguised dark figure, its face hidden under a black hood.

My heart jumps into my throat. I recognize the repulsive and powerful magical ripples emitting from the figure—the new Ankhar. Hiding behind the smoke disguise of Acerbus—the anti-element of my own magic, Lume.

"We meet again," it says in a distorted voice. "How fortuitous."

CHAPTER 2

I wipe the sweat off my face and try to shake exhaustion as we enter our vast compound near the black foreboding Teryn ship.

We spent the morning hours in the Cathal jungle, training with laser weapons, then moving on to tactical marches and scenarios. My pack weighs at least forty pounds, but Callum—our unit's leader and my beloved husband—insisted on getting accustomed to carrying it.

Caderyn—praelor or emperor of the lethal Teryn Praelium, and my father-in-law—wasted no time in creating this compound. In the three weeks since we arrived on Cathal, he established a well-functioning center of operations with room for everyone to stay outside the humongous spaceship which could house a small city.

The Archgoddess of the Eternal Light and Order—or The Lady, as I like to call her—ordered us to come to this uninhabited jungle world, but She never explained why. The Lady has not been in contact with me since, leaving me guessing.

Caderyn demanded camouflaged orange-green tents to be manufactured in quick order—they have a whole area in the spaceship designated for this very purpose—then had his Teryn warriors set them up as barracks, mess halls, medical centers, command centers, armories, and storage. Luckily, my friends got a separate barrack. Since Callum and I are married, we got our very own tent at the edge of the compound. Not that it provided much privacy.

The overgrown jungle soon gave way to a military city run tightly by the praelor.

Caderyn also enacted strict security measures and sent many of his warriors off on reconnaissance. The only information they brought back was that of wild animals and strange ruins overgrown with plants throughout most of the jungle.

My friends, Isa and Bella, fall in step next to me. The two twenty-year-old and nearly identical twin princesses glance around with their emerald green eyes. In unison, they swipe at their sweaty black hair—both styled in a bob—off their foreheads. "I'm glad we spent seven weeks training and acclimating to the heat of the jungle. It's almost bearable now."

Belthair, the six-armed ex-rebel captain and ex-boyfriend of mine, shoves a thumb over his shoulder. "Speak for yourselves. Not everyone can handle the humidity."

I glance at my friend, Arrov, the tall seventh prince of the wintery world of A'ice. His light blue skin looks too pale under his shoulder-length midnight blue hair. He stumbles on his own feet and curses.

A popping sound makes me turn back.

On my left, blond Ivy, crown princess of the Marauders' Syndicate, chews her pink hexagonal gum open-mouthed. "You know, on my home world, someone as weak as Arrov wouldn't last a minute. He would be mugged to death, then stabbed to death, then poisoned to death."

"Isn't that the definition of overkill?" I ask.

Ivy shrugs her thin shoulders under her orange-green military jacket. "One can never be sure when your enemy is truly dead. Best to overkill then regret it later."

Rhona marches next to Ivy, nodding. The Teryn colonel and younger sister of Callum says, "I concur with the Marauder. Heedfulness is vigilance in battle." Then she cuts me a look, as if implying that she considers me someone who wouldn't last on the Marauders' world.

Moira chuckles. *Rhona just used two synonyms for* caution, *dear. Now that's* overkill.

I thought Rhona and I had overcome our differences in the Spirit Realm. It seems I was wrong.

"How do you poison someone who is already twice dead?" I ask.

Ivy flicks an elegant hand in front of my face. "There are many ways."

Belthair raises his eyebrows. "I have questions."

Teague strides up between Ivy and me. "Wasn't today a jollity?"

"I see you've been hanging around Rhona too long," I mutter.

Teague grins, puts his arms around Ivy and me. "We practiced shooting our way out of many different ambushes. Then we waded through the swamp and shot those foot-sized leeches. Then we engaged in close combat shooting and sparring. Then we—"

Ivy covers Teague's mouth with a mud-stained hand full of bleeding leech bites. "We were there, you know. No need to remind us of that *torture* your best friend and our unbeloved commander put us through."

Callum overhears Ivy's words and strides back to us. "This is no joke. Pay attention, learn, and grow up." A reddish-orange light flashes across his blue irises, a clear sign of his anger.

Ivy recoils from Callum's stern words. Even Rhona glances at her brother with eyebrows pulled together.

Callum crosses his arms. "At ease."

Nobody moves.

"What are you waiting for?" Callum snaps. "Get out of here!"

My friends jump, and head toward their tent, grumbling.

I wait until they are out of earshot. "That was a bit harsh, don't you think?" I study his clear blue eyes in his tanned face framed by short black hair.

Callum puts his hands on my shoulders. "It's not a laughing matter to me. Not when it's your life and their lives on the line. Jungle terrain doesn't allow us to have heavy artillery or laser tank support. We have to rely on each other. Danger lurks behind those trees or in those swamps."

He is not wrong, dear.

I nod.

Moira, the true queen of all Teryns and my melded spirit, has a lot more experience than I do. She has been alive and leading her people for hundreds of years, even if she had to rule many of those years in the Spirit Realm.

Callum slides the heavy backpack off my shoulders, taking it.

I smile in thanks. "We haven't seen any danger for almost two months now, outside those jungle predators. I doubt that will change any time soon. Maybe The Lady directed us here with the Teryn armada to teach me a lesson of obedience and patience."

Callum shakes his head. "I doubt that. There is something vital about this planet for the Era War; we just don't know what." He leads us toward our tent.

This Era War—the seventh one between the two ruling archgods—broke out because of the imbalance of power in the Seven Galaxies. I had one chance to stop the Archgod of Chaos and Destruction—or as I like to call Him, DLD—from advancing the war when He was in a mortal form on my home world, Uhna, but I only managed to injure Him.

My gaze snags the neat rows of latrines to our left. Not that long ago it was a beautiful clearing where Callum and I got married. It feels like it happened a lifetime ago.

Don't let Caderyn's antics rile you up, dear. He can't ruin your memories.

At the word "memories" a flash of images full of anguish cross my mind. When I try to focus on it, severe pain shoots from my temples.

I misstep.

Callum glances at me. "Are you okay? Is the heat getting to you? Do you feel dehydrated? When was the last time you drank from your flask?"

I raise a hand. "I'm fine." At his concerned expression, I add, "Really, it was just a small headache and now it's gone."

Callum purses his lips, clearly not believing me, but turns his attention to our tent.

It's orange and green, much like the jungle around us, with its roof shaped like a heptagon.

We step into a small area covered only with nets to keep the bugs and rodents out. We leave our boots there with the socks stuffed in them. Then we enter the main area.

Callum closes the fabric door with ties and checks for any gaps.

Muted light comes through the fabric walls of the tent just enough to see without having to turn on the green gaslights fueled with the same gas as the spaceship. There is not a lot of clutter in the spacious area. On the left, a portable sonic shower stands big enough for two people. Across from it awaits a waterproof mattress with dark green bedding. On the right, a green fabric armoire stores our military clothing.

The furnishings might be bleak, dear, but very effective.

At least it's bigger than our living quarters on the spaceship. The only problem is that it provides much less privacy.

That's true, dear, and—

I cough.

Oh, right, dear! Privacy! I'll be taking a nap and . . . Moira falls silent, retreating somewhere in my mind.

Callum places the bags by the door. Then he pulls me into his embrace. His strong arms bracket my back, his hand caressing me.

"I've missed you," he murmurs and kisses the top of my head, which is easy for him, being over six feet in height, while I am five-and-a-half-feet tall.

I laugh into his muscular chest. "We spent all morning together. How could you miss me?"

Callum steps back. "I couldn't do this, for example." He unzips my jacket, then drops it by our feet.

I grab his jacket, wrestle it over his head, then throw it behind him. "Yes, I can see how that would have been quite inappropriate. Anything else you missed?"

Callum chuckles, his blue eyes full of desire. "I couldn't do this as well." He helps me get out of my pants.

"That also would have been *very* inappropriate," I say, acting as if he does not ignite burning passion in my veins. "Is that all?"

Callum clasps my hand and pulls me into the sonic shower. "Well, there is *this*, of course."

"Of course," I say and close the plastic door behind us. Then I thread my arms around his neck while he turns on the shower. "Question is, can you keep quiet?"

He steals a heated kiss from my lips. "If I recall correctly, that was more of *your* problem than mine."

CHAPTER 3

Freshly showered, dressed in black military shirts and pants with matching boots, Callum and I duck into the closest mess hall. The tent is spacious enough to serve thirty people but mostly empty as usual. My fingers curl around my mom's journal. I plan to read the worn pages again later.

We walk past a dozen green metallic tables with matching benches, heading toward my group of friends all wearing the same military outfit as us.

Arrov sleeps at the table, his head braced on his elbows. Snoring lightly, his midnight blue hair falls around him. Next to him Belthair whittles three small pieces of wood, holding them in his three left hands. On the tabletop by Belthair perches blond Ivy, picking under her long pink nails. Across from them, black-haired Rhona sits with the twins. When Rhona's gaze connects with mine, her smile disappears, and she looks away before I can nod at her in greeting.

I stare at the back of Rhona's head. I don't remember offending her.

Isa and Bella busy themselves with wires and fragments of a device that was probably a round digital galactic clock above the tent entrance.

I glance back. Sure enough, the clock is missing.

Putting the purple journal on the tabletop, I sit next to Isa. Callum takes the spot next to me, his body so close I feel the heat emitting from him. Which reminds me of the fun we had earlier . . .

Oh, dear! Please don't think about that.

Blushing, I say, *Sorry, Moira.*

Belthair blows on a piece of wood. "If you are here, Callum, to berate us because we dared to take a break from your precious jungle . . ."

Callum raises an eyebrow. "Then what?"

Belthair lifts up his head, his dark brown eyes glinting dangerously. "Then I—"

"Then we will eat," I cut in, "and enjoy our break." This stubbornness is what made Belthair a great captain in the rebellion against my father, the ma'ha of Uhna. However, he won't win against Callum.

Ivy scoffs. "Having dirt under my nails is not the Marauder way."

She is right. The Marauders, a Tier One faction under the Teryn Praelium's control, are famous for their thieving, fast ships, and favoring methods like poisoning or backstabbing. They took part in a conspiracy and coup attempt against Caderyn, kidnapping him and his family and killing his two sons from a previous marriage—Callum's older brothers.

Isa drops a screw but catches it before it could roll off the table. "I have dirt in my ear." Bella adds, "And in my bra."

I stifle a smile. The twins love talking in tandem, but I've seen them act differently when they are without an audience.

The twins giggle at their own joke then turn back to the device they are building. Not only they are great inventors and scientists, but they are also talented hackers.

"I abhor dirt," Ivy declares.

Rhona rolls her eyes. "Why do you have to be so capricious all the time?"

At least Rhona gets along with Ivy if not with me. When we were stuck in the Spirit Realm, they bickered a lot.

I dislike contradicting you, dear, but they still bicker.

I should have said they get along better.

Ivy glares at Rhona. "Don't pretend to be flummoxed. You should know me by now."

The others laugh.

And there it is, dear. They are nothing if not predictable.

Using his middle right arm, Belthair wipes a small knife on his leg. "Ivy, did you just borrow a big word from Walking Dictionary?"

"Don't call me that," Rhona says. It's a nickname she got from me because of all the big words she likes to use.

Ivy grins. "It's hard not to call you Walking Dictionary when you always show off."

That is true, dear. Rhona seems to be compensating for not having a melded spirit.

And whose fault is that?

Moira ducks her head.

"Does anyone else feel strange around those ruins?" Belthair asks, then blows on another wooden piece. "They feel . . . haunted."

Ivy slaps his shoulder, making Belthair cut a thin line across his top left hand. "Don't be silly! They're just ruins."

Isa twists a few wires together. "Belthair is right. There is something about the ruins that makes me feel sad. Someone spent a lot of time building those structures only for them to end up empty and overgrown by nature." Bella adds, "It's clear that those buildings were magnificent a long time ago—you can see the delicate architectural details under all that vegetation."

Ivy tilts her head. "I wonder what happened to them."

"I don't," Callum declares, then glances around the empty table. "Where is the food? Did you already eat?"

"No, we didn't," Belthair says without looking up.

Isa lifts a hand. "Wait," she says, and Bella adds, "Three, two, one, and—"

Teague strides in, whistling. His black hair—with scarlet, white, and blond streaks—glints freshly washed. His black shirt has spots of wetness on it. He heads to the wall of counters with cabinets on top of them. Then he lifts a vertical cabinet door to reveal trays upon trays of sliced meats, rolls, savory pies, dried fruits, and desserts. He piles four trays laden with meat and rolls on his muscular arms, then heads toward our table.

Teague puts the trays in front of him but before he can dive in, Ivy distributes the trays to the others—handing one to Belthair, one to Rhona, another to the twins, and one for herself.

Teague throws his hands up. "Every godsdamn time! Why can't you lazy rogues serve yourselves?"

Ivy drops to sit on the bench. "Why should we? You do such a great job."

The others laugh.

I study Arrov, who still hasn't moved despite the noise and the smell of food. "Shouldn't we wake him?"

Muttering, Teague heads back to the counter, perusing the selection.

Ivy shakes her head. "Nah, I wouldn't wake him. He was caught trying to sneak inside the spaceship without permission, and Caderyn made him wash all the beaked salamanders as punishment."

"That's horrible," I say. The beaked salamanders clean the spaceship's green gas fuel. Supposedly, the animals have a temper when they are removed from their favorite place—the gas. They fight back—and even bite too.

Teague chooses four more trays and sits next to Ivy. He passes two trays to us—one with sliced cured meat and one with fresh crescent-shaped rolls and creamy butter. I put my mom's journal to the side to make room and dig in.

Belthair frowns. "Hey! How come you give the food to them, but not to us?"

Teague shrugs. "Because I like them."

Ivy snickers. "Does that mean that you don't like us?"

Teague shoves a bunch of sliced meat into his mouth. "I can't talk . . . mouth full. . ."

Ivy shakes her head. "You're such a Marauder!"

Rhona scoffs. "That's gobbledygook and also the worst compliment I've heard."

Ivy beams. "I know."

I sigh, missing my best friend Glenna and elementalist mage Ragnald, who mentored me in magic. He tried to convey hundreds of years of knowledge in bite-sized lessons. Glenna, while a highly skilled healer, needed the mage's help with the growing corruption in her. Only Ragnald's magic kept that dark-ness in check. But when we were on Pada, trying to uncover a conspiracy and find a murderer, her condition worsened. Now they are at the Academia of Mages to seek help from the archnemesis of healers. I hope Glenna got there in time.

I'm sure she'll be fine, dear.

A soft touch on my knee makes me look under the table. S'affi leans on my knee with her two front paws. Her large green eyes glint mischievously as she stands by my leg, sitting on her two chubby legs. Her red-violet-colored fur, with green vines and small white flowers, has a few wet spots, as if she went swimming in one of the nearby lakes. Her long bushy tail wags.

I scratch the silky fur on her head between the two small pedicles.

She twitches her button-like nose with long whiskers, then she vanishes.

She is adorable, dear.

S'affi, who is mostly magic, decided to join me when I was on the Pada world. She likes to appear and disappear at her whims. I'm surprised she followed me to Cathal.

Picking up a crescent-shaped roll, I nod. I take a bite of the still warm and crusty end, savoring how good the food tastes. Caderyn might be stubborn about many issues, but he knows how to take care of us.

Isa puts her device on the tabletop. "Isn't today your day of birth?" Bella's head snaps up, and she adds, "Yes, it must be. Let me check the galactic calendar." Bella pulls out a flat rectangular card from her pants pocket. With Isa, they study the lines of writing and numbers that scroll on the surface.

Callum glances at me. "Why didn't you tell me?"

I swallow the bite and wipe my mouth. "I forgot about it." Celebrating in the middle of a war also seemed a bit silly. "It's just another day."

"Nonsense," Isa says, and Bella adds, "Today is your twentieth day of birth."

Everyone raises their water flasks, shouting, "Happy Day of Birth!"

Moira claps her paw-like hands. *Much happiness to you, dear.*

Callum puts an arm around my shoulder. "Happy Day of Birth, my love and life." Then he kisses me.

The others cheer even louder.

"Thank you," I say, blushing, "but we have more important things to worry about."

The smile disappears from my friends' faces.

"Like what?" Ivy asks.

I pick up my mom's journal. Then I caress the burned yet still velvety cover, seeking comfort. All the questions, worries, and doubts bubble to the surface. I open my mouth but struggle to say a word.

Callum squeezes my shoulders. "Take a few deep breaths."

Inhaling and exhaling, I relax my body, then say, "Why are we here? Why didn't The Lady tell me the purpose of this mission? Who are we going to face? When will the danger come at us? How am I going to win the Era War when I can't even convince Caderyn to listen to me? Why am I so different from other Lumenians? What if I am the worst Sybil in the history of Era Wars? What if—"

Isa puts a hand on my arm. "Oh, sweetie! You worry too much." Bella adds, "You're not alone. We are all here for you."

The others chime in, murmuring comforting words.

Being a Lumenian is still new to me. Lumenians are a legendary magical race, created by The Lady to fight against the armies of DLD. However, DLD managed to decimate them until only I remain—even if I am not the typical Lumenian. I don't even look like one—they all had golden-white hair with matching eyes and beautiful golden-brown skin.

"It means a lot to me, really," I say and tap the cover of the journal. "I just wish I could be more like my mom. She always knew what to do." She also didn't look like a stereotypical Lumenian. I wonder why.

Rhona gets up from her seat and squats by Callum, then reaches across him to grab my hand in an unusually kind gesture, even if it's an awkward one. "We all want to be like our parents, godsknow it's true for me as well. They are our heroes. It's easy to forget that it took them years or even decades to get where they are now, especially since we didn't see them faltering. Don't be too hard on yourself."

That's nice of her. "Thank—"

A loud horn sounds.

We groan, then push to our feet.

Isa and Bella point at the sleeping Arrov. "Should we wake him now?" they ask in unison.

Callum grins. "He'll figure it out."

Teague adds, "By then it will be too late, and he'll have to do laps around the compound."

Seeing my frustrated expression, Callum adds, "It's a lesson we all had to learn at one time or another."

He is right, dear. Arrov needs to be more careful.

When none of us move, Callum growls and points toward the exit.

With more groans, we shuffle around the tables.

"Oh, how fun! We'll get to spend the whole afternoon with more torture," Ivy says, then glances at Callum, and adds with a sly smile, "I mean training, of course."

CHAPTER 4

"You are too slow," Callum shouts at us, his eyes burning with orange-reddish light. Standing over seven feet tall, his body vibrates with strength from his bulky and corded muscles. His usual black uniform has turned into a bodysuit that accommodates his new powerful shape. Short black fur with steel-colored stripes covers his lion-like face. Sharp white fangs glint in his wolfish muzzle.

After lunch, Teague took my friends for more jungle warfare training while Callum and I went to a glade to practice sparring in our battle forms. We've been practicing like this for weeks now.

We'll show him, dear, who is slow.

We turn with our three heads to follow him circling us. From our ten-foot-height we tower over him, but we've learned not to underestimate him. He can leap six feet in the air in an instant. He has agility and speed that should not be possible for someone his size.

"Today, please," Callum taunts.

He is impatient, dear. That's a mistake on his part. Get ready.

We smile from three heads—one wolfish, one eagle-like, and one dra'agon-ish. The muscles tense in our dra'agon legs. Then we snap our thick scale-covered tail that ends in a scorpion stinger at him.

Callum jumps over it and kicks at the wolfish head.

We lean back and spread our twenty-foot-wide wings, flexing the claws at the ends.

"Looking scary," he mocks, baring sharp fangs.

We punch him with our right wing, then swipe at his legs with our tail.

Callum ducks under our wing, then jumps up, avoiding our tail.

Before we can attack again, Callum grabs our right arm, checks us with his hip, and we go flying over his shoulder.

We land on the ground, out of breath.

Moira growls in my head. *We need to work better together, dear. He's right. We are too slow. You are still fighting me for control, slowing us down.*

I am not doing it on purpose.

Callum squats by us. "I think that's it for today."

He straightens and spreads his arms out with palms up. The reddish-orange blaze spills from his eyes, encompassing his whole body. Heat radiates from his strange light-cocoon, making the air shimmer around him as if he is on fire. From one second to the next, the cocoon implodes, sucking all the reddish-orange light back in. Then Callum, in his black uniform, stands.

We get to our feet and shake dirt off our body. A rainbow-colored shimmer washes over us, gone by the time I blink. Then I stand in front of Callum, naked.

Callum picks up my pants and shirt, holding it in his right hand, but doesn't hand it to me.

"See something to your liking?"

Callum blinks. "What did you say?"

I laugh and take the clothes from him.

He locks his arms around me, nuzzling my neck. "We are not in a hurry to get back."

"Yes, we are." I pull out of his arms and get dressed. "There are Teryn warriors everywhere, and I do not wish to entertain them as well."

Callum chuckles. "It would be a show they won't forget."

I slap his shoulder. Then I look for my boots. They are near a bush with spiky leaves. I shake them out in case any insect decided to make its home in there, then shove my foot in one, then the other. Unlike Callum, I do not have a uniform that can survive my transfiguration into my battle form.

He smirks. "I would have heard them from a mile away."

"That's comforting to know." Not.

He clasps my hand in his, and we head back toward the compound.

For a second, it's only Callum and me. A newly married couple. Walking side by side and in love with each other. There is no war. No obligations. No jungle. Just us.

The thicket rustles on our right.

We step to the side to make way.

A huge brown animal on four legs rambles out. Six long horns curve around its triangular head. On top of it, a warrior woman sits and nods at us. Then she leads the k'beast, the Teryn war tank, away.

After it, two six-foot-tall gray boars, k'hogs, follow, pulling armored guns on two wheels—the Teryn artillery.

Then three dark green lizards, k'iguanas, five feet tall at the shoulders, lumber after the boars, smoke curling from their maws. Teryns use them as flamethrowers as they can spit fire.

Lastly, six round creatures, k'turtles, ten feet tall and wide with bone ridges all over their bodies, stroll behind the lizards. Their long tails, ending in sharp spikes, act as catapults.

Something shrieks above us.

I glance up.

Soaring overhead in a two-column formation are two dozen flying manta-ray-like k'birds with warrior men and women on their backs.

I release Callum's hand, all feeling of normalcy gone.

"You are getting better sparring in the Cymmerion form," he says.

I grimace. "I still can't defeat you."

Callum grins. "No one can defeat me."

I snort. "You're so humble." Then I sober up, and say, "I worry that I am running out of time to figure it out."

What is the Cymmerion form good for, if I can't fight in it effectively?

Callum puts an arm around my shoulders. "We'll practice again tomorrow. And again. Until you're unstoppable. Believe in yourself, Lilla."

I sigh.

Easier said than done.

CHAPTER 5

ANKHAR

The Archgod of Chaos and Destruction stabs the small brush on the painting with such vehemence that green paint splatters on the pristine white walls and polished white floor—only to vanish the next instant. On the canvas, a tall blond woman argues with a younger one. The first woman resembles The Lady with Her ethereal beauty while the latter young woman looks a lot like the Sybil with her dark violet hair.

Anger burns seeing the Sybil so spiteful and getting away with it. I do not have such freedom.

With effort, I squash my temper. I do not have the freedom to act like the Sybil, but if I follow my plan, then I will become more powerful than the archgods.

Softly exhaling through my nose, I let my gaze roam the seamless white room. In this pocket realm created by the archgod, there are no visible windows or doors, yet I was able to enter.

My vision swims from disorientation and I shut my eyes.

Why the archgod loves this room is a mystery to me, with all its whiteness and cleanliness standing in such sharp contrast to Him, the ruler of Chaos and Destruction.

Inhaling the scentless air, I center myself. I've become better at controlling the animalistic urges of the powerful yet faulty body I gained when I ascended to the role of Ankhar. I lock my muscles, holding myself still like prey in the presence of a lethal predator who has not taken notice of it. Though being preyed upon is only a pretense. I am anything but a victim. I have ambitions and patience. I will strike when He least expects it.

Waves of untamable and limitless magical power pulse from the six-foot-tall archgod, nearly sucking the air from the stark room. As one of the ruling archgods of the Seven Galaxies, it is not a surprise to feel such power in His presence. It is suffocating just the same. Electric-like ripples cascade over His black shirt tucked into black pants, all the way to His bare feet. Long black hair frames a divinely stunning face with highly intelligent black eyes and a straight nose. A long black beard—a new addition—reaches his muscular chest.

Fear lights up my dead veins. Any second now, He'll punish me for my failures. Frantically I make up rationalizations that could save my life.

My gums ache, and I retract my elongated canines. Constant blood hunger rages in my not-so-alive body—the price I have to pay for all my new powers.

The slight paintbrush breaks in the Archgod of Chaos and Destruction's hand. Acerbus zaps out of the archgod, burning the pieces of the paintbrush into smithereens. The dark element is the most dangerous one of the twelve elements. These twelve elements were broken into six light and six dark elements by the Omnipower: A'qua for water and its counterpart Murky A'qua; Fla'mma for fire and Black Fla'mma; T'erra for soil and Barren T'erra; A'ris for wind and Dusky A'ris; A'nima for all things living and Diseased A'nima, then Lume for light and energy, with its counterpart Acerbus for darkness and chaos. Each archgod has control over six elements—The Lady rules over the light elements while the Dark Lord of Destruction, as He is often called, controls the dark ones.

Any time the Balance shifts between the ruling archgods, an Era War breaks out. The Dark Lord of Destruction has not won a single Era War, but He has plans to change that. Once He wins, eliminating The Lady, then I will strike.

Frowning, the archgod looks up, noticing me.

He has the ability to skim the surface of my thoughts, but not the deeper ones—those I am able to hide from Him, using my inborn skill that—

A dark stream of noxious Acerbus magic snaps out of the hand of the archgod, shaping into a snake. Within an instant the magical serpent wraps around my body.

My muscles freeze, pain screaming from every inch of my skin. I open my mouth to shout, but the dark element contorts around me, cutting off my air.

"You are late, Ankhar."

I gasp for air, fighting the urge to panic.

The Acerbus snake burn white hot, stinging my skin. The air suddenly smells sickly sweet with a tinge of rot.

Desperate, I look at Him, begging to be released. His unrelenting gaze connects with mine.

A vast, ancient power slams into my mind, pressing me to my knees as He towers above me, the firstborn and true leader of the Seven Galaxies.

Black blood leaks from my eyes and ears. Darkness threatens to devour my conscience.

The archgod sneers and glances away.

The pressure vanishes.

Panting, I put my head on the ground, not daring to move, lest it encourage Him to do more cruelty.

"Get up," He commands.

I scramble to my feet and hide my shaking hands behind me. The archgod despises any sign of weakness in His presence.

Watching Him from the corner of my eye, I wait in silence. My oozing wounds heal sluggishly. I will need blood. Soon.

The archgod looks back at His painting. "I have an intriguing new power, thanks to the carelessness of The Lady."

I stay silent.

"Every time The Lady breaks the rules and acquires a new power, so do I gain its equivalent. I always knew She underestimated me, but this level of ignorance on Her part confirms my suspicion. Winning all those era wars must have made Her arrogant. It will be Her undoing."

Then He turns to me, and I flinch, earning a smirk from Him. "I have a divine new power that will come in handy. Later."

He picks up a thicker paintbrush from the edge of the easel and paints over the golden-haired woman until the younger one is left. "The Lady has made many blunders that will allow me to finally win. She always thought that She was the favorite of the Omnipower, our Creator. She did get away with everything, including the creation of the Lumenian race. But I corrected that mistake, and now there is only one left—the weakest one."

He studies His painting, then points His paintbrush on the younger woman.

"There is something about the last Lumenian, the Sybil, that sets her apart from the others. I tasted something familiar yet unique in the Sybil's power when I syphoned magic from her. I must take another look . . ." The archgod's voice trails off. He rubs His right shoulder, where the Sybil's Lume spear injured Him, almost killing Him in His mortal form.

He winces in pain, though there is no sign of wound or injury.

The painting explodes into shards, showering around Him. The falling particles disappear into thin air before they can shower on the white floor.

"I will not let anything or anyone stop me now, especially not that annoying Sybil. Which reminds me of the conundrum you caused." The archgod strides toward me.

I raise my chin but avoid looking directly in His eyes this time, focusing my gaze on His chin. The archgod rewards me with a rare smile of approval. There is a precarious line He allows me to walk between arrogance and insolence. A fine line that tends to move at His whim.

As the archgod nears me, I back away until my foot hits the wall.

"I wonder whether I should skin you first before I kill you, or just kill you and be done with you. My previous Ankhar would have done a better job than *you*."

"I . . ." All thoughts of explanations and reasoning escape from my mind.

The archgod shakes His head, then His hand shoots out. His long fingers, ending in black claws, curl around my throat, tightening.

Pain shoots down my spine. I try to inhale but only manage to gurgle.

I can't die again!

My fingers grapple with His but can't pry them off.

The archgod lifts me off my feet, dangling me in the air. "You promised the cooperation of the Guardian Goddess Laoise. You promised control over the Teryns. You promised to capture the Sybil—not once but twice. Did you accomplish any of these things?"

I turn my head an inch to the side in answer, my mouth gaping uselessly.

"You also gave Laoise the extraction wand and lost thirty-three Turned mage elders from Raghild."

My lungs strain for air and cold sweat runs down my spine.

This is it; He will kill me for these failings.

"Answer me," He says, shaking me, but I cannot. "Or better yet, I will find the answers I need."

Agony bursts in my mind as the archgod rummages through my memories. Using most of my skill, I hide the thoughts that would betray any insurrection or defiance against Him.

"Nothing interesting there," the Archgod of Chaos says, then He opens His fingers.

I fall to the floor, leaning onto the wall for support, and lock my leg muscles to stay upright. Every time my skill works, it's always a relief mixed with disbelief. The archgod might not be as powerful as He thinks if I can trick Him so easily.

"Explain yourself," He says.

"The Lady interfered on Teryn, giving the Sybil an unfair advantage when She—"

His face distorts in disgust. "The Lady had no right interfering! She might think She will win, but I have been preparing for this moment a lot longer than Her."

The archgod steps toward the closest white wall and waves a hand in front of it. A large screen opens to space, showing an orange-green planet floating in the vast blackness of Galaxy Seven.

"You may redeem yourself by completing this mission."

I rub my throat to ease the pain, and a patch of skin dislodges. "Are we attacking the planet?"

The Archgod of Chaos and Destruction kneads His right shoulder, and a chilling smile appears on His face. "I have waited for this. Now I have everything I need in place to win."

CHAPTER 6

LILLA

After the sparring and another brutal training session right after dinner, I fall onto the green bed in our tent, still clothed and exhausted. Callum hugs me to him, and I drift to sleep in his arms.

The dream starts out pleasant—Fearghas and I gallop down the red sands of Frida Bay on Uhna, one of my favorite beaches. Cool mist showers us from the Fyoon Ocean as the two suns set on the horizon, painting the water with streaks of orange, red, and pink. My lungs fill with brine-scented air, recharging my soul, as I lean over my horse's muscular black neck.

Then it morphs from one moment to the next into a nightmare.

Beathag faces me in the blue parlor. She holds my mom's journal.

"I did it all for you, Lilla," she says. "I tried to be your friend, but you pushed me away."

I shake my head. "No."

"It is your fault that I had to resort to desperate measures," she continues. "You left me no choice."

"You lie!"

"Now I am dead because of you."

I squeeze my eyes shut. "No!" When I open them, the blue parlor has vanished.

Instead, I am in the dungeon deep underneath the Crystal Palace.

Darkness presses down on me. Cobwebs stick to my face that I cannot wipe away.

Then the Archgod of Chaos and Destruction strides out of a tunnel across from me.

Fear tightens my muscles, nearly paralyzing my body. My heart races in my throat.

Even in mortal form, disguised as an average-looking man with short brown hair and dressed all in white, He cannot hide His suffocating power—a power that chokes me even now, cutting off my air.

Then the dream morphs again, and I am facing Him on that hovering platform fifty feet above a gaping dark canyon. I throw my Lume spear, aiming for His heart, but miss, injuring only His right shoulder.

The archgod brushes blood off His white shirt—so unlike what He did on that horrible day—and the dream turns again.

DLD faces me. "You are weak and pathetic. How could you ever think you had a chance of defeating me?"

His laughter mocks, and dread washes over me.

This is not what happened.

The last of His words echo in my mind: *Defeat me? Defeat me?! Until they sound: You will never defeat me!*

Panic raises goosebumps along my body. Cold sweat breaks out on my skin, as if He dumped me into a barrel of frozen fish. I try to yell back that I am not afraid, but no sound leaves my gaping mouth.

The archgod waves His hand. An image of my brother, his neck covered in blood, appears on the cave wall. Then the pompous and purple-faced Ma'har Irvine appears just as he is falling to his death, followed by Beathag's ghostly pale face as she tumbles over the ledge of the hovering platform.

DLD points at me. "These innocents died because of you." More images play on the wall. Images of hundreds of thousands of Uhnan citizens, refugees and rebels, ma'hars and ma'haras flash too fast until they all become a blur.

I'm blinded by tears. Their deaths weigh heavily on me. I should have stopped Him when I had the chance.

"Stop!"

I fall onto my knees. Closing my eyes against the agony, I sob.

"My beautiful girl," I hear my mom's voice say, "this is not your fault."

I open my eyes, and I am five years old again, holding a broken piece of pitcher. When I grabbed it in haste, the ear of the pitcher separated from its clay body and the rest shattered by my feet.

My mom, a tall, dark, violet-haired woman in a black pantsuit, squats by me. Her dark violet eyes are full of love as she smiles.

She brushes my hair and helps me sit down, taking the broken handle.

"I should have been more careful. Now a refugee won't have their mineral drink."

My mom gestures toward the refugees behind her. "Our job is to protect the innocents who cannot protect themselves. That's the most important thing for you to remember. Promise me you'll do that."

I nod. "I promise."

Mom hugs me, her arms closing over my thin back. I bury my face in her long hair, inhaling her flowery scent. "I love you."

"I love you too," she murmurs, then pulls back and waves goodbye.

I reach out for her with my small arms. "Please don't go! I cannot do this without you!"

Sobs wrack my body as she retreats into the darkness.

"Lilla?" Callum's voice breaks into the dream, shattering it.

I open my eyes and blink against the near pitch darkness of our tent.

"You were having a nightmare. Again."

I turn in his arms and brush short black strands of hair off his forehead, revealing an old scar that runs down the left side of his face. "This was different from the others." There is a nagging and foreboding feeling that won't relent.

"You kicked me, multiple times," he says with a smile, then his expression sobers as he adds, "It's getting worse, isn't it?"

He studies me with his blue eyes. I detect worry and frustration in their depths.

"It was just a dream," I say, and poke him in his corded bare chest. "There is no need to overreact."

In a second, he turns me until I am on my back. Then he is on top of me, caging me in with his arms. "I'll show you overreaction," he says, then tilts his head down. He takes my lips with so much passion, as if he could erase any remnants of the nightmare.

I kiss him back, holding onto him like he is my lifeline in the raging Fyoon Ocean of my home world.

After a long moment, he lifts his head. "I love you, my love and life."

I smile at him and touch his cheek. "I love y—"

Agony and fear bursts in my mind.

My chest bows, and I gasp in pain.

"Lilla! What is it?"

Waves of anguish and dread choke me but I fight through. "He is here!"

CHAPTER 7

Callum and I cut across the sleeping compound, heading toward the Teryn spaceship. At its entrance, two warriors stop us. "You cannot enter, General Callum. The praelor ordered—"

Callum raises a hand. "Step aside. I have critical information to deliver to the praelor."

The warriors look at each other. One shrugs, and they let us enter.

We hurry through the narrow and mostly windowless corridors. Sectioned and angled panels form a trapezoid shape around the perimeter with soft yellow lights glowing behind them. The dark blue surface of the walls looks velvety, almost like a hide of an animal. Metal grates cover tubes with green gas and beaked salamanders, alternating with regular metal flooring, all pristine. The powerful hum of the engines provides a strange background music to our footsteps.

My claustrophobia rears its ugly head. I break out in a cold sweat.

Remembering Glenna's advice, I take a few deep breaths of the clean air scented with a hint of mechanic grease. Focusing only on my steps, I shove the panic down.

"You're getting better at it," Callum says and brushes his hand against mine, knowing I don't always like to be touched in the midst of a claustrophobic attack.

I clasp his hand and squeeze it. "Practice helps." My mind still whirls with the ramifications of my nightmare. Not to mention I am not looking forward to facing Caderyn. The praelor barely tolerates my presence on good days. What if he refuses to see me?

"It will be fine," Callum says.

What will I do if Caderyn doesn't listen to me again?

"It will be fine," Callum repeats.

What if I can't convince Caderyn that—

Callum halts, turning me to face him. "Stop worrying, Lilla."

"How did you know that I was worrying?"

He grabs my hands, his thumbs rubbing circles on top of mine. "You tend to hold your breath when you're anxious. Also, I'm not blind. I know how difficult it can be to talk to the praelor. Now take a deep breath."

I do, feeling better already.

Callum releases my hand, and we resume our trek through the inclining corridors.

"How come you call your father 'praelor'?"

He looks at me. "Because he is the praelor, the leader of the Teryn nation, its armies, and its factions."

"But that doesn't stop you from arguing with him," I say, reminding him of how he and Caderyn had an "argument" that was a physical fight governed by their ten Ground Rules.

Callum bares his white teeth. "No, it doesn't. First and foremost, I am your husband, who loves you and would die for you, and then the second war general of the Teryn army."

"Which puts you in struggle with Caderyn."

"Correct. Also, I see you as the Sybil, right hand of the Archgoddess of the Eternal Light and Order, and my true general, whom I support even if it means treason. Last but not least, I see you as the mother of our future children."

I gape at him, speechless.

Callum laughs. "Don't look so surprised."

I close my mouth. "I am not."

Callum grins wider.

I clear my voice. "How many of these future children are we talking about?"

"A dozen," Callum says with a nonchalant expression.

"A dozen?!" I squeak. "That's a lot!"

He chuckles. "You should see your face."

I hit his shoulder with my fist, then shake my hand out. It's like hitting a wall.

"I hope we'll have as many as we can," he says, then we stop in front of two inward angled metal doors guarded by a bearded warrior. "But I got you to stop worrying, didn't I?"

I shake my head.

Moira yawns in my head, *What is going on, dear?*

Callum points at the guard and a reddish-orange light flashes across his irises. "We are here to see the praelor."

The bearded warrior shrugs. "The praelor does not want anyone to—"

Callum growls.

I tune out their argument.

Not much, other than the nightmare I had.

Moira rubs her eyes with an elegant paw-like hand. *Oh, yes. I can see it in your memories. That must have been awful, dear.*

I thought we decided that you won't be reading my memories.

Moira shrugs and yawns again. *It's a much more efficient way to catch up, don't you think?*

Fine, but only when it's absolutely necessary. I don't want her to read all my memories. Then I ask, *Are you feeling well?*

I am a bit tired, dear. Must be the, uh, aftereffect of the meld, I'm sure. You and I are not exactly compatible. Though I am surprised how long it's taking me to adapt. Again, probably nothing out of the ordinary.

Are you sure that's all?

Moira combs through her long black mane with her claws, getting the knots out. *What else could it be, dear? I am sure it will resolve on its own soon.*

Callum pushes the bearded warrior to the side. "Enough! Don't get in my way."

The guard glares at Callum, who returns the stare with his steely blue gaze. After a long moment the bearded warrior looks away.

Callum slams his fist on the control panel. The two doors open with an audible swoosh.

With his hand placed on the small of my back, Callum and I enter.

Most of the cavernous two-story room is made of tinted glass panels that show the overgrown, wild orange-green jungle in the reddish-pink light of dawn. We stride across a metal grate, past warriors working in front of transparent sections of screens with lights and Teryn language running on their surface. Across from the ship's viewscreen, a narrow corridor runs along a tall metal wall where even more warriors sit in front of built-in screens.

Callum and I climb the stairs of the raised metal platform. Caderyn paces before us, barking orders at his warriors in Teryn language.

An older and burlier version of Callum, his father the praelor fills the vast room with his authoritative energy. Standing over six feet tall with wide shoulders, Caderyn glares at us with his blue eyes. "How did you get in here?"

Moira laughs in my head. *The "not permitted" part is loud and clear.*

Caderyn, used to ruling the vast Teryn Praelium with an iron fist, raises an eyebrow while his fingers drum on the metal railing. He still hasn't come to terms with my status as his "leader" since I am the Sybil to The Lady. Now I am also his daughter-in-law, a twenty-year-old, who is much too inexperienced to his sixty-five years of hard-earned knowledge.

"Never mind," Caderyn says. "Why are you here?"

Before I can answer, ear-bursting alarms go off.

CHAPTER 8

In mere seconds, thousands of red dots appear on the screens, surrounding the five hundred blue dots representing Teryn ships.

I whirl to Caderyn. "You said you brought the entire Teryn armada."

Caderyn grunts. "Don't take that tone with me, *Sybil*. I've tolerated your so-called leadership long enough. I brought enough spaceships for your supposed mission, whatever it entails. These warriors are well versed in jungle warfare. Besides, we've been stranded on this godsforsaken planet for months without any sign of danger. I'm glad I didn't order the rest of my ships away from fighting in the Era War elsewhere in the Seven Galaxies—a much more vital task."

"But The Lady commanded you," I insist. Technically, She ordered *me*, and I relayed Her order to Caderyn. She was adamant to have the whole Teryn armada over Cathal.

"What if you misunderstood the archgoddess?" Caderyn asks.

I sputter.

Moira crosses her fur-covered arms in front of her red dress. *Did he just question your intelligence?*

"You are too young and have a tendency to daydream," Caderyn says. "I wouldn't be surprised if you misinterpreted what the archgoddess said."

"I didn't misunderstand the order. You promised—"

"I did no such thing," Caderyn says. "You made the mistake of hearing what you wanted to hear. Again, part of being inexperienced."

I gape at him.

Is he serious?

I'm afraid he is, dear.

I clench my fists. "You purposefully obeyed the bare minimum—"

Caderyn grunts. "I made a judgement call—as usual. My ultimate goal is to keep the safety of the Seven Galaxies. I can't do that when the majority of my warriors are idling on this jungle planet. But you wouldn't understand what I'm talking about anyway."

I count in my head slowly. "You're not the only one protecting the Seven Galaxies. Just admit that you're the one who is responsible for this debacle and—"

"I don't care whose fault this is," Caderyn says. "Now is not the time to be childish."

"Who's childish? You won't even listen to me—"

"I've just about had enough of your insolence," Caderyn interrupts. "I've changed much to accommodate you in the Teryn hierarchy even though you are an outsider. But sleeping with a general won't make you one—that takes hard-earned experience."

Callum narrows his eyes and a reddish-orange light flashes across his blue gaze. "Do not talk to Lilla like that."

My fingers curl into my palms. "How dare you!"

Moira growls in my head.

Caderyn steps closer to his son, his eyes flashing reddish yellow. "Or what?"

Rhona climbs up the stairs and pushes the two men apart. "Both of you, stop it. Remember Ground Rule Number Nine."

"Yes," I say, trying to recall the details of that particular rule. "It forbids arguments between family members."

Rhona rolls her blue eyes. "Not even close. Ground Rule Number Nine prohibits fights on spaceships. It was a necessary stipulation after too many command ships exploded due to heated arguments. You should learn the rules, seeing how you are a Teryn, or so you claim."

Moira chuckles. *The Teryns do love their fights.*

It's not that amusing when you *are the one in the middle.* I'll never forget how I almost died on the Teryn home world, when I stumbled into a fight circle.

If I remember correctly, dear, it was Ivy who pushed you.

I shrug. *She never admitted to it.*

Rhona turns to me. "What did you do now?"

I point at my chest. "Me?"

Rhona crosses her arms, making her biceps bulge. "Yes, you. Who else has the uncanny ability to bring trouble wherever she goes?"

I glare back. "I didn't invite DLD's army to Cathal, nor was I the one who refused obey The Lady's order to the letter."

Caderyn focuses on me. "How do you know whose ships those are?"

"Who else would bring such a force? Why don't you check with your spaceships. I'm sure they've gotten a good look by now."

Caderyn touches his right ear, activating the k'bug communication device nestled behind it. I have one too, though it never works for me when I need it.

Caderyn crosses his arms. "They're the ships of the Archgod of Chaos and Destruction." He adds, "I don't understand why you insist calling Him DLD."

Rhona nods. "It's juvenile and naive."

"It is not," I insist. "It's better than constantly calling Him the Dark Lord of Destruction, or the Archgod of Chaos and Destruction, giving Him all the power. This knocks Him down a few notches." I'm actually proud of coming up with that diminutive nickname.

"You should *never* underestimate your enemy," Rhona says.

Caderyn inclines his chin toward me. "And she is supposed to be *my* general."

Rhona and Caderyn share a laugh.

I grind my teeth.

Callum brushes his hand against mine in support. "How are you planning to fight an enemy who outnumbers us four to one?"

A warrior from the right chimes in, "It's ten to one, General."

Callum shakes his head. "Who outnumbers us ten to one."

"I owe you no explanation, son. Moreover, you always take Lilla's side over your family."

"How can you be surprised?" Callum asks. "If you want to argue—"

"No!" Rhona and I yell at the same time. She glares at me then turns away.

She is unusually upset with you, dear. Did you do something to her?

You mean outside of marrying her brother? That would be a no.

I turn to Caderyn. "Why aren't you attacking the archgod? We must order reinforcements, moving them from the nearby galaxies and—"

"We won't make the first move," Caderyn says, "and I won't listen to your novice prattling. Your fear will not dictate my next move. I've faced bigger enemies and won."

"I doubt it," I mutter.

"We are done here," Caderyn says, then turns his back on me. "Son, you stay. We have much to discuss."

Buckets of fishguts! When will the praelor listen to me?

I throw my hands up, then march out of the command center, wishing I could slam the automatic doors. I don't care if that's childish.

CHAPTER 9

I exit the spaceship, fuming about Caderyn's pigheadedness. I pause for a moment to allow my eyes to adjust to the near pitch darkness of the night.

Moira yawns. *He is a lot like you, dear.*

I am nothing *like Caderyn.*

Moira yawns wider and rubs her eyes. *I'm too tired to have this conversation, dear. I'll see you in the morning.*

But—

Only a soft snoring is my answer.

Moira wasn't kidding when she said she feels tired.

I glance around the tidy compound. Guards patrol the perimeter. Scented by sweet yellow flowers that bloom on vines, the hot and humid jungle air presses down on me. I don't want to go back to the tent alone.

With a deep exhale, I stride around the black rectangular ship. I have no idea where I'm heading. Then I hear a soft neigh. A black silhouette gallops toward me.

"Fearghas," I whisper to my battle horse, who has once again escaped the special barn set up for him. The horse, standing eighteen hands or six feet at the withers, bares his fangs. A few wooden shavings fall to the ground by his clawed hooves. He shakes his long black mane over his dark hide that even laser shots cannot penetrate easily. Then stomps his front webbed foot.

"We shouldn't go for a ride this late." Though I am feeling overwhelmed by the idea of staying locked inside the compound.

Fearghas huffs, clearly disagreeing with me.

"Maybe a short ride," I concede and jump on his back. Then I grab the end of his mane and turn him toward the metal fence.

Fearghas hurdles over it with plenty of clearing left between his belly and the spear-like fence posts.

I urge my horse to pick up his pace.

"We'll be back before they miss us."

We enter the dark jungle with the moon's white-bluish light barely illuminating the path the Teryn warriors have cut into the thick vegetation. I duck under low-hanging branches and vines covered with yellow flowers.

Fearghas flicks his ears, letting me know that a predator watches us from afar. The Cathal jungle is full of feline-like beasts that hunt small animals.

"No need to fear," I say. "It's just us."

A scrub rustles on my left.

I whirl toward it.

A small critter darts out of the brush, and up a vine, disappearing in the crown of a tree.

With a shaky exhale, I turn away as we continue our trek.

"See? Just small nocturnal animals."

"Lilla," an ethereal voice says. "Find me!"

Shocked, I pull on Fearghas's mane, halting him, while searching the jungle for the source of the voice.

Nothing moves around us. The varied insect life, encouraged by our stillness, picks up their nightly serenade until all I can hear is the usual buzzes, ticks, clicks, whirrs, and trills.

"Maybe I imagined it." I pet Fearghas's muscled neck and add, "Maybe we should—"

"Find me!" the ethereal voice orders, originating from deeper inside the jungle.

Fearghas shakes his head and neighs.

"I don't like it either. Yet, I want to investigate it."

Fearghas whinnies.

"I'll be careful, I promise."

I turn him toward the voice. The battle horse steps over roots, veering off the path into the wilderness of the jungle.

The insect noise dies out. The hair stands up on my neck. Branches and thorns cut into my arms as we fight through the vegetation.

Suddenly, the thick undergrowth opens to a small pasture with the bluish moon shining above.

Bushes rustle on my right.

I turn toward the crackle and gasp.

CHAPTER 10

Fearghas rears, neighing and clawing the air in front of him. Holding onto him, I watch monstrous dark fiends—eight feet tall and resembling *grotesque* bears—shuffle out of the trees, surrounding us in seconds. Then my horse kicks out in a warning while he bares his long fangs at the dark fiends in front of us.

Moira, I need your help!

But Moira does not wake.

Buckets of fishguts!

I gulp, pushing the rising panic down. I stare at the dark fiends, stifling my gag reaction at their rotting smell.

Black viscous liquid oozes from gaping wounds on their bodies that the long black fur does not cover. Menace saturates the air around them; their burning red gazes lock on us.

Fearghas dances around in a circle, keeping a distance from them. I gather a Lume thread from my magical bright white orb, holding it at ready. The familiar hot-and-cold-and-hot-again feeling envelops my body. My skin glows.

None of the dark fiends advance. It's as if they are waiting. But for what?

A hooded figure wearing a long black cloak and smoke-like disguise made out of Acerbus waltzes toward us.

Repulsion from the Acerbus raises the hair on my arms. I glower at the figure, but I can't make out any distinguishing features.

Without a doubt, I know that I am facing the new Ankhar—the right hand, avatar, and general of the Archgod of Chaos and Destruction. My counterpart in the Era War.

"Finally, we meet in person," the hooded figure says in that ethereal voice I heard before. "Happy twentieth day of birth, Sybil."

I gape at it.

How would the Ankhar know about my day of birth? Also, how did DLD find a new Ankhar so fast? The last one died on Uhna in the battle between the archgod and me.

"What do you want?" I ask as I tighten my fingers in Fearghas's mane to hide the trembling of my muscles. *Why does the Ankhar wear a disguise?*

"Same thing you do."

I frown. I have no idea what it means.

I glimpse graying skin and black veins on the Ankhar's hand for a moment, then the smoke-like disguise shifts to cover its skin. Yet, I know that whoever the new Ankhar is, it is not alive; just like these dark fiends are not alive.

I wish the Ankhar would release the disguise for a second, revealing its true identity. I wrack my brain to figure out who this new Ankhar could be. Someone that I may have met before. But who?

So many died in that battle when I faced DLD. Any one of them could have become the new Ankhar due to the high levels of corruption the archgod inflicted on my world. But how many of them would know about my day of birth?

Unfortunately, a lot, as my father had celebrated those days with world-wide feasts and announcements. At least he did in the beginning, when my mom was alive. After that he forgot more than he remembered.

I shrug, hoping the Ankhar will elaborate. I know from personal experience how frustrating it is when someone only offers silence in a conversation. The need to fill the awkward void is nearly unbearable.

"Why aren't you afraid?" the Ankhar asks.

"Should I? There is only you and seven dark fiends. I can take them in no time."

The Ankhar snaps its fingers.

Thirty more insectoid dark fiends along with dark servants—once humans but now mindless creatures—shuffle out of the jungle.

"How about now?"

I lock my jaw to hide my frustration. Then I gather more threads of the raw elemental magic, preparing for a fight.

"Don't bother with your weak magic," the Ankhar says. "I will overwhelm you in mere seconds."

Fearghas neighs and stomps his front leg.

"Then what are you waiting for? Even if I die, the Teryns won't let you have Cathal."

The Ankhar tilts its head. "Cathal? Why would I want this unpleasant planet?"

I frown. "Isn't that why you're here?"

The Ankhar laughs. "Are you telling me that you have no idea why Cathal is so important?"

"I—"

The Ankhar laughs even harder. "The Archgoddess of the Eternal Light and Order didn't trust you with imperative details about the portals?"

I school my face to hide my surprise. "She trusted me enough to tell me to be here."

"But did She tell you that these seven portals will be opening soon?"

Buckets of fishguts!

"If you know so much about these portals," I say, "then why are you here, pestering me in the middle of the night?"

The Ankhar shrugs. "Maybe I enjoy seeing you suffer."

My eyes go wide. "You have no idea *where* these portals will open." Which means DLD doesn't know where the portals will open. Could it be that The Lady has no clue either? Is that why She didn't tell me more about this mission?

The Ankhar slashes out with a hand. "It is only a matter of time before I will figure it out. Then my master will have what He needs to win the Era War."

Chills run down my spine as if I've been dunked into a barrel full of frozen shrimp. "I will never let Him win the Era War."

The Ankhar laughs. "You can't stop us now."

I shape the Lume magic into a short spear. "We'll see about that!" Then throw the magical weapon at the Ankhar.

A dark fiend lunges in the way, shielding the Ankhar.

The Lume spear pierces the dark fiend through its chest, and only grazes the Ankhar's forearm.

"You will regret this!" the Ankhar screams. "Kill the Sybil!"

CHAPTER 11

LARR-NA

Larr-na, leader of the proud Neath clans, paces up and down in her underwater cavern, deep below the surface of Cathal.

She feels the presence of an ancient power. It fills her with trepidation thanks to the spoken tales repeated generation after generation. She suspects that one of the ruling archgods must be nearby—probably the Archgod of Chaos and Destruction, who is infamous for instilling fear wherever He goes. However, she doesn't know why the archgod would come to Cathal.

Larr-na takes a few more steps until she reaches the curved wall of the cavern. She puts a webbed hand on the natural surface that has never seen a tool's mark.

Her instincts tell her that the archgod doesn't present any threat to her people at this moment, but that doesn't mean He won't threaten them later.

And if there is one thing I dislike, it's being unprepared for the worst. I learned my lesson the hard way. Many, including Kerr-no, had to pay the price for my mistake.

She gestures to her closest sentry. "Go to the surface and keep an eye on Kerr-no. Wait for further orders."

The guard bows and exits the cave. She inclines her head at the other two guards, giving them permission to leave.

She picks up a spiced crab claw from a large shell nearby—her dinner— and chews it.

Kerr won't like it, but I still worry about him. It's my job as his matriarch.

She glances around the empty cavern decorated only with purple plants that grow naturally in the crevices. Their fluorescence provides ample light; their scent fills the air with a sweet perfume. She dares not delay any longer.

With a deep exhale, Larr enters the inner chamber of her cavern. A chamber she rarely uses. Only in emergencies, like now.

Near pitch dark greets her. Her leather sandals slip on the wet surface of the rocks. Faint light emanates from a few dozen plants growing on the rocky wall, lighting her way. In the middle of the chamber waits a woven kelp blanket, spread out. A small bowl sits atop the blanket, holding a wet mixture of mud. The mud is fungi growing at the bottom of the deepest cavern mixed with the ashes of the previous matriarchs of the clans.

Larr sighs, then lies down on the blanket and closes her eyes. Preparing for her soul to journey into enlightenment, she dips her fingers into the small bowl. Swirling the mud and water together, she smears the mixture onto her face.

"We are made of Lume; when we die, we return to Lume," she murmurs the traditional prayer. Then adds, "Ancestors, hear my plea. Our clans needs your guidance."

She repeats this over and over, letting a familiar numbness spread through her body.

I really dislike this part.

Pain spreads through her body, paralyzing every muscle. Her breathing slows down to a sputter. Her mind enters the state of soul.

Blackness envelops Larr. It's neither welcoming nor threatening—just cold, dark blackness.

Don't think about the many tribe leaders who never came back from their soul journeys. Don't think about . . .

Larr exhales. She lets her eyes roll back and focuses on one thought: *How can I protect my clans?*

Darkness whirls around her, faster and faster until colors and impressions enter her mind. They journey with Larr for a few moments and thus dispense some meaning—but not enough for her to be satisfied with it.

She forces her soul to travel deeper into the darkness.

A newcomer appears next to her, not quite visible but not quite a silhouette either. Almost like a sense of a presence. Possibly a soul who already passed into Lume.

That's the most dangerous of all! What if—

Warmth spreads through Larr, reassuring and safe.

Larr relaxes a bit. "Who are you?"

The presence ignores her question, and says into Larr's mind, "Someone who should have never come to Cathal is here."

"Who?" Larr asks, worried.

The presence does not answer. Instead, instructions appear in her mind.

But that's not possible!

The presence swirls and golden sparkles shower around the edges. "You must do exactly as I told you. Everything, including the safety of your clans, depends on it."

Larr frowns. "What if this fails?"

"Then all is lost."

"Tell me more," Larr demands.

The presence edges closer. "I'd rather show you."

Something warm touches Larr's forehead. Images flood her mind, too fast to make sense of them.

Distress lights up the nerve endings in her body. "It hurts!"

The presence retreats. "There was no other way to tell you what you must know."

"I don't understand any of this."

"Not yet." Something burning touches Larr's scalp, and she hisses. "You will not remember any of it when you wake. But everything you need to do will come to you at the right time."

"How will I know the right time?"

The presence twinkles. "Don't worry about it."

Then soft warmth touches Larr's forehead almost like a kiss.

Golden light bursts behind Larr's eyes, ending her Journey of Soul.

Larr sits up and rubs her face, feeling confused.

This was such a waste.

She hits the ground with a fist. "None of this makes sense!"

CHAPTER 12

LILLA

"What are you waiting for?" the Ankhar screams. "Kill her!"

Dozens of dark fiends and dark servants advance on us.

There are too many monsters to try to subdue them with Lume. They would overwhelm me in seconds. My best bet is to fight them with elemental magic until I can escape.

Without hesitation, I release the elemental magic threads I gathered previously in their raw shape.

Fire, ice, wind, and fangs batter the ursine dark fiends. Fearghas kicks with his back legs at two monsters who get too close while I gather more Fla'mma threads to me. I need to cut an opening among the horde of dark fiends before it's too late.

The Ankhar exclaims in pain. "Take her down, now!"

A hundred more dark fiends and dark servants pour out of the jungle, their maniacal red gaze locked on me.

We have to get away before they completely surround us!

I let go of the Fla'mma thread, clumsily shaped as a torrent of fire. The dark fiends shy away, many burning and rolling on the ground to put the fire out.

"Fearghas, retreat!" I shout the command we practiced many times under the tutelage of Captain Murtagh, back on Uhna.

Fearghas rears, then jumps over the head of the dark servants.

Claws reach for us, scratching my legs and sides.

Then Fearghas lands, breaking into a gallop. I hold onto him, kicking out at the dark fiends trying to latch onto my left foot. They drop away.

A group of ten dark fiends give chase, darting after us on six insectoid legs. One of them leaps and grabs Fearghas's tail, trying to slow us down.

I turn back in the saddle, holding on with my thighs and gather thick threads of A'qua. Shaping the threads into icicles, I shoot the magic into the gaping maw of the dark fiend.

The magical icicles cut its mouth. It shrieks and drops Fearghas's tail.

I turn back in the saddle and lean forward over my horse's neck, urging him to go faster.

Screeches and yelps follow us.

I gather various threads of elemental magic, preparing for any surprise attack. My gaze darts around us, expecting danger among the vines and leaves of the dark jungle.

Branches get stuck in my hair, scratching my face and neck. I resist the urge to look back until all I can hear is Fearghas's huffing and my panting.

We escaped!

I slow Fearghas. "Let's go home, boy."

He neighs, then changes direction, instinctively knowing the way back.

My heart beats in my throat. I release the magical threads. They vanish back into my bright white orb. The glow on my arms recedes as well.

The three moons' light filters through the thick canopy of the tree crowns, illuminating our way.

Why did the new Ankhar trick me to a meeting? I do not know.

I recall the previous Ankhar, Loch Ramor.

In the battle with DLD, Loch kept asking for power until the archgod gave it to him, transforming him into a huge monster. It took all of my power to defeat it.

What kind of powers does this Ankhar possess? Why did it have all that knowledge about the portals? Was it truthful that The Lady doesn't trust me?

I shake my head to stop the line of problems I cannot solve.

Suddenly, exhaustion takes over, and I doze off.

Explosions sound high above us, waking me. I careen my neck, trying to see the sky, but the tree crowns are too vast.

Did Caderyn decide to attack DLD's ships? If yes, what made him do it now?

Moira, are you awake? But she still snores in the back of my head.

Slapping my cheeks, I fight sleepiness.

I wish I could talk to Moira, or Callum, or Glenna. I miss my best friend so much. Not only is she a talented healer, but she always knew how to comfort me. I hope she and Ragnald are doing well.

Fearghas trots through the jungle until we reach the closed entrance of the Teryn compound.

I heave a sigh of relief.

Then it gets caught in my throat as the metallic gates open to reveal a furious Caderyn with Callum behind him.

CHAPTER 13

"Follow me," Caderyn orders. Then he whirls on his heels and marches toward the Teryn ship.

I get off my horse's back and pat him. "Why don't you go rest, boy?"

Fearghas shakes his head and whinnies.

"I'll be fine," I mutter to him, eyeing Caderyn up ahead. If I keep repeating it often enough, maybe I'll believe it too.

Buckets of fishguts!

Fearghas neighs and trots toward his barn at the back of the compound.

Callum touches his fingers on my cheek, avoiding the scratches. "Are you okay?" His gaze is full of concern and questions.

There is no time to tell him what happened; how I almost didn't make it back to him.

I manage a nod.

Callum gestures toward the spaceship. "We should go."

I fall in step next to him.

In silence, we stride through the waking compound with the sky lightening pinkish-yellow at the edges. Then we enter the spaceship and pick up our pace to keep up with Caderyn.

The monotone hum of the powerful engines mixes with the sound of our boots clanging on the metal floor.

Chewing on my lower lip, I try to figure out how much trouble I am in with Caderyn. Judging from the stiffness in his back, a lot.

Then we arrive at the command center.

Caderyn climbs the metal steps of the raised platform with three transparent screens. Callum and I follow after him.

The praelor turns his back on us with his hands clasped behind his back.

"Do you know why I brought you here?" Caderyn asks.

I shake my head.

"The Archgod of Chaos and Destruction attacked one of my ships and terminated it an hour ago. There were five thousand veteran warriors on that ship. I knew every one of them, trained most of them. Now they are gone. Care to explain why?"

I sway on my feet.

So many died as a punishment!

"An hour ago," I say in a weak voice, "I fought with the new Ankhar and injured it."

Caderyn turns back to me. "Why would you engage our enemy without my permission?"

"I wasn't planning on doing it; It just happened."

A muscle twitch under Caderyn's left eye. "That is the most irresponsible and immature answer I heard. You failed those Teryns. And you claim to be their general?"

Suddenly, there is not enough air to breathe.

Callum clasps my hand, wrapping his fingers around my cold ones. "They all knew we were at war. They died with honor."

I squeeze his hand and take a deep breath. The panic retreats, leaving grief behind.

Caderyn points at me. "This is the kind of recklessness I warned you about. Now we are down by one space vessel and—"

"Nobody understands the stakes better than Lilla," Callum cuts in.

"I don't believe that she does," Caderyn responds.

"This attack was a fluke," Callum says. "They have not attacked again." Then he points at the screen showing the map of Cathal. "However, they have deployed hundreds of troop carriers all over the planet. Seemingly without any logic. Those troops are staying in place and not engaging us—a strange strategy from the archgod."

"He is showing us that He doesn't care about the loss of His troops," Caderyn explains, "because He has a lot more forces to deploy. Or it's a trap."

"There is a reason why He placed His troops near those random locations—this planet has some kind of portals that will open in seven days' time.

The good news is that DLD has no idea where they will appear." I don't tell them that it's highly possible that The Lady doesn't know either.

"What kind of portals?" Callum asks.

"I am not sure. That's all I was able to learn from the Ankhar."

Callum nods. "That would explain why we had to come here. Still, more information would have been better."

"You know how cagey The Lady can be about these missions," I say. "When do the reinforcements arrive?"

Caderyn frowns at me. "What reinforcements?"

"Are you saying that you did not arrange for reinforcements when those enemy spaceships arrived? You know, the ones that outnumber us ten to one?"

Caderyn narrows his eyes. "Don't be disrespectful with me."

Callum steps between me and his father, but I push him to the side. "It is not disrespectful to state the obvious that we need more ships."

Caderyn points at me. "I'll be the one who makes the—"

A tremendous explosion sounds.

One of the young Teryn warriors working at a screen leans back and says, "Sir, another space vessel has exploded. It was T-6973 carrying—"

"I can see that, Caporal Mitchell," Caderyn growls.

"Are you willing to request reinforcements now?" I ask. "Or are you waiting for another ship to be destroyed? How many more of our warriors must die before you act?"

"They are *my* warriors," Caderyn snaps, then drags a hand through his short black hair. "Caporal Mitchell, send out a signal to all space vessels available in Galaxy Two and order them to join us."

The young warrior nods and taps on his screen with efficiency. After a few moments of strained silence, he says, "Praelor, sir, our signals are blocked. I have not found a way around it."

Caderyn grabs the metal railing in front of him. "Send a stealth drone with an encrypted message."

Caporal Mitchell works busily for a few minutes, then gulps. "Sir, they shot—"

"I know," Caderyn growls. "They shot down our drone. Send a Stealth Nine Automatic Starship with an urgent request for support to all available space vessels in the Seven Galaxies."

Caporal Mitchell inclines his chin and turns back to his screen. After a few minutes, he pales. "Praelor, sir, they—"

Caderyn slams his hands on the metal railing. "They shot down that ship too."

The pit in my stomach grows to an unbearable size. There will be no help coming.

I turn to Caderyn. "This is your fault."

Caderyn blinks. "This is outrageous—"

"I wasn't finished. You underestimated the enemy. Now we are floating seagulls in the ocean full of hungry deepwater sharks. All because you are too stubborn."

"That tenaciousness is what makes me a great praelor and—"

"What are we going to do now?" I continue. "We cannot let DLD win the Era War. When are you going to listen to me?" Red curtains descend in my vision. I lock my fingers into fists to control the shaking of my body.

Caderyn's eyes turn orange-yellow. "Nobody has spoken to me like this and survived. You have proven over and over that you are too juvenile to lead my armies. Therefore, you are banned from *my* command center until you learn your lesson."

I step forward. "You can't ban—"

Callum curses under his breath and clasps my hand. "Let's go, Lilla. We are done here."

With an exasperated sigh, I let him lead me out of the command center.

CHAPTER 14

Outside the spaceship, I let out a frustrated yell.

Moira jerks awake. *What was that? Where is the danger?*

Now *you've decided to join me?*

A few patrolling warriors glower at me in passing, then turn their heads away in disapproval.

Callum hugs my shoulders. "Let it all out, then let's grab something to eat. I find these things help in dealing with the praelor."

I nod.

Together, we head toward the mess hall tent, kicking up dust from the dirt path. The dawn already brings heat and humidity, typical of the Cathal jungle.

Moira rubs her whiskers. *Do I detect irritation in your voice?*

Are you okay, Moira? You slept through a lot.

Moira drops her paw. *I'm not so sure, dear. I do feel more exhausted with each day. Sleep does not help either. I hope it will go away soon.*

I try not to worry about Moira as we enter the mess hall.

My friends sit at their usual table in the back, sleepily gazing into their caffeinated drinks.

I settle at the edge of the long bench next to Isa and Bella while Callum takes the seat across from me by Arrov and Belthair. Rhona perches next to the twins while Ivy leans on the table across from Rhona.

Ivy raps her nails on the metal surface. "You two look . . . distressed. What happened?"

Teague gets up from the far end of the table and heads to the metal counters where food and drink are laid out. The others yell orders for him to bring back.

"While you were asleep, I had quite a confrontation with the Ankhar and Caderyn." I fill them in with the details. Then I cover a yawn—all the sleepless night's events catching up with me.

Rhona glares at me. "No wonder Dad considers you an immature child—you sure act like one."

I shrug. I am too tired to argue with her.

Callum cuts a glance at his sister. "That was redundant. Children are inherently immature."

Rhona shrugs her muscled shoulders. "If she wants to be our general, then she has to act like one. Otherwise, no one will take orders from her. Especially not Dad. Though she'll never be *my* general."

"I'm still here, thank you very much."

What has gotten into Rhona?

Teague returns with a multitude of trays and pitchers of dark red drinks. "Dig in."

We pick our favorite rolls and cold cuts, then spend the next few minutes eating in silence.

Rhona leans back from the metal table. "Are you sure the Ankhar didn't tell you more about those portals? Where are they going to appear? How will we know what a portal looks like? Anything else you can remember?"

I frown at Rhona. "I am not stupid; I already told you everything."

"Not as stupid as Dad thinks," she mutters.

Ivy grins. "Someone is in a hostile mood. Just like a Marauder!"

Rhona grimaces but doesn't look at me.

I wonder, dear, if Rhona might be a bit jealous of you.

Me? Why?

Since you met Callum, he spends more time with you than with her. I am not saying that it is not normal for a couple, but we both know how close she and Callum were. Not to mention, they both struggled with their older brothers' bullying. This could be a lot for her to deal with.

I study Rhona in this new light. *It's possible, but how do I fix this?*

You don't. Rhona must get over it one way or another.

Arrov wipes his mouth on his light-blue toned forearm. "I find it odd that DLD deployed so many of His ground troops, yet they are standing in place like some grotesque sculptures. Does the archgod think we won't attack His troops?"

Belthair drums his feet. "It seems like He is overly confident that we'll be too scared to do anything. Or maybe He is too focused on the portals to care about us."

Isa leans her head on her clasped hands. "I bet these portals facilitate some kind of instantaneous travel. Probably from another dimension." Bella adds, "That would explain why it's difficult to know where they appear."

Ivy tilts her blond head. "Where do you think they lead?"

Isa and Bella say in a unison, "Could be anywhere in the Seven Galaxies. How exciting!"

Belthair shakes his head. "It's less exciting if the portals fall into the hands of DLD."

We look at each other. Losing the Era War is not an option.

"I think DLD has a plan," I say to the others, "and that does not bode well for us."

Ivy wipes her hands on her pants. "Maybe we should see these troops for ourselves."

I get up from the table. "Who wants to go for an early morning stroll?"

Isa and Bella both beam. "And skip today's jungle warfare training? We do!"

CHAPTER 15

We exit the mess hall and head into the armory. We grab our usual gear—heavy packs full of rations, tools, survival kits, medic kits—enough for a week. Then we take laser guns and holster them.

Callum and Teague march our group toward the tall metal doors. Fearghas gallops from the barn on our right. He lines up at the back as if the horse has done this a hundred times.

Ivy eyes my battle horse. "Why do you bring that beast with you everywhere?"

Fearghas bares his fangs at Ivy, who takes a step back.

I hide my smile. "Because I don't want him to chew through the fence trying to follow me."

A bearded Teryn warrior raises a hand. "General Callum, where are you heading?"

Callum gestures toward the jungle. "We are going for a practice run while we still have a chance." He takes a step toward the doors.

The Teryn warrior doesn't move. "Are you sure that's a good idea? The praelor—"

Callum interrupts the other man, saying, "The praelor will be happy to know how seriously we are taking our training."

The bearded guard mutters, then steps out of our way.

Callum looks back at us. "Close that line and move!"

We stride out as a unit and keep marching deep into the jungle until the compound disappears from view.

Callum stops. "This is not a game. When we encounter the dark servants, you follow my lead."

Teague pulls out a meat jerky and bites into it. "Now remember to not use your k'bug communicator, or the praelor will know what we are up to. Which means—"

Rhona interrupts him, saying, "—which means stay close, pay attention to Callum, and don't try to be a hero." She glares at me.

I glare back.

Remember, dear, it's going to take time for Rhona.

Callum pulls his longsword from its sheath and cuts a path in front of us into the thick verdant foliage. Strong scents of undisturbed undergrowth with its slightly decaying aroma drift to my nose. My hair plasters to my forehead under my helmet. Sweat runs down my back in rivulets.

Vines and branches covered in green leaves scatter all around us.

I rub my neck.

My sybil talisman zaps my fingers as it usually does. The transparent oval talisman has two crab-like claws. It attached itself to my spine through long golden filaments, unremovable forever. It dislikes me as much as I dislike it— while it's supposed to heal me, often it only does a mediocre job of it.

We spend the next hour trekking through undisturbed areas of the jungle until Callum stops. He raises a fist, and everyone comes to attention.

Teague carefully pulls back a branch to reveal a clearing where ten horrendous dark servants stand around, twitching.

CHAPTER 16

Belthair shakes his head, watching the group of dark servants in the clearing. "It's surreal to see them do nothing."

Ivy shivers.

Isa and Bella step to either side of the Marauder crown princess and hug her.

Callum sniffs the air. "They are only a quarter corrupted."

"Which means DLD must have been in a hurry," I whisper, "to get to Cathal with them."

I concur, dear. This is a good sign for us.

Teague grins and unsheathes his longsword. "Let's go introduce ourselves."

On silent feet, Callum and Teague descend on the ten dark servants. They methodically attack them, slicing and cutting with their swords until the Teryns are the only ones left standing.

We stride up to the men.

A sharp smell of rot saturates the air, driving away the scents of jungle. I cover my mouth to stop heaving.

"Not one of them tried to fight back," Callum says and sheaths his longsword. "Not even to protect themselves."

Teague nods. "The archgod has unrelenting control over them."

I study the fallen. My heart breaks knowing that these dark servants were once living, breathing people until DLD infected them.

Remember, dear, that corruption can't take place in them unless they have set themselves up for it by their actions, like your friend Glenna did.

Somehow that doesn't make it easier to bear the loss of lives.

I hug my elbows. "Wouldn't that mean that DLD knows we slaughtered His troops?"

Callum exchanges a look with Teague. "Maybe. Attack position!"

We all line up, as we practiced, facing the jungle and waiting.

Minutes tick by.

Nothing happens.

"Stand down," Callum says.

"Maybe the archgod is not so connected to His troops?" I ask, and Callum shrugs.

Arrov dry heaves, then wipes his mouth. "Can we also step away from the bodies? I don't want to greet my half-digested breakfast if possible."

The others mutter agreement as they move to stand farther away.

Before I can join them, Callum gestures for me to stay. "We cannot allow the archgod to retrieve them."

I nod. I know what needs to be done.

I hand my backpack to Isa. Then I reach deep inside for my bright white orb of magic and select a thin thread of Lume. The magical tattoo on my back lights up on its own—a souvenir from the Aak Saage women—and vines from the magical tree slide into my magic, strengthening it.

The vines are unexpected, dear. Has this happened before?

In a way yes, when we were on Pada. Though I had to shape the Lume magic into vines from the tree. Now the magical marking joined with the Lume, making my magic stronger without prompting it.

Please be careful, dear.

The vine-like thread comes to my hands, willing. I send the magic into the corpses, eliminating the corruption from them.

A dark cloud lifts from the bodies, emanating a menacing vibe.

As I release the Lume thread back into my magical orb, I send a prayer to their souls, guiding them to their final rest.

"I just wish I could save them somehow," I say.

Teague cleans his sword with a rag, then sheaths it. "This is us saving them, Lilla." Then he winks at me.

Isa hands me my backpack. Bella pats my forearm. "Sweetie, once the corruption sets in, you know they are gone."

I choke on an inhale, thinking of Glenna, who struggles with corruption as well.

Belthair points at the twins with his right three arms. "What they meant to say is that you did your best and took care of their souls."

Arrov nods. "That's a very important job."

Fearghas neighs and places his head into the crook of my neck. I run my fingers through his mane.

Callum inhales. "I scented another group, maybe a ten-minute walk from here."

Teague raises his finger and makes a circle in the air. "The rest is over people. We have a job to carry out."

Hiking through the jungle, we duck under low hanging vines full of tiny insects. We push aside long fluffy grasses with orange moths perching on the blades. We slide down a rocky path until we reach another clearing, this time with thirty dark servants.

Rhona, Teague, and Callum lunge at the dark servants from the left, cutting them down in mere moments.

Rhona wipes her sword on one of the corpse's pants. "This is not as fun as I thought it would be. They don't fight back at all."

Teague shrugs. "I have no problem making them into tiny—"

"Do not finish that sentence," Callum growls, interrupting the colonel. "We have women among us."

The others laugh as Teague ducks his head.

Engaging my Lume magic, I free the corpses from the corruption's grasp and guide their souls to Lume. I try not to notice how young some of them had been. They had so much life ahead of them.

Numbness spreads in my body. I'm unsure why I'm even doing this anymore.

Don't let DLD's malevolence infect your soul and rob you of your kindness. You are saving their souls. That's why you keep going.

Callum points to the right this time. "Another group about twenty minutes from here."

My friends curse, but we all get in formation again.

Callum leads a fast-paced trek through the jungle cutting through the vegetation until we reach another small field with the largest group of dark servants yet—sixty of them.

"I wonder if there are more of them because we are cutting their numbers down," I say, studying them. "Shouldn't we be more cautious?"

Rhona shakes her head. "Don't be silly. They were deployed before we started eliminating them."

Silly me for trying to be safe.

Callum raises his hand, but Teague strides past him, whistling and twirling his longsword.

Callum scowls. "What are you doing?"

Teague walks backward and wiggles his eyebrows. "I'm going to have a great time."

"It's not like they mind it," Ivy says.

Callum curses. "Teague, get back here."

Teague shakes his head. "What are you afraid of? That they bore me to death?"

The trees across the field rustle.

Hundreds of dark fiends in all shapes and sizes rush out with claws and fangs bared.

CHAPTER 17

Hundreds of dark fiends stream at us, ignoring the dark servants who still have not moved an inch.

Callum and Teague jump in front of me while Arrov and Belthair protect the women behind me. Fearghas lunges into the fray, biting and kicking anyone who tries to get too close.

I fire laser shots at the approaching dark fiends—long-necked monsters on six legs with gaping wounds that ooze black fluids—but it takes more than one shot to take them down. They tower over the dark servants by five feet, knocking a few to the side as the monsters barrel across the field.

Foot by foot they gain on us.

Arrov yelps from my left, staring at his furry blue left arm with a horrified expression. It seems he is about to transform into his A'ice giant form—in which he was stuck before for quite a long time.

A dark fiend swipes at the distracted Arrov, sharp claws raised to deliver a lethal strike.

"Arrov, move!" Ivy shouts, but he doesn't react.

The twins and I fire into the advancing humongous fiend, managing to deter its strike from Arrov's head, but the monster's claws cut deep cross his chest.

Gushing wounds open under his shredded shirt, dark blue blood spreading quickly.

Belthair shakes the dazed Arrov. "Snap out of it!"

Arrov blinks. The fur recedes from his left arm. Then he touches his chest and notices the blood on his fingers. His face pales, and he stumbles.

Rhona shouts at Belthair, "Get him out of here before he bleeds to death!"

Belthair nods and lifts his top right arm with a worn leather gauntlet that opens Umbrea, or shadow portal, for traveling short distances. His fingers tap on the gauntlet. He shakes his head and says, "It won't work! DLD must be jamming it as well."

Two feline dark fiends with spider-like mandibles leap at Belthair, one from the left and one from the right.

The twins fire their laser guns, taking down the aggressive dark fiends. But more pour out from among the jungle trees.

"We cannot stay here," Ivy yells, backing away from the clearing.

"Working on it," Callum snarls.

Teague puts his longsword away. "I can use my skill to move Arrov out."

Callum, fighting three fiends, says, "Do it!"

Teague closes his eyes, moving his arms in a circle.

A dozen ursine dark fiends with beaked heads veer off from the main group, loping toward the colonel.

"Teague, watch out," I shout, dropping on my knees to fire at the monsters, trying to cut their legs out from under them, but they shake off the shots that barely penetrate their thick hides. The first one pierces Teague in the shoulder with its sharp claws and lifts him up in the air, biting into his neck then throwing him backward.

Teague lands on the ground at our feet, dazed and bleeding profusely from his wounds.

Four feline monsters with huge maws gallop toward us from the right.

Callum takes the first two while Rhona attacks the other two. We pepper them with laser fire but can't hold back the rest. More than a dozen simian monsters with horns attack Teague, piling on top of him.

Do something, Moira shouts.

Anger surges through my veins.

Reaching for my magic, I call up Fla'mma, A'ris, and A'qua threads. With quick motions, I shape Fla'mma into fireballs, A'ris into air tornadoes, and A'qua into water spears. Then I release the torrent at the dozen dark fiends covering Teague.

The magical miasma burns, pummels, and cuts up the monsters until an unconscious and badly injured Teague remains.

Callum, Rhona, Ivy, and the twins push back the fiends by laying down covering laser shots, buying us a bit of time.

I look for Fearghas. My horse trots to me. "I need you to take Arrov and Teague—"

"And me," Belthair interrupts, holding his right three broken arms to him as he limps over. "I'm useless as well."

I sigh. "And take Belthair too."

Callum helps the three men onto my horse.

Fearghas, unburdened by the weight, breaks into a fast trot, heading back toward the compound.

Callum wipes blood from his cheek, then turns to me, searching for any injuries.

"It's my fault," I say. "I shouldn't have encouraged us to go look for the dark servants. Now Arrov, Teague, and Belthair are severely wounded and—"

Callum disappears from my view.

In his place, a beautiful meadow appears.

"Yes, it is your fault," The Lady says from behind me.

CHAPTER 18

CORRIGAN

Corrigan stares up at the ten-foot-tall teal-and-gold-veined white marble counter that takes up most of the luxurious room where the Eldryan Elders rule.

Behind the half-moon-shaped counter, six elders sit with the middle seat belonging to Corrigan empty. Floor-to-ceiling windows, with delicate white lace curtains parted to the side, reveal a carefully manicured green lawn with colorful flowers blooming around it. Arranged in a swirling pattern, they strike awe in any observer. The room's golden-white marble floor shines in the setting sun. Three sparkling crystal chandeliers hang overhead.

Corrigan shifts his weight from one foot to the other, resisting the urge to check on the state of his stylish gray suit.

I never thought I would ever have to stand here, in the petitioner's place. It is not an experience I care to repeat.

The first elder on the left, a new member of their ranks at the age of seventeen, Youngest Elder Christen, clears his throat.

"Together, we are happy," Youngest Elder Christen says. The others, including Corrigan, repeat the greeting. "We have gathered here at the bequest of our Esteemed Elder Corrigan, who will turn forty years old in two days' time."

Youngest Elder Christen's gaze pauses on the other five elders, all of whom wear white robes with metallic ropes dangling from their shoulders and across their chests signaling their age and thus their rank: gold for seventeen to twenty, ranking Youngest Elder; gold and silver for twenty-one to twenty-five, ranking Young Elder; silver for twenty-six to thirty, ranking Honorable Elder; silver and bronze for thirty-one to thirty-five, ranking Old Elder; and lastly, bronze for thirty-six to thirty-nine, ranking Esteemed Elder—on their way out of the ruling elders.

For godssake! Enough with the power play and get on with it.

Youngest Elder Christen continues, "As we all know, according to the Eldryan constitution, no elder who reaches their fortieth birthday is allowed to continue as a ruling elder to guide our society. They must enter the second and largest phase of their lives—becoming an Esteemed Grandfather to disperse wisdom to their family unit and neighbors, serving our society till they draw their last breath, then finally returning to the bosom of the Archgoddess of the Eternal Light and Order."

Corrigan looks away before his fellow elders can see his exaggerated eye-roll at the newest elder's self-importance.

The elders converse among themselves, murmuring quietly.

I was not arrogant like him when I first entered my elder rank.

Corrigan takes a deep breath and faces the elders. Each of the men he knows from working side-by-side for many years or, as in the case of Youngest Elder Christen, many days. He took painstaking efforts to learn all about his fellow elders.

That's how I knew which one of their dark and hideous secrets or hidden desires I could exploit to get this constitutional amendment that will allow me to stay as a ruling member. Now if they could get onto the voting part, before I turn old and gray. . .

Black-haired Esteemed Elder Carther, who has a bronze rope on his white robe since he is thirty-eight years old, clears his voice. "Before we vote, I would like to address the Worthy Elders for consideration. When our constitutional amendment was voted in, almost seven hundred years ago, the Eldryan lifespan was very different from what we enjoy today. Chaos and madness afflicted the then-Acclaimed Elders, especially those who were past their fortieth birthday. It was a necessary and crucial addition to our constitution. However, we have not seen such madness cause issues anymore. Therefore, I would like to move forward to propose an extension of service eligibility for elders from forty to sixty."

The other elders gasp and mutter under their breath.

"Thank you for the history lesson, Esteemed Elder," Youngest Elder Christen says wryly. "However, you are trying our benevolence with your proposal."

Corrigan doesn't bother to hide his eye-roll this time.

Such theatrics! I've talked to every single one of you. This is not a surprise to you at all.

Twenty-two-year-old blond Young Elder Cronnor raises a hand. "I disagree with Esteemed Elder Carther. The threat of madness has never left us, although we have not experienced any outbreaks of it recently. But to declare that we are beyond its reach is a clear proof that the madness still lurks in unexpected corners of our thoughts. No one is safe from it, not even Esteemed Elder Corrigan."

Corrigan narrows his eyes. *That's not what you told me yesterday when I gave you half my fortune.*

Red-haired Honorable Elder Colter, who just turned twenty-six, leans forward. "Seven hundred years is not long enough to breed out the madness of our society. I am not sure we should be so brazen as to put such risk on our beloved Eldryan society only because Esteemed Elder Corrigan is too selfish to give up his seat—"

Esteemed Elder Carther hits his open palm on the marble counter, interrupting the other elder.

Corrigan grunts with dissatisfaction. *How can he challenge me so openly?*

Honorable Elder Colter stares back as if to say, *Go ahead, let everyone know my secrets, I don't care anymore.*

Corrigan inclines his chin. *I might just do that, just to see you humiliated.*

Corrigan searches the gaze of his two allies—Old Elder Carper and Old Elder Clint—who promised they would help him, as they often did before, but both elders avert their gaze in shame.

I don't like where this is going.

Quiet settles on the elders. "We will not disparage each other, Worthy Elders," Carther says. "We will treat each other with benevolence. Am I clear?"

The others reluctantly nod.

Youngest Elder Christen clasps his hands. "Now that we have heard points and counterpoints, it is time to cast your vote."

A small screen rises from the edge of the marble counter in front of each elder. It is palm-sized with only two symbols on it: a flower in bloom for a yes vote, and a flower torn in half for a no vote. Each elder presses one of the two buttons, then the screens retreat into the counter.

I should win this four to two . . .

Corrigan turns to face the opposite wall to the right of the floor-to-ceiling windows where a marble panel flickers, turning orange—a unanimous no.

Corrigan curses under his breath.

How dare they refuse me? I'm broke from bribing them. Now I will lose my rank and status too. I have so much to offer to our society. I am not done yet!

Youngest Elder Christen claps his hands. "The Worthy Elders have spoken. There will be no amendment to the Eldryan Society's Constitution."

CHAPTER 19

I turn around in the gorgeous meadow amid sweet-scented flowers. My fingers brush against silk-like flower stems. A warm breeze plays with my hair. The striking blue sky with fluffy clouds makes this pocket realm feel like a surreal landscape painting.

"It is your fault we are in this situation," The Lady repeats, standing with Her hands clasped in front of Her white gown. "You are too willful when it comes to completing my missions." She smiles sadly, yet it only makes Her divinely beautiful face even more stunning. Ancient and endless power shines in Her golden bright eyes. Her bare feet do not disturb the plants around Her, as if She is not physically present.

Whatever you do, dear, please don't antagonize the archgoddess. Remember the consequences.

I cross my arms. "I am not willful."

"My child, you failed to take care of the archgod when you had a chance."

"I was not fully in control of my magic then; I am now. Besides, I recruited the Teryn army as you asked."

"While you achieved recruiting the formidable armada, you failed to bring the whole of them to Cathal, didn't you, my child?"

Argh!

Just say something diplomatic dear. Be polite and respectful.

"I completed that quest to the best of my ability. Caderyn brought five hundred ships."

I won't admit to Her that Caderyn fooled me as well.

"You also almost allowed L—" She looks away.

"I almost did what?" I ask, but The Lady only shakes Her head. Her golden hair, like sunlight infused into the strands, flares out around Her.

"My child, you are not the best Sybil when it comes to carrying out my orders. I expected more obedience from you. Especially since you were raised as a princess in the Uhnan court."

"If you wanted a meek and demure sybil you should have never picked me. Not that there was anyone else vying for the job."

Suddenly, happiness and love bursts from the sybil talisman, cascading down my spine, robbing me of air.

Gasping, I claw at my throat and fall to my knees.

Moira grasps her furry head. *Make Her stop!*

The Lady steps around me. "I am tiring of your complaining and disrespect, my child. I am stuck with you—that much is true, however, this stubbornness of yours will be your undoing. Learn your lesson before it's too late."

Joy bursts behind my eyes and my vision turns black. "I . . . am . . . doing . . . my best . . . without any . . . training."

Shrieks of pain are torn out of me, turning my throat raw.

Moira screams in my mind too.

"Your mistakes can cost me the Era War, and I will not let Him win. Do you understand?"

Moira claws at my mind. *Just say yes, for the love of gods!*

Choking for air, I incline my head.

The overbearing happiness and pressure recede.

I gulp in blessed air, glaring at The Lady. How can someone so beautiful be so cruel? Clenching my teeth, I keep my thoughts to myself.

The Lady smiles. "That's much better, my child."

Moira bares her fangs. *We will have our chance to repay Her in kind, dear, but that time is not now.*

Getting up, I wipe grass and dirt off my knees. Then I look around, frowning. Something is amiss. "Where is Acolyte Aisla?" The petite blond goddess enjoyed seeing me suffer and was always by The Lady's side.

The Lady purses Her lips for a moment, then says, "I have a new mission for you, my child."

That was not an answer, dear.

I try to remember the last time I saw the petite goddess, but my reward is a severe headache that jabs into my temples but brings no memories forward.

The Lady continues, "You are to hold this planet, Cathal—"

"Don't you mean that I should protect the portals on Cathal instead? Aren't they most important part?"

Why must you always be so direct with the archgoddess, dear? I'd recommend not pushing Her too far. We've already suffered enough today.

I will never back down, no matter how much She punishes or lectures me. Besides, She has no one else to take my place. I am the last Lumenian, remember?

Moira laughs. *I do admire your bravery, dear.*

The Lady narrows Her eyes and studies me. "How do you know about the portals, my child? Who told you about them?"

Notice, dear, how She avoided to answer again. Instead, She turned the question around to you.

I spread my hands. "I'd love to ensure the portals don't fall into the wrong hands—those of the Archgod of Chaos and Destruction, for example. All I need to know is where they'll appear."

"You must find them and protect them, my child. They will appear soon, in seven days' time, starting now."

The Ankhar was right, Moira. Neither of the archgods know where the portals will appear.

"How will I—"

The Lady and the meadow disappear, dropping me back into the middle of the battlefield with the dark fiends.

CHAPTER 20

DAY 1

The jungle replaces the meadow in an instant. Humidity and heat press down upon me. All around, large feline-like fiends battle with my friends.

"Lilla, You're back," Callum shouts but cannot come closer. A dark fiend springs at him, poised for a deadly strike. Callum cuts the creature across the ribs, then whirls on his heels and stabs another one in the middle of its back.

What are you doing? Moira shouts. *Move!*

I try to lift my feet, but pain shoots down my spine from the sybil talisman, paralyzing me.

I can't!

Three insectoid dark fiends with scorpion-like stingers spot me and change direction. They scamper toward me on four disjointed legs.

Moira shouts, *They are six feet away!*

My body stays frozen no matter how I fight the talisman. Sweat trickles down my face, my heart beating as fast as the dark fiends' claws drum the jungle floor in their hurry.

It's The Lady's doing. Moira, can you take over?

Moira strains, then growls. *I can't reach you. The talisman is blocking me.*

Suddenly, Caderyn shoves me to the side. He slashes at the two fiends with his longsword, cutting one's throat and the other across the chest. The third scorpion-like fiend grazes him on the shoulder with its nasty-looking stinger. Caderyn slices its legs out from underneath it, then stabs it in the back.

Six more awful dark fiends turn their head toward Caderyn, sniffing the air and scenting blood. The largest ursine dark fiend howls and charges.

Finally, the talisman's hold disappears. I shake off the paralysis.

Without waiting, I engage my Fla'mma and A'ris magic, mixing the threads and creating a torrent of fire. Then I aim the deluge at the fiends, burning four of them badly while two run away. Callum picks them off with his longsword, cutting them in half.

Black spots dance in front of my eyes.

Moira shakes her head. *You're overusing your magic.*

I'll be fine for a bit longer if I am not using Lume.

"Thank you," I say to Caderyn.

The praelor studies me with his cool blue eyes, his beard twitching with disappointment. After a long second, he grunts, then wades into the fray, ensuring no dark fiend can go past him.

I have no idea how he found us, but I sure appreciate his help.

Rhona and Callum hack a path to us, followed closely by Isa and Bella, and lastly, Ivy, who looks like she rolled in mud. When Ivy notices my glance, she raises a hand. "Don't bother to ask; I won't tell you what happened."

Rhona shoves her sword into the ground and points a finger at me. "We are in this conundrum because of you! You are too irresponsible, Miss Let's-go-attack-dark-fiends-without-a-plan!"

"First of all, it's *Mrs.* Let's-go-attack-dark-fiends-without-a-plan," I say. "Second of all, you were right next to me, agreeing with my idea."

Rhona raises her chin. "I've changed my mind. Now I disagree with you."

I cover my face with a hand. What is her problem?

Caderyn grunts. "We will discuss this matter later—and don't think there won't be severe consequences for your actions—but right now we have a battle to fight. Our goal is to make our way back to the compound. Alive. Callum, you are on point. Rhona, you guard our back. The rest of you, shoot at anything that moves. Now go, go, go!"

We line up as Caderyn instructed.

For the next hour, all we do is shoot, slice, cut, as we make our way, inch-by-inch, closer to the compound. I can see the humongous black spaceship through the branches of the overgrowth. But the direct route toward it is blocked by hundreds of dark fiends.

"Keep right to avoid the monsters," Caderyn orders as we veer off the path.

We reach the second clearing on our way back with dark servant bodies scattered around.

Ivy stops, bending over her knees. "How much longer? I'm exhausted."

Rhona points at Ivy. "This is exactly why we ran all those conditioning exercises, so you'd get in shape."

Ivy straightens up. "You underestimate a Marauder's ability to eat their weight in food and thus avoid being in shape."

Rhona shakes her head. "You always have an answer to everything, don't you?"

Isa and Bella, supporting each other by the shoulder, stop too. "We were just here hours ago, yet it feels as if this all happened ages ago."

"Who gave you permission to stop and gawk?" Caderyn barks. "Keep going or die here!"

Before we can take a step forward, scores of horrendous dark fiends emerge from the trees.

CHAPTER 21

A horrible putrid smell from the monstrous scorpion-like dark fiends saturates the air. Their growling reverberates throughout the jungle. They scurry to get around us.

Caderyn, Callum, and Rhona form a protective barrier in front of us women.

"Don't let them surround us," Caderyn barks, matching the pace of the closest dark fiends, preventing them from flanking us.

Using Rhona as a shield, Ivy shoots at the few dark fiends who manage to get close. "As if that's an easy feat . . ." The injured dark fiends limp back a few steps, snarling.

Isa's laser rifle clicks repeatedly. "I'm out!"

We cannot stay here, dear. Soon we'll be overrun.

Cursing, I reach for my pulsing magical orb. I grab onto A'qua, A'ris, and T'erra threads, combining them into a torrent of blasting wind, icicles, and shards of rock. Then I spray the corrupted beasts with the magical miasma.

The first row of fiends falls to the ground, severely injured and shrieking. The rest back away.

Next, I grab a thick thread of T'erra and shove it in the ground in a semi-circle.

A wide trench opens up between us and the rest of the dark fiends. The trench separates us from them, giving us a temporary reprieve.

"Retreat," Caderyn orders.

We follow the praelor.

Suddenly, my vision turns black. I stumble.

Rhona glances back with a disapproving expression.

Callum steadies me by the forearm. "You must stop using your magic, Lilla."

"I'll be fine," I say, while increasing my steps. I hope I sound more convincing than I feel.

Rhona scoffs. "I despise retreating. Where are we even going?"

"How about toward that rocky outcrop about two hundred feet to the west?" I ask, recalling the terrain I glimpsed on one of the screens in the command center. "We could climb it, and then go around the dark fiends blocking our way to the compound."

Rhona frowns. "Since when do you give directions, when you can barely find your way back from the mess hall to your tent?"

That's not funny.

"It only happened once," I grumble.

Callum snorts. "Don't worry Rhona. I'll make sure she'll never get lost."

Rhona glares at me, then turns away, hurrying forward.

Caderyn grunts. "Enough with the chitchat. We are not on a family outing. We will head west and go the long way around middle of the jungle. That trench won't hold them for long, so pick up the pace. We are slower than a k'sloth! Ivy, Isa, and Bella, move your feet faster. That's an order!"

The twins hold on to each other but limp quicker. Ivy groans, then shuffles her feet, with chunks of mud falling off her.

Caderyn keeps a brutal pace, cutting through the foliage with ease, belying his age of sixty-five.

We hike across roots and jump over fallen trees. Caderyn and Callum cut a path through the dense vines and other flora. The heat of the midday becomes nearly unbearable.

I wipe the sweat off my forehead, but still more moisture pools at the waistband of my pants.

Rhona swipes away a large green leaf.

Insects shower the twins and me as the leaf passes over our heads. Grinding my teeth, I fish out my flask, but it's empty.

After a while, we reach a mostly dirt field full of dark fiends with six-foot-long necks standing around on two legs. Their head is a strange cross between a horse and a wolf.

Caderyn raises a hand.

We halt and drop our backpacks at our feet.

I resist the urge to bend over my knees from exhaustion. The last thing I want is to give Rhona fodder to pick on me even more.

I'm telling you, dear, she is a bit jealous of you.

Somehow that's still not helping.

Ivy paces around, panting. "They . . . don't look . . . too dangerous." She pokes one with her short sword in the neck.

The closest dark fiend whips around and snatches Ivy's weapon. Then it swallows it whole. The sword protrudes across its neck as it makes its way toward its belly. Then the long-necked fiends turn their heads toward us and breathe fire.

We retreat a few steps, only to find the six-legged insectoid monsters advancing from behind.

"I've had it," Caderyn barks. "Battle form, now!"

CHAPTER 22

Callum raises his arms to the side, palms up. His blue eyes blaze with a reddish-orange glow, which soon encompasses his whole body. From one blink to the next, a seven-foot-tall battle form appears, wearing his uniform stretched over his more muscular and bulkier body. Short black fur covers his wolfish face. Steel-colored stripes run down his cheekbones. A black mane cascades over his head. His hands end in long black claws.

Caderyn's battle form has more dark gray fur than Callum's. His head is more bearish than wolfish, with white stripes across his cheeks. He, too, stands seven feet tall next to Callum.

Then they look at me from nearly black, orb-like eyes.

Moira laughs. *Finally, it's our turn.*

The transfiguration lifts me a few feet off the ground. I hover in a vertical position, suspended in a cocoon of energy. Then the next instant I drift back down in my Cymmerion battle form, a gift from Moira. Dra'agon legs support our ten-foot-tall, strong, and bear-like body, covered in iridescent black scales. A thick black mane frames a wolfish head, black feathers cover an eagle head, and multi-hued scales cover a dra'agon head. Twenty-foot-long leathery wings spread wide as we raise our scale-covered tail ending in a scorpion stinger.

"Keep going to the rock formations," Caderyn says. "There we make our stand with our backs protected."

Callum and Caderyn plunge their longswords into the necks of the monsters, slicing them up.

Bella and Ivy lay down cover fire.

Using my Fla'mma magic, I spray the beasts with a burning torrent. Isa throws rocks at the monsters.

We battle for each step toward the rocky hillside until we finally reach it.

Moira and I face the horde of dark fiends with our back protected. From our height, we see hundreds more simian-like creatures hurtling toward us.

We're never going to win against such numbers, I say to Moira.

Then we die fighting, dear, with honor.

Caderyn slashes the beasts to our right with the twins and Ivy while Callum and Rhona battle up ahead, keeping the scorpion monsters from reaching us.

A flicker coming from the side attracts our attention.

We turn the eagle head toward it.

A nine-foot-tall and two-foot-wide crack appears on the surface of the rocks, showing a vision of a city.

A force field! The rock formation must be a disguise of a force field.

We should enter through the opening, dear, before it closes.

We yell, "This way!" Whatever waits beyond the force field must be better than hundreds of dark fiends.

The twins and Ivy jump through the fissure without hesitation.

Caderyn turns toward his children. "Callum, Rhona! Move now!"

However, both of them are surrounded by a dozen scorpion-like beasts along with long-necked dark fiends, unable to break away.

Caderyn curses, hesitating.

With our left wing, Moira and I push him toward the opening. "We must go now!"

Caderyn grumbles but strides through the force field as well.

We turn to Callum and Rhona. "Hurry!"

Our heart breaks watching Callum being pushed farther and farther away from us.

We cannot keep waiting. We must go, dear!

More dark fiends press on until we have no choice but to backtrack.

Callum looks up, his eyes full of rage, clawing and cutting his way toward us, but barely making any headway.

Strong hands grab our tail, yanking on it hard.

Moira and I stumble backward, falling through the opening. We lose our battle form immediately.

Whirling to face the fissure, I raise a hand. "No!" But the force field closes in my face.

CHAPTER 23

I stare at the closed force field showing a blurred image of the jungle. I can barely make out Callum and Rhona still fighting the monstrous fiends beyond it.

"Callum!" I shout, but he can't hear me.

He'll be fine, dear. Not to stress you more, but you are naked.

Oh! I cover the important bits with my arm and a hand, then turn around.

Caderyn's military uniform has changed back into its usual size. Avoiding looking at me, he hands me his jacket.

"Thank you," I say with cheeks burning hot. "I don't understand why I keep losing my clothing when we transfigure."

Caderyn clears his throat. "It's probably because your battle form is nothing like the others."

That's right, dear. We are unique.

I would prefer having clothing after we change if it's all the same to you.

Moira chuckles. *I'm sure they've seen it all by now.*

At least the banter distracts me from worrying over Callum. I must stay calm so I can think logically. But my heart aches with physical pain from being separated from him. Again.

Isa and Bella look around. "Where are we?"

Ivy picks out a broken stick from her blond hair. "I'd like to know that too."

I look at the nearby cloudscrapers covered in green plants, stretching toward the domed yellowish-blue sky. Narrow streets weave between the elegant buildings, full of mechanical coaches that roll by without the help of any animal. How strange that this city is here, hiding under a force field. The Teryn ship's sensor didn't pick it up at all. Do these citizens even know about the Era War? How long have they been living here?

A shadow passes over me.

A few mechanical coaches glide by above the cloudscrapers.

Isa points to the far left. "Look at those sculptures." Bella adds, "Aren't they amazing?"

I turn to see.

A thirty-foot-tall sculpture depicting a female warrior with long braided hair, pointed helmet, and armored dress stands about a hundred feet to my right. Behind her, in the distance, another massive sculpture stands, this one a male warrior holding a spear and wearing light leather armor and boots. He too has his eyes closed.

They seem historically important, dear.

I survey both sculptures. There is something ancient and powerful about the two warriors. They look as if they could wake from their slumber at any second and burst into action.

Suddenly, there is an urge to go toward the female warrior. I take a few steps, but Ivy puts a hand on my shoulder, stopping me. "Where are you going, Lilla?" she asks.

I tear my gaze away from the warrior. "I'm not sure."

There is something familiar about that sculpture, though I swear I have never seen anything like it in my life.

I felt its pull, too, dear.

Caderyn crosses his arms. "We are attracting a crowd. Best to get going."

Several passersby have stopped to gawk at us in shock and dismay. They are all elegantly dressed in colorful outfits—the women wear long skirts with jackets and hats, all of it adorned by lace and ribbons, while the men wear a three-piece suit. They all have a slight yellowish or reddish tint to their skin tone, probably from the force field's effect.

I pull the jacket's lapels closer to me. "That's a good—"

"Together, we are happy!" a man in his forties with dark brown hair shouts. The other six men with him shout, "And your happiness matters to us!" They are all dressed in the same style yellow jacket and pants with matching boots.

We gawk at them.

"Do not move, please. We are the Protectors of Peace. Disobeying us will have consequences." He lifts a thin black metal baton with wires running around the top and electricity dancing on its polished surface.

Caderyn opens his arms with palms out and inclines his head at us.

We follow his example.

My borrowed jacket parts a bit. The yellow-clad men avoid looking at me, preserving my dignity, or what's left of it.

They take the weapons from the others, though Caderyn does not want to let go of his longsword, ensuing in a tug of war before the praelor finally relents.

The leader of P.O.P. nods. "Good. Now after you, please."

CHAPTER 24

Caderyn scowls at the P.O.P. men. The praelor falls in step, leading our group with the yellow-uniformed men flanking us. "Where are we, and where are you taking us?" he asks.

"Do you know that we are in the midst of a new Era War?" I ask.

"How long have you been here?" Isa asks, and Bella adds, "What technology allows you to have a milder climate inside of the force field than outside of it?"

"What are those sculptures?" Ivy asks.

"Do you ever leave the force field?" I ask.

"Did you leave those ruins in the jungle?" Isa asks, and Bella adds, "And to what purpose?"

The leader of P.O.P. raises the black baton. "Your questions must wait. Now please keep moving."

We cross the street, heading toward a road. As we near the other side, the leader of the P.O.P. points at a puddle by the curb and says, "Avoid these as if your life depends on it."

I frown. "Why?"

But none of the P.O.P. answers as they keep their pace.

Shouldn't we attack these P.O.P. and escape? I ask Moira. *They're all pretty old. We should be able to overtake them easily.*

Moira shakes her head. *Not right now. It's best to lay low, hide our strength, and gather information about this strange place. We may convince them to help us against the archgod as allies.*

Then that's what we'll do.

I try not to stare too much at the technologically advanced buildings that seem to be in harmony with nature or the flying coaches above us. Yet the weaponry of the protectors does not seem that advanced. My pirate ancestors had better laser rifle-swords covered in deepwater shark teeth than those simple bats these elderly men carry.

Maybe they don't have to deal with much crime, dear.

Ivy puts a piece of purple gum into her mouth. "Look at this bustling city. Caderyn, how come you never knew about this place?"

Caderyn glances at Ivy. "Are you suggesting incompetence on my part?"

Ivy blows a bubble and bursts it with her tongue. "You did miss it, didn't you?"

The twins clap their hands. "We can't wait to explore the city."

Caderyn shakes his head. "Don't expect much. We are intruders in an advanced society who put painstaking effort into staying out of view. We are as good as dead."

"That's a bit harsh," I say, taken aback.

Caderyn turns to look at me. "I'd rather prepare you than lie."

He does have a point, dear. Albeit he could have delivered it nicer.

"How do you know?" Ivy asks and hugs her elbows. "What if you're wrong?"

"I am never wrong," Caderyn says. "I know because that's what happens to anyone who sets foot on Teryn."

"Yet my friends and I survived," I say. "An exception to your harsh rule."

Caderyn makes a face. "You survived against my better judgement. Whoever rules this society might make a smarter decision."

"Is this the first time you admitted that there might be others smarter than you?" Isa asks innocently. Bella adds, "Do you feel any heart palpitations? How about increased sweating?"

Caderyn lets out an exasperated sigh. "Why did I have to get stuck with you four? You are nothing but—"

"Here we are," the leader of P.O.P. says.

We stop in front of a pristine white mansion. Wide but low, it squats on a cobblestoned street, with quaint flower beds around it. Tall transom windows cover the front of the building. Dark red double doors complete the look. The structure sticks out among the high-tech cloudscrapers with its stockiness, elegance, and lack of plants growing on its walls.

The leader of P.O.P. climbs the three steps toward the entrance and opens the door. "After you, please."

"Is this a prison?" Ivy asks, unmoving.

"Why are we here?" I ask.

"I demand to see whoever is in charge!" Caderyn snaps.

Isa and Bella don't say a word. They ogle the cloudscrapers with their back turned.

The leader of P.O.P. sighs. "Now I asked you politely," he says and raises his electric baton, "but if you make me repeat myself, I won't be as polite."

We enter.

CHAPTER 25

The double doors of the mansion slam behind us with a bang, leaving only the leader of P.O.P. as our guide.

Shiny white marble with teal veins covers a massive foyer with doors branching off on the left, and an elegant marble staircase going up on our right. Sunlight pours in from the tall windows, illuminating the emptiness of the hall.

I inhale the clean and cooler air.

It's a beautiful place but without any personality. I wonder if this is some sort of government building.

It could be, dear.

Ivy whistles, careening her neck. "Fancy place. It would even make a Marauder proud."

Caderyn scoffs. "I never cared for pomp—"

We roll our eyes. "We know."

"—and I am not impressed at all," Caderyn continues as if we didn't interrupt him. "Why isn't someone here to receive us? Why are we being kept waiting?"

We turn to look at the leader of P.O.P., who shakes his head and strides toward the stairs.

I guess we used up his patience, dear.

After a few seconds of hesitation, we follow him.

On the second floor, corridors branch off in three directions. We take the first corridor on the left. The white marble continues on this floor too, with windows on our left and a wall of doors on our right.

The leader of P.O.P. gestures toward five doors. "Please select a room of your choice. Dinner will be waiting for you there."

Caderyn takes the first one, the twins the second one; I take the third one, and Ivy the fourth one.

Each room has the exact same furnishings: a large and comfortable bed at the back wall, white plush carpet on a dark hardwood floor, a small white table and chairs, and a bathing area behind the bed. There are no weapons, scrolls, tomes, or any other objects in the room. Not even a single painting.

On each table waits a platter of fruits and sliced meat.

At least they are consistent, dear.

I stride around the room, touching the soft beige blanket on the bed and the dustless table. I glance out the window and notice that the yellow-uniformed men still linger around the mansion.

No matter how nice the room is, dear, it still feels like a prison. I wonder if they locked the door.

With my heart beating in my throat, I check the door by pushing down on the cold silver handle.

It opens smoothly.

That's a good sign, dear, right?

I shrug. *What if this is a false sense of security?*

I leave the room, keeping the door open, and step into the corridor. The leader of the P.O.P. has vanished.

My companions step out of their rooms as well.

Isa rubs her right arm. "We are free to wander." Then Bella adds, "I bet we are not allowed to leave the building."

"Should we chance it?" Ivy asks.

"No," Caderyn and I say in unison.

"The P.O.P. are still out there," I explain.

"Now what?" Ivy asks.

Caderyn gestures for us to come close into a huddle. Then he whispers, "I do not know if there are any listening devices around, but it's best not to risk it. Whatever happens next, do not volunteer any information to these strangers. Do not reveal who we are or why we are here. Allow me to speak. Nod if you understand me."

"But—" I say, only to receive a harsh glare from Caderyn.

My shoulders hunch, and I nod along with the others.

We straighten up.

Caderyn gestures to the window on our left. "It seems we are spending the night here."

Darkness spreads as the sun sets. Electric lights mounted on the walls come to life, pushing the shadows away.

"But won't we be murdered in our sleep?" Ivy asks. "Or at least poisoned?"

Isa shakes her head. "Being poisoned would still result in being murdered." Bella nods.

"What if this is a test?" I ask. "To see how we behave?"

Caderyn grunts. "It could be. However, to answer Ivy's question, I do not see the point of politely escorting us to this place—clearly a high-ranking person's home or office—only to kill us in such barbaric ways. If they are going to kill us, it would be probably in the morning, in a public execution—it's killing two k'birds with one axe. Instill fear in the citizens while getting rid of us. That's how I would do it."

"You have some strange ruling techniques," I mutter.

"But they are effective," Caderyn says.

I open my mouth to debate him, but Moira says, *You won't win this quarrel.* I snap my mouth closed.

The twins cover their throats. "That's horrible."

"Go back to your room," Caderyn orders. "I have chosen the first one to guard the rest of you. I will hear if anyone tries to enter this corridor. Do not fret."

"It's a bit too late for that," Isa grumbles, and Bella adds, "Especially after you scared us."

Ivy makes a grimace. "I always preferred poison over execution. Now that I've joined Lilla's side, the Dowager Queen will have me executed in the most spectacular public scene. In her eyes, I betrayed her and the Marauders. Yes, in that order." She goes back in her room.

The twins sigh, then enter their room.

Caderyn stops me before I can return to mine. With an eye on the closed doors, he asks, "Can you access your meld?"

I strain to transfigure but nothing happens. I shake my head.

Caderyn rubs his beard. "I cannot access mine either. How about your magic?"

I search for my magical orb, but it seems out of reach.

My eyes widen. "What kind of force field is this that blocks our meld and my magic?"

Caderyn exhales forcefully. "A powerful one. Watch yourself." Without waiting for an answer, he ducks into his room.

I wonder if he worries about Callum and Rhona. He sure doesn't talk about them.

I retreat into my room. The bed beckons with its warmth, offering a much-needed rest. Though it will be strange to spend a night without Callum when we've been inseparable for weeks now as a married couple.

Pressing my eyes closed, I force the tears away.

Gods, I hope he got back to the compound safely.

I'm sure he did, dear.

I pick at the colorful fruits and sliced meats on the platter without enthusiasm, eating just enough to stave off the hunger.

Finished, I head to bathing area with a mirror and a metal tub in the middle already full of hot steaming water, and a bar of soap on its ledge. Someone anticipated our needs.

I drop Caderyn's jacket to the floor.

Looking in the oval mirror, I examine my body, turning left and right. My skin is peppered with bruises in various stages of yellow, purple, or black, showing that at some point the talisman did try to heal me, but not the recent ones that I suffered just before coming through the force field.

There is no doubt now that it's not just my magic that doesn't work—the sybil talisman lies dormant too.

Buckets of fishguts!

CHAPTER 26

The next morning, a polite knock wakes me up. Rubbing my eyes, I sit up in bed, trying to shake the remnants of a nightmare.

In that horrible dream, I was on the Teryn home world in front of the Senatus—but suddenly I was deep underwater. I couldn't move, I couldn't breathe. I was paralyzed. Fear saturated my body in a warning, but I didn't know what the danger was. Then a sharp headache jabbed into my temples and the dream shifted into the usual nonsensical collage of jungle, peppered with dark fiends.

I feel as if a memory is trying to surface, but I cannot put my finger on it.

Having dreams like this is completely normal, dear. Your mind is just trying to cope with the past day's events.

Warm sunlight blankets the room from the tall windows. It is so unlike the tent I called home with Callum in the Teryn compound. How I wish I could be back there with him.

With a sigh, I get up and step to the discarded black jacket on the carpet. I really don't want to wear it again. Then my gaze catches a dark purple lace dress with matching undergarments on the closest wooden chair.

Thank the gods!

Don't be so happy, dear. Someone came into our room while you were sleeping and placed this dress here. They got past Caderyn and me. I never sensed anyone entering.

With my heart beating in my throat, I examine the room, searching for other signs of whoever entered. But outside of the clothing, they seem to have touched nothing else.

With a deep exhale, I pull on the dress. Not only is it comfortable but the fit is great too. Near the chair, a pair of low-heeled leather slippers wait. I slip them on my feet.

Another knock sounds.

I open the door.

An elderly man with almost all-white hair and bony shoulders steps back from the doorway. His outfit—a simple gray shirt and pants with a dark gray apron—suggests that he is a servant of sorts.

"Together, we are happy," he says in a barely audible voice. "Follow me, please."

"It's quite a strange greeting," I comment. "What is the meaning behind it?"

The older man averts his eyes.

I find it outlandish, dear, that they employ the elderly in such difficult positions as servants. Makes me wonder what their young people are doing.

I leave my room, shutting the door behind me. In the corridor, Caderyn, Ivy, and the twins wait.

"Took you long enough," Caderyn growls.

"And a sunny morning to you as well, dear father-in-law."

He winces, clearly not relishing his new role.

The elderly servant coughs, and we fall in step behind him.

He climbs down the white marble stairway, then takes a left turn, heading to the back of the mansion until he reaches two large doors.

Without looking at us, he bows and shuffles away.

Caderyn turns to us. "Whatever you do, don't ramble and follow my lead."

"Yes, sir," Ivy and the twins say in a mocking tone.

Caderyn pushes the doors open with such force that they bang into the wall.

He marches to the middle of the vast room. On our left, floor-to-ceiling windows take up most of the wall while on our right, a white-and-teal marble counter towers over us. Behind the counter, seven men ranging in age from late teens and early twenties to late thirties gaze down at us.

"Together, we are happy!" they say in unison.

We don't respond.

These men must be the ones who rule here, dear. Some quite young to have such responsibility.

Caderyn takes a step forward. "I don't know who you are—"

The youngest man, wearing a white robe with golden ropes on the front of it, interrupts him. "The Esteemed Grandfather has no voice in front of the

Worthy Eldryan Elders. He does not receive our benevolence."

I stifle a laugh, but the twins and Ivy don't bother to hide theirs.

"I imagine that hurts," Ivy says.

The youngest man points at Ivy. "Women have no voice in front of the Worthy Eldryan Elders either and thus won't receive our benevolence as well."

This is highly unusual, dear.

We women frown at the so-called Elders while Caderyn smirks.

Another man, this one at the end of his thirties with bronze ropes adorning his white robe, raises a hand. "Young Elder Cronnor, it seems we are at an impasse. We cannot talk to the Esteemed Grandfather, but we also cannot talk to the women, for their place is with the children."

Young Elder Cronnor grimaces. "I have noticed our conundrum, Esteemed Elder Corrigan. I think we should just—"

"Before we make any hasty decisions," Esteemed Elder Corrigan interrupts, "I propose to show our benevolence to these outsiders and nominate a stand-in speaker for them. That way we can learn how they managed to enter our society, and what their purpose is. If you are in favor, raise both of your hands."

Most of the elders raise both of their hands, then Young Elder Cronnor joins them too.

"Your benevolence, Esteemed Elder Corrigan, is vast," another man says, then stands up. "I volunteer to be their proxy speaker, if that's suitable for all of you."

Esteemed Elder Corrigan smiles. "It is. Thank you, Youngest Elder Christen."

The other elders hesitantly nod.

Youngest Elder Christen strides behind them, then down a hidden staircase until he stands in front of us. Intelligent dark brown eyes shine in a rectangular face framed by short dark brown hair. He too wears the white robe with gold-colored ropes.

Youngest Elder Christen turns to us. "Only one of you," he looks us over, then points at me, "is allowed to talk." He gestures at the others and adds, "Do not converse among yourselves. Do not attempt to address the Worthy Elders, nor should you attempt to speak to me as your words will not be considered."

Ivy sneers.

Youngest Elder Christen gestures at the others. "Please go stand by the windows."

They obey, dragging their feet.

Caderyn's expression darkens. "How is three feet of distance going to make any difference?"

Youngest Elder Christen turns his back on Caderyn, and gestures for me to stand next to him, facing the counter.

"Lilla," Caderyn says, "do not tell them anything."

Youngest Elder Christen glances at me. "I trust that you are going to ignore that unwise advice. We extended our benevolence to you; do not refuse it."

I manage a nod.

Be careful what you reveal, dear.

I was planning to but thank you.

Youngest Elder Christen clasps his hands in front of him. "We are ready to proceed."

"But you don't even know my name," I say to him.

He shrugs. "It won't matter, but if it makes you feel better, do tell me."

"Lilla." It *should* matter.

Esteemed Elder Corrigan raps his knuckles on the marble countertop. "How did you get here?"

Youngest Elder Christen turns to me. "How did you get here?"

"I heard the question the first time."

Youngest Elder Christen waits in a cool silence.

Just ignore their antics, dear. It will be over sooner.

"There was a crack in the force field and—"

Youngest Elder Christen interrupts me to relay my answer to the other elders.

"Why did you come here?" Esteemed Elder Corrigan asks.

I wait for Youngest Elder Christen to repeat the question.

"The Archgod of Chaos and Destruction has sent His armies to Cathal, a crucial location in the Era War, and we were fighting Him when—"

Youngest Elder Christen repeats my words.

Esteemed Elder Corrigan steeples his hands under his chin. "We have all the information we need to make our decision."

"I have questions too," I say.

Youngest Elder Christen sighs, then relays what I said.

"There was no mention of questions," one of the elders retorts.

"This is outrageous," another elder snaps.

Esteemed Elder Corrigan claps his hand to silence his fellow elders. "It is only fair to allow her to ask a question or two."

The other men raise their chins or murmur under their breath.

Youngest Elder Christen looks at me. "Ask your questions but choose wisely. Do not waste our valuable time."

"Do you know about the Era War, and will you join us fighting the archgod?"

Youngest Elder Christen repeats my words.

"Yes, we are aware," Esteemed Elder Corrigan responds. "No, we will not join. We simply do not have enough manpower to make a difference. Every one of our citizens is needed to maintain our society."

That's an excuse, dear, and a poor one at that.

I wait until Youngest Elder Christen finishes speaking.

"When can we leave?" I ask.

Esteemed Elder Corrigan listens to Youngest Elder Christen, then says, "Soon."

That's not a real answer either, dear.

Youngest Elder Christen inclines his head. "If that is all."

Turning, I take a step back to return to my friends when I hear a throat cleared.

Youngest Elder Christen leans forward. "Is any of you a Lumenian?"

Before I can respond, Ivy says, "No."

I gape at Ivy, and she looks away. Caderyn inclines his head as if to reaffirm Ivy's answer.

Youngest Elder Christen turns to me, waiting.

I shake my head. "No."

Aren't you glad, dear, that you don't look like a real Lumenian?

Thanks, I guess.

Esteemed Elder Corrigan listens to Youngest Elder Christen, then says, "Please return to your rooms and rest. We will assign each of you a guide so that you won't get lost in our mansion."

I believe he meant "guard," dear.

"That's it?" I ask, but six yellow-uniformed P.O.P. appear at the door. Having no choice, we leave.

CHAPTER 27

After the odd meeting with the Eldryan Elders, I enter the room assigned to me and shut the door. I lean my head on the cool surface of the white door, replaying the bizarre conversation, and worrying over the inexplicable parting question about a Lumenian.

Not to interrupt your legitimate concerns, dear, but there is someone here.

I turn and look around.

At the far corner, to my right stands a six-and-a-half-foot-tall man with his hands clasped in front of him. Long, teal-colored hair falls over his wide shoulder in a braided ponytail. A tight green bodysuit covers his muscular body, complete with decorative shell and fishbone chest plate and gauntlets. Long pinkish fins lay flat on his arms and legs. His light-gray-toned skin shimmers as if it's made out of millions of tiny scales. His dark teal gaze takes my measure, glinting harshly in his handsome rectangular face with strong cheekbones, lush lips, and a straight nose. On his neck, I glimpse three gills.

"Who are you?" I ask.

"May you swim in clear water," the man says coolly, flashing a pair of sharp fangs among his white teeth. "My name is Kerr-no from the clan of Norrek of the Neath people. You may call me Kerr. I am your assigned *guide*." Hostility saturates his tone. He clearly does not like his assignment.

The feeling is mutual.

"What does *guide* entail?"

Kerr's gaze turns even colder. "I follow wherever you go inside the mansion."

Meaning we can't leave the building.

We must get out, dear. We'll hide somewhere in the city until we find another crack in the force field.

What about the others?

We'll come back for them later, of course.

"You can go now. I plan to spend the rest of the day in my room."

"I stay where you stay." From his mocking tone, it's obvious that he questions my intelligence.

He won't leave.

Then find another way to get rid of him, dear. Think!

"I am hungry and thirsty," I say, trying my best to look innocent.

Kerr growls. "I am not your servant."

Buckets of fishguts!

I despise deploying my ex-ma'hana court voice, but I have no other options. "I don't see anyone else here, do you?" It's never failed me before.

Kerr curses under his breath. "I'll be right back." He stomps out of the room and slams the door.

Now get to it, dear, before we run out of time. You do want to get back to your husband, don't you?

I dash to the bed and yank off the blanket, then pull the sheet under it, tying them together. Then I hurry toward the window and push open a glass panel. A low metal barrier guards the bottom third, more for decoration than for function. I thread the blanket through the metal bars and make a break-knot one of my pirate ancestors invented.

Hurry up, dear! I hear footsteps approaching.

Gulping, I lean over the railing while holding onto the bedsheet. I risk a look down and shiver.

We are too high up!

You will be fine, dear. Now go!

I'm not so sure that this is a good idea anymore.

Moira growls. *We are running out of time!*

Alright, alright!

I step over the metal barrier when I hear the door to my room bang open.

"Stop!" Kerr shouts.

I step over with my other leg and turn to slide down.

Strong hands grab my forearms. "I must insist that you come back inside," he says, his polite words in stark contrast with his threatening tone.

Moira growls. *Shove him away and run!*

I push against him, but he doesn't budge. His dark teal eyes glint threateningly.

Muttering a curse, I climb inside.

Kerr's gaze slides to my neck and he inhales sharply. "What is that?"

The blood drains from my face. "Nothing."

"I've seen that before. It's, uh, what was it called? Some kind of talisman, isn't it?"

I glance away. "I really don't want to talk about it. Besides, it doesn't work."

Kerr nods. "I must taste your blood."

I choke on air. "What did you say?"

This is getting interesting, dear.

I can assure you that it's not.

Kerr reaches out a hand. "I cannot guard you without bonding with you."

I put a hand out. "Bonding?" Callum would *not* be happy to hear that! I add, "What kind of bond do you mean?"

"The bond is for me to you, and not the other way. It is what parents have with their children, to find them easier. It is not a marriage bond; that requires three bites. You won't even notice it, I promise."

I hesitate.

Dear, my instincts do not warn against his bond. How about yours?

I don't have a bad feeling if that's what you mean, just a bit of repulsion.

That's to be expected, dear.

With a deep exhale, I place my hand into his. He curls his cold fingers around my hand and turns it until my vein is visible. Then he bends his head over my wrist.

Sharp, needle-like pain originates from my wrist.

I gasp, expecting more pain, but it does not get worse. Warmth spread from the bite, his breath like a feathery touch on my skin. After a few moments he lifts his head and releases my hand.

I pull back my hand and examine my wrist. Two small red dots are visible near my vein, but no bruising.

Kerr closes his eyes. His irises dart side to side behind his eyelids in a fast-paced motion as if he is dreaming.

I wonder, dear, if he can read your blood.

My eyes go wide. *Read?*

There are races, dear, who have the capability to skim others' life experiences or even thoughts through a blood exchange.

Eek! I didn't know about that part!

Kerr raises his head. His gaze seems less cold, but his expression remains blank.

I don't think he learned anything from my blood, I say to Moira with relief.

Suddenly, he turns his head toward the door. "I hear footsteps. We'll have a visitor soon."

CHAPTER 28

Our Kerr has some impressive skills, dear. I did not hear any footsteps until he mentioned it.

The door to my room opens.

Caderyn enters, followed by a tall and even burlier man dressed in a dark green bodysuit. Caderyn's guard has teal-colored hair like Kerr, though this man keeps his long strands loose around his strong shoulders.

Caderyn looks at his guide, who stands down.

Kerr inclines his head in greeting to the other Neath man, then comes to stand next to me.

Caderyn points at me. "You got us into quite a mess."

Me? "How?"

"First, you ignored my order to stay away from the archgod's army," Caderyn says, counting it off his fingers. "Second, you attacked first, dragging my children into it."

I cross my arms to hide my hands in fists. "They're adults and made their own decisions."

"Third, we almost got captured by those dark fiends."

I roll my eyes. "It wasn't even close."

"Fourth, you trapped us behind a force field, in an ageist society with no way out."

"Don't forget patriarchal too."

"This is not a joking matter."

"If you want an apology, I'll give you one, right after you apologize to me."

Caderyn looks taken aback. "Apologize? For what?"

Now it's my turn to count off his transgressions. "First, you didn't listen to me about bringing the full Teryn armada to Cathal. Second, you didn't obey The Lady's orders to the letter. Third, you told me you did, but it was not the whole truth. Fourth, you didn't listen to me about the reinforcements until it was too late."

Caderyn takes a step closer, but Kerr cuts in front of him, pushing me behind him. "Why would I listen to you?" he asks, peering at me from around Kerr's muscular body. "You are too inexperienced for this Era War. You were raised as a spoiled princess. You cause trouble everywhere you go. And *you* never listen to *me*!"

"You didn't bother to give me a chance. If Callum were here—"

"But my son isn't here, is he now? He followed you until he got ambushed with those dark fiends while we got separated from him. Whose fault is that?"

I swallow down the urge to cry. "It was my fault. Is that what you want to hear? Is that what makes you happy?"

"That is not a proper apology."

"How would you even know what a proper apology looks like?" I ask. "When did you ever apologize to me? For treating me like an outsider—"

"You were an outsider!"

"—when I arrived on Teryn. Then you denied my Bride's Choice on Callum while insisting that Ivy had one on him earlier, which we both know was a lie. Then you set me up by demanding that I get Guardian Goddess's, uh . . ." My voice trails off as harsh pain jabs into my temples as I try to remember her name to no avail. Rubbing my forehead, I continue, "your goddess's blessing, which I did. But that was not enough for you. I had to prove myself by fighting your executioner, the Teryn man who almost killed me. But I fought him and won. You still didn't accept me. What more do I have to do?"

"I didn't ask anything more from you than I would ask from anyone else in your position. I told you before that I don't do special treatment, especially not for princesses raised on rich worlds, pampered, and entitled."

I am none of those! "Did I not prove my worth to you, when I uncovered that coup one of your consuasors set up to overthrow you? Consuasor Finigal made a deal with . . ." My voice trails off again, due to another bout of headache as I fail to remember the name. After blinking the pain away, I continue, "He made a deal with the leaders of Tier One factions to kidnap you, killing two of your older sons in the process. I uncovered the truth. And how did you repay me? You lied when you said you brought the Teryn armada to Cathal."

Caderyn crosses his arms. "I know exactly what you did. Rubbing it in my face will not earn my respect."

Ugh! He is too stubborn, dear.

"You are too willful to be a good leader. I have much to teach you. Here is your first lesson: respect is earned, not demanded."

"I wasn't demanding your respect. I simply wanted . . . Never mind."

Caderyn nods. "If you want to get out of here, you'll do exactly what I tell you—stop interfering and stay put!"

Without waiting for my response, Caderyn and his guide march out of the room, closing the door behind them with a click.

CHAPTER 29

*G*laring *at the door won't change anything, dear. Caderyn doesn't know what you are capable of. But we proved him wrong before, and we will continue to prove him wrong until he appreciates you.*

With a sigh, I slump down in one of the white chairs. Kerr sits across from me.

"I brought this earlier but didn't have a chance to offer it to you," he says, and hands me a glass of blue liquid from a tray on the table.

"What is it?"

"It's a brew that refreshes and calms. We make it from a plant that grows where I live."

"Thank you," I say and sip the pleasantly sweet drink. "Where do you live?"

Kerr sits up straight. "I am not allowed to reveal it without the permission of my matriarch."

I wonder why. "I see."

"Earlier today, when I took your blood, I sensed another sentient being. Who was that?"

"Her name is Moira. She is the queen of all Teryns, my melded spirit and mentor."

Kerr nods. "Fascinating. You must never feel alone or lost. I imagine she offers great comfort and wise guidance."

Moira grins proudly. *He got that right, dear.*

Just don't let it get to your head.

"It took some getting used to sharing my mind with Moira." Not as much time as getting used to the powerful Cymmerion form—three heads are two more than I possess or ever imagined having.

"Who was the angry man?" Kerr asks.

"It was my father-in-law, the praelor and ruler of the Teryn Praelium. I thought you would know, since you tasted my blood."

"Everything related to you is the clearest. Others come in and out of focus, but mostly remain a blur, as what we share is not a true bond lovers have."

Good to know.

"Why was he so upset?" he asks.

I place my empty cup on the tray. "He and I have different views of how we're supposed to handle many things." Things like the Era War or leading an army.

"Elders often do have such a differing view."

"Sounds like you had a personal experience."

Kerr shrugs a muscled shoulder. "It's in the past now."

We fall into silence.

"You don't belong here," Kerr says, with an eyebrow raised.

"I know." I appreciate him being circumspect, ensuring if someone listens to us, they wouldn't know what we're discussing. However, I do wonder just how much I can trust him. He was ready to protect me from Caderyn. But can I trust Kerr when it comes to the elders?

Dear, he mentioned a matriarch as his leader. I didn't see any among the elders, did you?

Kerr stands up. "I need to check, I mean bring you fresh food. I will be back."

I nod and get to my feet as well. "Sounds good." This gives me plenty of time to visit my friends and come up with a plan.

CHAPTER 30

I open my door, then poke my head out. I look side to side down the empty corridor, then hurry to the twins' room.

Isa and Bella, lying on their bellies on the carpet, fiddle with wires and other equipment pieces scattered in front of them. Across from them, multiple sections of the wall gape open with dangling wires and other technology visible.

"What are you doing?" I ask, hoping they're not going to pull a prank here, as they did with the Teryn spaceship's lights.

Bella puts her finger to her mouth.

Isa holds up a small black card. She presses a button on it until a click sounds.

"Now you can speak," Isa says, and Bella adds, "They were listening to our every word."

Moira growls. *I should have sensed it!*

"Where are your guides?" I ask.

Isa blushes. "They left to bring us some food." Bella adds, "They are *very* handsome, but sadly mated."

They both sigh in disappointment.

I hide my smile. The twins love flirting with men—and sometimes with women too.

Isa runs her fingers through the pile of debris. "The elders locked us in our room all night. We heard our guides open it in the morning." Bella adds, "But we made a key."

"That is why Kerr came only in the morning," I say. "The elders were not in a hurry to assign anyone to us. They knew we would have no choice but to stay put."

Isa stands and picks up another black, rectangular card-like object from the table. She hands it to me. "Keep this in your room. It will prevent them from listening in on your conversations. The others already have theirs." When she sees my doubtful expression, she adds, "Don't worry; it scrambles your words, yet still makes it sound as if you're talking."

Bella giggles. "It's one of our best inventions."

"Thank you." I put it in my pocket.

Isa hands me a small, transparent, round object, full of colorful wires. "We made everyone a key. This is yours. All you have to do is to hold it near the door handle, and it will unlock or lock your room."

"Good job," I say and put the orb in my other pocket. "We cannot stay in this force-field-protected society for too long. The Lady tasked me with a new mission of protecting the portals that open in five days' time. She was adamant that these mysterious portals cannot fall into the hands of DLD."

"Five days is not a lot of time," Isa says with a solemn expression. Bella adds, "Especially when we have no way out of here."

"I need your help."

The twins perk up. "What do you need us to do?"

"I need you to find out about the technology that operates this society. How do we turn off the force field? We must leave at our first chance and rejoin the others."

The twins nod. "We can help with that."

"I knew you'd be up for this task." I turn to leave when a thought occurs to me, and say, "I'd like you to examine the sculptures as well."

Isa raises an eyebrow. "Intriguing." Bella asks, "Why?"

"I am not sure how to explain it, but I think they are . . . important and . . . there is this feeling I have . . ." My voice trails off. "Maybe I'm wrong about them."

Isa steps to me. "We'll look into them." Bella adds, "Don't worry, Lilla."

It's hard not to worry when I'm running out of time, and the fate of the Seven Galaxies depends on my actions. "Please remember to be careful."

"We will," they say in unison.

I slip out of the twins' room, then enter Ivy's next door.

Ivy lays on top of her bed with her chin in her hands and her feet hanging off the edge, singing to herself. When she notices me, she scrambles to her feet. "What are you doing in my room?"

Closing the door, I ask, "Does that mean that I can come in?"

Ivy shrugs, then perches on the edge of the bed. "You are already inside."

I sit next to her. "I wanted to check on you."

Ivy lifts a shoulder. "I doubt that. Nobody ever comes to check on me. They either want something from me or want to reprimand me for my earlier actions. Let me guess. You're here to ask why I denied that you are a Lumenian."

She is a lot smarter than she lets on, dear.

"That's not the only reason, but yes. Now that you mention it, I would like to know why."

Ivy crosses one slim leg over the other. "There was something suspicious about how they waited to ask such an important question until the very end of our hearing, almost as an afterthought—yet the way they watched us told me how much your answer mattered to them. Besides, I make it my life's goal to disappoint people; just ask my mother. When people underestimate you, they don't see you coming."

"You are doing great on that front. Are you up for some spying?"

"I am a great spy! It's one of my many talents as a Marauder, outside of poisoning, of course, or lying. But it doesn't count as lying when you do it to save your life."

"I guess." I fill Ivy in on the details.

She twirls a strand of blond hair around her finger. "The elders will never let us leave. I could tell that the second they called us 'outsiders.' One of them probably wanted us dead, but the other elder, Corrigan, stopped him. There is dissent among these elders, who are barely older than us. Which makes me wonder why they use such rank. Anyway, I'll learn their secrets. Then we won't be locked in this mansion any longer."

She looks away, but I detect vulnerability and pain in her green eyes.

Moira shakes her head. *Just how many times has this poor girl experienced being imprisoned to get such a haunted look in her eyes?*

I cannot imagine, but I am not brave enough to ask her, or she'll poison my food.

"Don't tell Caderyn," I warn her.

Ivy scoffs. "As if I would tell him *anything.*"

She rolls back onto her belly, ending our conversation.

I sneak back into my room.

Kerr paces up and down. He opens his mouth to speak but I raise a finger. Then I press the rectangular card-like object in my pocket until it clicks.

"It's safe to talk now," I say and tell him what I learned from the twins.

He nods. "I have talked to my clansmen. They are willing to ensure our—that includes your friends—absence won't be detected as long as needed. You can go freely through the servants' entrance—one of us will help you to sneak out or back into the mansion. Do you accept my help?"

For a second, I wonder if I'm making a mistake trusting him. Even with the room keys Isa made for us, we still would need help to leave the mansion undetected. Which means our safety is literally in the hands of Kerr and the other Neath men.

There is something about Kerr, dear, that reminds me of my Edan and your Callum. He seems trustworthy.

I nod.

"I trust you."

"Good. It's too late to head out. I'll be back for you in the morning."

CHAPTER 31

The Archgod of Chaos and Destruction, in his average-looking mortal form, stands in front of me in my dream. "You are weak and pathetic. You have no chance against me!"

I face DLD on the platform, alone.

Debris falls from the ceiling of the cave underneath the dungeons of the Crystal Palace, scratching my arms and drawing blood.

Fear petrifies me.

"You are nothing," He says with disgust. "The Lady only chose you because there was no one else."

I want to take a step back, but my feet stay rooted to the rocky ground. Dark tunnels branch off all around me. From their black depths, lethal and menacing silhouettes snarl.

"No!" I yell but no sound escapes my lips.

DLD points at me. "You are the worst Sybil. Trillions will die because of your incompetence."

Glenna and Ragnald appear on my left, their faces pained. Then Callum and Teague writhe in agony, followed by Caderyn, Rhona, Belthair, Arrov, Isa and Bella . . . then innocents I've never met, all flash in front of me until their suffering becomes a blur.

"Stop!"

DLD laughs. "I've only just begun."

With a muffled scream, I sit up in bed.

What is it, dear? Why are you shouting?

A sob breaks free from my throat. "He was in my dream again."

Moira rubs her eyes. *It was only a nightmare, dear. Go back to sleep.*

But all sleepiness has escaped me. My light gray nightgown—one that our host provided—sticks to my sweat-covered body. "DLD is right; I am a nobody." I don't even look like a Lumenian.

Now, now, dear. Do not give into the archgod's lies. He is the master of wreaking chaos. He manipulates and threatens until you're stupefied and in fear of Him. Remember, He has one goal—to win the Era War. He will go to any length to achieve that.

"First, he has to go through me."

Moira laughs. *Exactly, dear! Why do you think He intimidates you in your dreams?*

"To keep me afraid of Him."

Exactly! Remember, fear prevents you from thinking logically. Otherwise, you'd realize that it is He *who is afraid of you.*

"That's hard to fathom. I am a twenty-year-old princess-turned-sybil while He is tens of thousands of years old archgod."

And yet, He is apprehensive of you.

I wipe the sweat off my face, trying to rid myself of the remnants of the nightmare. Then I notice dried blood on my forearms from where the rocks scratched my skin.

Oh, how I wish I could talk to Callum or Glenna about this! How I miss them. I even miss Ragnald, with his overconfident magic lessons.

I worry about Teague, Arrov, and Belthair. Did they make it back safely? Did their injuries heal fine? Did Callum and Rhona escape the ambush? What is happening on Cathal? How are the Teryn warriors faring?

I have so many questions, but I am stuck here, unable to do anything.

Suddenly, I cannot keep my worries at bay anymore. All the anxiety and dread I pushed deep down come back with a vengeance. Tears burst out of me.

I cover my face in my hands, my whole body shaking.

Let it out, dear. It will make you feel better.

After a long moment, my tears ebb.

I cannot know what you are going through, dear, but I can imagine your pain. Lean on your fears and embrace them. Let your emotions fuel you. Let your desire to get back to your husband and friends strengthen you. You are not alone, no matter what the archgod wants you to believe. We will get back to the Era War and fight Him.

"How am I going to succeed, if I am trapped here?"

Moira yawns. *We'll figure it out, but not tonight. Sleep and recuperate your energy. Tomorrow is another day.*

"Tomorrow I will find a way out."

CHAPTER 32

ISA

"Are you up?" Bella asks.

"Yes." I turn to my side on the bed, looking at her across from me. I can barely make out my sister's shape in the darkness of our room at the mansion.

"Why are you still up?" I ask.

Bella turns to her back with faint ruffling of the bedding and stares up at the high ceiling. "Did we make a mistake?"

I snort. "You have to be more specific than that."

"You know what I mean. About *that*."

I know what Bella is referring to—our inheritance. "It's a bit late to worry about stealing it."

Bella sighs. "I regret trusting Xor. Now it's all gone. Aren't you sad about it?"

We never told Lilla that we gave all our inheritance to the rebellion leader as opposed to a little bit. She was already upset with us for stealing it.

"I do feel sad about it," I respond. "But at the time, we both agreed that we were doing the right thing. Remember?" We also wanted to prove to everyone, including our family, that we were capable of anything.

Bella rolls to her side and tucks her hands under her cheek. "It was quite a feat, wasn't it? Seventy layers of interconnected firewalls with traps all over the place. But we hacked it. I wish I could have seen whether Mom and Dad were proud of us. I hope they don't hate us."

"It doesn't matter. They'll never know it was us who did it." We left a bit of a surprise in the Barabal central network to cover up any clues we may have inadvertently left behind.

I recall my mom's smiling face whenever she mixed chemicals in her beakers. How my dad used to punch the air with his fist whenever he solved an equation. How our siblings, two sisters and two brothers, used to huddle around us every time we broke a complicated government code.

"Do you miss them too?"

Bella nods. "Yes, more than I thought I would. I was upset with Mom and Dad for so long, but now I know that they raised us to the best of their abilities, even if we never liked their methods."

They had an interesting parenting style, like reciting the prime numbers for hours while standing on one foot or going to bed hungry. But never corporal punishment.

"They did," I agree. "I thought joining the rebellion with Lilla was following their principles." Granted, in a roundabout way. Our parents raised us to be honest and to use science for the greater good. At the time, the rebellion on Uhna felt like the noblest cause I could have imagined. Now I know it was a huge mistake.

"At least, in the rebellion, we had an active part to play. Unlike in this Era War."

Bella swipes a few strands of short black hair away from her eyes. "Lilla needs us and you know it."

"I know but I wonder if all she'll ever see us as hackers and nothing more."

"Isn't that what we are? The best hackers in the Seven Galaxies?"

It's a bit of a self-proclaimed title, but still counts. "Yes, and that's an important role. But, Bella, don't you want to be more? Lilla was a princess, then a rebel, and now she is a sybil to the archgoddess. I wonder if we can handle such a big change."

Bella nods. "We made the right choice when we decided to leave behind the generational job of scientist. For me, that was enough. Besides, whenever we are with Lilla, we're always having fun."

"There is more to life than fun." Like being a general of an army. Or being the first inventor of Acerbus-infested technology used for good. Doing anything that makes me feel less of a follower and more of a leader.

Bella sits up. "What do you mean?"

I get out of the bed. "We'll discuss it later. Right now, we have a job to do." I shuffle to the chair and pick up black pants and a shirt—we made it from the black sheet that covered the bottom of the mattress—and pull them on. The black leather slippers our hosts provided complete my attire.

Bella yawns and gets dressed too. "Don't worry."

I glance at my sister. "About what?" Does she know how much I worry about wasting my life by not knowing what I truly want? How difficult it is to motivate myself some days because this burden weighs a ton? How difficult it is to put on a face so that no one will know the churning storm of emotions inside of me?

"About the device," Bella says. "I think it's ready."

Oh, that. "But what if the wiring starts to smoke again? I don't like the risk."

Bella crosses her arms. "You know I am the best at building holograms."

That's true. Bella has been building them since we were three years old.

My sister activates the hologram—two pillowcase-looking objects—one on each bed. It will create a life-like appearance of us resting, fooling anyone who comes to check on us.

Then she picks up the transparent orb key and opens the locked door.

Using a small mirror I pried off the bathroom wall, I check outside.

Dimmed lights show an empty corridor, with darkness beyond the tall windows.

"It's safe to go," I whisper to Bella.

The two of us tiptoe out of our room.

We stop at Lilla's door.

Muffled voices sound, as if she is carrying on a conversation.

Bella tilts her head toward the door. "Should we talk to her?"

I shake my head. "She must have a lot on her mind with worrying about Glennie, her husband, and the Era War. When we have something to tell her, we'll talk to her."

We hurry down the corridor.

"Remember all those nights we sneaked out of our rooms in the Crystal Palace to prank Nic?" Bella asks in a low voice. "This reminds of those times."

Poor Nic, Lilla's half-brother. "We pranked him so many times, and he never once saw it coming." He always assumed the best of everyone.

Bella's expression turns mournful. "He didn't deserve to die."

I nod. "So many perished in the battle on Uhna."

We creep down the stairs on silent feet until we reach the entrance of the mansion.

Bella uses her orb-key on the door. The lock clicks, and we slip outside. We lock it after us. Then we take the stairs and head to the right.

We barely manage a few steps when we hear the front door of the mansion open again.

For a second, I hesitate, then Bella grabs my hand and pulls me to the side. We squat by a tall bush with large pink leaves. Just in time too, as seven men, the Eldryan Elders, stride down the steps of the mansion.

Bella twists her fingers of both hands in a quick motion—our secret language we developed when we were young. *We must follow them.*

I cross two fingers. *I agree.*

The men take a left around the building. We jump up and trail them.

The elders don't go too far. They enter another building, located behind the mansion.

One of the elders glances up.

We plaster our backs to the wall and cover our mouths.

After a moment, I use my small mirror to peek.

The elders are gone.

"That was close," I whisper, and Bella adds, "Thank goodness for your freakishly good reflexes. It has saved us many times."

We look at each other. "We should find out where they went."

We creep to the metal door.

Bella uses the transparent orb again and a click sounds. I open the door to a crack and verify with my mirror that it's safe to proceed. An empty corridor comes to view.

Together, we enter. Straight ahead, a narrow tunnel with a low ceiling covered in dark gray brick waits.

Bella signs, *I don't like tunnels.*

Me neither. Nothing good ever comes from tunnels.

I reach out and pat her shoulder, then sign, *We are in this together.*

We hurry down the tunnel. It twists and turns for a few minutes, heading downward until it reaches an archway with elaborate symbols carved into it. The archway opens into an oval cavern. A few workstations stand on the left, covered in cobwebs.

Bella signs, *How come there is a cave when we entered a building?*

I sign back, *Isn't that the question.*

Then we notice the elders talking to someone we cannot see, far on the right. They gesture toward the many levers built into the cliffs with buttons and other high-tech features that stand out among the ancient rocks.

". . . It's our duty to preserve the force field . . ." one of the elders says.

". . . we still have a few days before the seven years are up . . ."

". . . why do we always have to play this game? Let's just get over it now. . ."

". . . too soon. Elder Christen is in a hurry to learn how to operate the force field . . ."

". . . we will in five days as the instructions specify . . ."

". . . after that we'll be ready to reaffirm the force field for another . . ."

The elders drone on, their voices mixing together.

I nod at Bella.

Hunched, we sneak back up the tunnel to exit the building.

Outside, Bella shakes her head. "It's not going to be easy to leave, is it?"

"No."

We hurry inside the mansion, not stopping until we are inside our room. After I lock the door, we undress, hide our black clothing, and quickly pull on our nightgowns. Then I deactivate the hologram and we dive into our beds, pulling the blankets all the way to our chin.

"Isa, this is bad. Really bad. What are we going to tell Lilla?"

I reach out and grasp my sister's hand. "Nothing for now. Besides, we have to first—"

"—examine the sculptures. I agree."

CHAPTER 33

LILLA—DAY 3

Kerr and I come to a stop.

He came to get me at the crack of dawn, and we sneaked out of mansion together.

The beautiful city that I glimpsed when I first entered this society looks even more stunning in the early light of dawn.

"Are you sure your clansman won't tell anyone that we left?"

"Their word is trustworthy, unlike the Eldryans'."

Careening my neck, I stare at the white buildings with greenery covering their sides, balconies, and rooftops. They do not look as new as they did from afar. There are long cracks visible on many cloudscrapers, and some balconies have chunks of plaster missing.

"What have they done to you and to your clansmen?"

Kerr guides me on a sidewalk between two cloudscrapers. "They tried to eradicate us. But we prevailed."

I wonder, dear, if they had a civil war. Considering that Kerr is in a servant-type role, I assume his clansmen did not win.

I nod. "Rulers often make the mistake of underestimating their subjects. Then they have to pay a hefty price for their mistake." I should know. Father treated the refugees on Uhna with little to no respect, bribed his way to be the leader of the Pax Septum Coalition, causing a rebellion to revolt against him—one that I was part of as well.

"Sounds like you speak of personal experience," Kerr says, quoting my own words back to me.

"The monarchy on my home world made many mistakes, and now there is no more of it left. Instead, they have a fledgling democracy."

"I cannot imagine a day where my clansmen and the Eldryans will live in peace."

I want to know more, but he glances away.

Many civilians, older men and women of all ages, stare at us.

"Is this going to be a problem?" I whisper to him. "My presence?"

Kerr curses. "It's not you who they are staring at."

I study the well-dressed citizens. Many do not bother to hide their disdain for Kerr. Others whisper behind their hands, laughing mockingly.

Moira taps a claw on her furry chin. *I wonder if societal rank is the issue, or something else.*

"I don't understand." I never grasped such contempt, even when I lived on Uhna. The way the court treated servants with such haughtiness that only emphasized the disparity between the ranks, or how they disregarded the refugees and their peril.

Anytime, dear, a group decides that they are better than another group based on monetary, racial, religious or any other consideration, they regress that society. Often such societies encounter civil unrest to right such wrongs.

Kerr raises his chin. "You are not the only one who doesn't understand."

We pass by a sixty-story-tall building, with tangles of foliage growing on every available surface. "It's impressive how the Eldryans cultivate plants," I say to change the topic.

Kerr grunts. It's so much like the sound Callum makes when he is not happy that my heart aches. I blink quickly. Now is not the time to get emotional.

"There are no farms in the City of Enigma," he explains. "The buildings are the only available surface for any agricultural means. The Eldryans have no choice but to take advantage of it or starve to death. We clansmen have no such problems."

"Is there any significance of who lives in what building?"

Kerr glances at me as we take a left on the cobblestone street. "The building itself in this section at least does not matter. However, which floor one lives on does. The civilians who are considered the top rank of society occupy the ten highest floors, often including the roof terrace. The next twenty floors are the middle class. The tradesmen occupy the rest."

"What made them do this?"

"Necessity," Kerr says. "But not everyone lives in this side of the city. There are areas with lower buildings that have little to no resources."

"We'll be seeing any of those?"

Kerr shakes his head as he comes to a stop next to a puddle in the middle of an alley. "We won't have time to explore the city much I'm afraid," he says, then points at the puddle. "This is our destination."

I recall the yellow-suited P.O.P. telling me to avoid the puddles at all costs. I back away. "I don't think so."

Kerr extends a hand. "I promised to help you."

I do trust him more than the P.O.P.

"Follow after me," he says, and jumps into the puddle, feet first, disappearing under the water.

I frown at the rippling murky water that cannot be deep enough to swallow up a six-and-a-half-foot-tall man, yet Kerr does not resurface.

Moira grimaces. *It seems we only have one choice here, dear.*

Holding the skirt of my dress close to me, I take a deep breath and jump in too.

CHAPTER 34

CADERYN

Caderyn strides through the city, heading toward a pub his guide Borr-ak recommended for gathering information.

Borr-ak stayed in the mansion, not wanting to risk discovery. Caderyn does not fault the honest man, who is much like a seasoned Teryn warrior—both have little to say, but when they speak it's important.

Caderyn spares a glance at the white buildings festooned with greenery on their sides. *Fancy living, overly luxurious—it stinks of weakness and softness. Where are the barracks? Where is the military? Those yellow-dressed Protectors of Peace, hurrying around like buzzing bees, are nothing but a joke.*

To his left, the upper part of a massive sculpture is visible.

Caderyn studies it.

Long braids fall around a scarred face of a warrior man with closed eyes. The mustache and well-kept braided beard make the sculpture's face radiate with an air of authority. Muscular shoulders with long arms crossed over powerful chest covered in light armor further emphasize the warrior's strength and power.

There must have been a model for that sculpture. A warrior leader perhaps. What happened to him? What happened to this society that ended up so pathetic? Unlike the warrior depicted by the sculpture. What a shame.

Shaking his head, he crosses the street. Many Eldryan civilians study him, but when he glowers at them, they scurry away in a hurry.

Good. That will show them who is in charge.

Caderyn clasps his hand behind his back.

Why can't Lilla respect me as easily as these people?

Caderyn searches for the tall tree with white blooms and vines as per Borr-ak's instruction. When he sees one growing to the left of a tall building, he heads toward it.

Lilla reminds me so much of my first wife, Korhina. She was willful and stubborn, always dismissing my advice or commands. She too ran into danger headfirst, causing a bigger problem than helping to solve a situation.

Caderyn reaches the tree. Next to the tree, a narrow alley waits. It is barely visible through large leaves of intercrossing green vines that grow from the tree to the building. He checks for any passersby, then he stoops under the oval leaves. He takes ten steps and turns toward the vine covered wall. He pulls the plant to the side to find a green door.

Borr-ak's directions were precise and methodical, leading Caderyn here unerringly. Otherwise, it would have been challenging to find this place.

He pushes the door open and marches in.

A typical pub greets him with the fumes of beer, both fresh and regurgitated, mixing with the acidic smell of wines, unwashed bodies, and fear.

Caderyn marches across the sticky stone floor, passing rickety wooden tables with plastic chairs around them full of desperate and pitiful people.

He heads toward the counter where a single man sits, one that he recognizes, and the origin of the other patrons' fear—Esteemed Elder Corrigan.

How suspicious to find the pretentious elder here in this disgusting, sandcursed place.

Caderyn takes a seat next to the elder, making sure not to touch the grimy metal counter.

Corrigan slams down his wooden mug, spilling a foaming green beer. Then the elder mutters, his voice rising to a shout, which scares the patrons even more. Yet Caderyn cannot smell alcohol on the elder's breath.

Corrigan is pretending to be drunk and putting on quite a show. But why?

Caderyn gestures to the cowering bartender, pointing at the green beer and showing two fingers. "Next round is on me."

The thin bartender gestures toward a woven basket full of root vegetables and packets of seeds. "No need. He paid enough for a few rounds."

Caderyn inclines his head. "Much appreciated." Especially since he has nothing to pay with. Interestingly, they seem to employ a rudimentary barter system.

The elder turns to Caderyn. "You recognize me," he says, slightly slurring his words.

"I make it my business to remember those who are in charge."

Corrigan perks up, then his expression sours and he gulps from the green beer. "I am not in charge anymore."

Caderyn waits until the bartender places two foaming mugs in front of them, then asks, "How come?"

Corrigan chugs down the rest of his first beer, then pushes the mug away and reaches for the fresh one. "I made a mistake."

Caderyn leans forward. "I'm listening." It never ceases to amaze him how much people enjoy complaining when someone has an ear to lend. Lots of useful information can be gained from such venting.

Corrigan lifts his second mug and gulps it down. "I hired some of the V-maids to take out one, maybe two, but no more than three elders. Nothing serious, really; just a bit of incapacitation like a few broken bones."

"V-maids?" Caderyn asks, hiding his amusement at how quickly the other man forgot about pretending to be drunk, and how he is now well on his way to be truly drunk. Another reason Caderyn never took to drinking alcohol. Once you start, it's hard to stop, or easy to forget how much you had. Giving up control over his thoughts and actions was not something Caderyn allowed—ever.

Corrigan hiccups, then gestures toward the other mug. Caderyn helpfully places the beer in front of the ex-elder.

"We call your guides many names, like: V-maids for vampire-mermaids—I mean they take your blood to bond with you, for godssake, and live in those puddles like some kind of mermaid, which is, um, the other name we have for them, puddle people, but *shhhh!* It's not very nice to say." Corrigan tries to place his finger on his lips, succeeding only on the third try. He burps, smiles at Caderyn, and asks, "What were we talking about?"

"About what you did to get here."

Corrigan drinks some more green beer. "Well, not only did the V-maids fail, somehow the others found out about it, and they kicked me out. I would have resigned anyway since I am too old to be an elder as per our laws. I turn forty at midnight."

Corrigan gestures for more beer.

The bartender grimaces and puts a foaming green pitcher on the counter in front of them. "This is the last one; you hear me? I don't want you to cause any problems."

Corrigan shrugs and reaches for the pitcher but misses the curving handle entirely.

Caderyn pours beer into the ex-elder's mug. "I don't see how turning forty is a problem. You are still young." The praelor does not feel his true age, sixty-five. He remembers that he was in prime shape when he was in his forties.

Corrigan grins, revealing teeth covered in a green sheen. "I am, aren't I? I have so much more to give. I am smart, and cunning, and . . . I forgot."

Caderyn frowns. "You are lucky you got away so easily."

Attempted murder of government officials is treason. Consuasor Finigal learned the hard way, but then again, that consuasor was too busy with his plans for a coup to realize the mistakes he made against me.

Caderyn chuckles recalling how it was Lilla who ruined the consuasor's plans. Though at the time, he was not happy with her interfering.

Lilla needs to learn what it means to rule decisively. How to be unfeeling for her own sake. Kindness is weakness; it is something others take advantage of. She needs to be more ruthless.

Corrigan shakes his head. "I told you already. I didn't want to leave the council of elders. But it doesn't matter anymore." He reaches for his mug and misses, then stares at his own hands as if he'd never seen anything so special.

Caderyn shakes his head. "What are you *really* doing here?"

Corrigan's eyelids close, and his head falls forward, waking him up. "Oh, I am here," he whispers, "because of the Grandfather Revolution." Then he adds in a raised tone, "But don't tell anyone!"

Caderyn strokes his beard with a cunning expression.

This is why Borr-ak wanted me to come here—to find the Grandfather Revolution. Now that's something I can use to my advantage to get out of this place. I despise being away from battle.

Caderyn studies Corrigan, who has fallen asleep again, this time with his head resting on his crossed arms.

He is not surprised that there is a revolution, though it does not have the most awe-inspiring name. The way these so-called elders—younglings all of them—rule this society leaves a lot of opening for insurrection. Yet more proof how important it is to rule with an iron fist. They did not stifle this revolution in the beginning. Now Caderyn can overthrow the elders and get back to the battlefield.

That will teach them not to imprison the Teryn praelor.

Caderyn pats the other man's shoulder—noting how little strength is in there—waking him up. "I'll keep your secret. Tell me all you know. Don't leave anything out."

Corrigan upends his mug, but only a few drips fall out. "I first heard about them, four—no, five years ago." Hiccup. "They were a small group, a fledgling revolution." Hiccup. "Nothing important to deal with." Hiccup. "I decided to not report them and keep them as a what's the word? Not primary plan but secondary . . ."

"A backup plan?"

Corrigan jabs his forefinger on the counter. "Yes! I kept them as a backup plan. I told you I was wily!"

"Yes, you did. You would have been a great consuasor."

Corrigan frowns. "I do not know what that means but thank you."

It wasn't a compliment.

Corrigan stares at the bottles longingly behind the bartender.

"Keep going," Caderyn prompts him.

Corrigan rubs his face. "Oh, that's about it." He points at a man with a graying mustache who must be in his fifties sitting all the way at the back of the pub near another door. "You have to convince him to let us join their ranks. He is their leader."

Caderyn turns to stare at the leader of the revolution. The man looks up, narrows his eyes, but after a moment glances away.

Caderyn grins. *That's not going to be a problem. I can tell they are in desperate need of a real leader like me.*

Caderyn gets to his feet, but Corrigan reaches out and stops him with a hand on his forearm. "Promise that you get me in as well."

Caderyn shakes off the ex-elder's hand. "Fine," he says. Corrigan's information might come in handy later. "Now sober up."

CHAPTER 35

LILLA

Cold water laps over my head, shocking my body. My dress flares out around me, but I push the soft fabric down. A line of bubbles escape from my mouth. I sink fast in the semi-dark, landing into a narrow but smooth stone tunnel.

I hope I won't run out of air.

Don't think about that, dear. I'm sure it's almost over.

Suddenly the tunnel widens.

Before me a vast, colorful cavern comes into view. The transparent water shines in soft bluish light, illuminated by sponge-like creatures that cover most of the cave walls. Many more caves open all around us. Above me more tunnels end, with others entering the cavern the same way I did.

I look down, paddling in place. Somehow, I lost Kerr, and now I'm not sure what to do.

The water around me bursts with activity from schools of fish, color-changing octopi hunting them, and more people like Kerr swimming nearby.

My lungs strain for air. I desperately scan for a place to surface but find nothing.

Relief floods me when I see Kerr swimming my way, carrying a glass orb with a black tube floating out of it. He hands it to me, indicating to pull it on.

I would hurry if I were you, dear. Drowning is not a nice way to go.

Quickly, I put it on. The bottom of the glass orb seals at my neck, and I gulp down air. A fan-like sound echoes in the orb, coming from the back tube.

It's probably filtering the water, dear. Nothing to worry about.

I nod.

Kerr signs with his hands while his bare webbed feet tread water. Fins spread from his legs and from his forearms, and his gills work at the sides of his neck.

I shake my head, not understanding his meaning.

Kerr points at fish with yellow tails and gives me a thumb up. Then he gestures toward fish with red stripes and shakes his head. He mimics biting by closing and opening his fingers.

I nod.

He points at the closest sponges on the wall. A round fish swims by it. The sponge shoots a few thorns at it, but the fish keeps swimming oblivious.

Best to avoid them, dear.

I nod again.

A brown mammal, no longer than three and a half feet, swims up to us with four dorsal fins and a large tail. Its round head holds curious black eyes with elongated beak full of sharp teeth.

Kerr grasps my hand and puts it on the back of the animal. It immediately turns on its back, showing me its lighter brown stomach.

Gently I rub its belly. "Look how much it loves it."

The animal lets out a series of clicks, sounding disturbed, and with a big swat of its tail it swims away.

"What did I do?"

Kerr shoves a hand into the middle of my chest, pushing me backward with a thunderous expression.

What is happening?

I flail my arms, avoiding the rock wall.

Three large men swim past, a hairsbreadth away from me.

I don't think everyone is as welcoming to our presence, dear, as Kerr.

Kerr throws a spike-covered rock after the men but misses. He looks back at me, the gills flaring on his neck.

Don't mind them, dear.

I'm starting to have doubts about what kind of solution Kerr might have.

It's too late now, dear, to change your mind. Let's hope for the best.

Kerr reaches for my hand, and we dive deeper.

CHAPTER 36

Scuffling my feet, I wander the streets aimlessly. But that's only a pretense. I'm observing the citizens of the Eldryan society that like to hide under the force field dome. Makes me wonder if they ever lived outside of it. If they did, could those ruins we encountered near the Teryn compound belong to their ancestors?

Probably. It doesn't matter now.

I turn my attention to my surroundings.

At first glance, the cloudscrapers are impressive but when you take a closer look, you notice that's not the case—many buildings are worn and in need of repair.

I listen in on conversations of the passersby, learning how the Eldryan citizens use puddle people—their derogatory name for the Neath—as servants. They justify the name because that is where the Neath people emerge from— those puddles the P.O.P. warned us about. But I have no doubt that they use the term to express superiority over the Neath clan members. It's their version of drawing caste lines.

My Neath guard—I won't call him a guide; even I am not that stupid to believe it—was just as uninterested in bonding with me as I was with him. He looked the other way when I slipped out of the lavish guest room—thanks to the hologram and key the twins made for all of us.

I cross the street, taking long strides as if I'm dancing. All those stares slide off once they classify me as crazy. No matter where I am, that trick never ceases to work.

I take a right turn when someone runs into me.

"Ow!" I exclaim.

The young woman lifts her head and blinks at me, as if she just realized that there are other people outside of her. How self-centered.

The woman tucks a strand of long chestnut brown hair behind her ear and steps back. "I am so sorry. I wasn't looking."

"Only someone with little intelligence would stare at the ground instead of where she is going."

The young woman blinks. "Are you saying that I am stupid?"

I scoff. "I don't have to say it; it's implied."

She stares at me for a long moment, then laughs.

It's the sweetest laugh I've heard in my life. It's disarming.

I extend a hand. "My name is Ivy, and you are?"

She places her delicate fingers in my hand for a handshake. "I'm Fiona. You are quite rude."

Her touch sends goosebumps up my arm. "Yes, I am, but at least I excel at it."

Fiona smiles. "Are you new to the City of Enigma?"

"Yes, though I can't say I ended up here on purpose. For poison's sake, I'm not even supposed to leave that fancy mansion where your snooty elders live." I don't know why, but I instantly trust her.

Fiona pulls her hand from mine. I squeeze it before letting it slip away.

She blushes. "I could give you a tour."

"I'd love that."

Shyly, she glances away and resumes her walk.

After a few moments, I ask, "Can you tell me why everyone uses 'Together, we are happy!' as a greeting?"

"Oh, it's a shortened version of 'Together, we have to stay under the force field—it's safe here, and it's the only way to live happily."

I grin at her. "That must have been quite a mouthful."

"It was. By the time my grandparents were marrying age, it was already out of fashion. Thank the elders for that!"

A strand of hair gets stuck on her cheek. I reach out and gently brush it off.

A blush darkens Fiona's face. She clears her throat and gestures ahead. "We should start there and make our way back."

"Fine by me." The more time I get to spend with her, the better. Who said I can't have fun while spying? I'm sure Lilla won't mind. She is much more flexible than her best friend, Glenna, who always regards me with suspicion.

Fiona gestures at a building and gives a long-winded explanation about it, but I tune out the words. I only listen to her sweet voice that makes me feel as if I am home, even though I have never really had one.

She grasps my hand when I am slow to follow her and drags me toward a fountain. She reaches into the water and splashes me playfully.

I laugh and scoop up a palmful of cool water, then flick it at her.

Fiona giggles, then gets to her feet and we resume our trek through the city.

A sculpture of a woman with closed eyes becomes visible between two cloudscrapers. Her braided hair hangs over her right shoulder. She wears a wrap-style long dress, with light armor protecting her chest. Her feet tucked into leather boots. She holds a mace with two hands.

"What is that?" I ask, squinting at the sculpture.

Fiona turns to look. "Oh, that? I don't know."

"Are you jesting?"

Fiona shakes her head. "I am not. The knowledge of those sculptures has been lost for many years now. There are only a few people who might know about it."

"Like whom?"

Fiona grimaces. "Like my mother. Anyway, let's keep going. There's so much more I want to show you."

I fall in step with her. I sense conflict with her mother. Or maybe I'm just projecting my own mommy issues.

After a few seconds, Fiona's cheerful mood returns. We cut through the city, stopping occasionally when she indicates something of interest.

I know I should pay attention to her, but I've never felt the way I feel in her presence. Happy. Joyful. Playful.

None are words that I would normally use to describe myself.

As the sun sets, we arrive back where started the tour.

Fiona glances at me then quickly away, biting on her lower lip.

I reach out and play with a long strand of her hair on her shoulder. "I had fun."

Fiona's cheeks turn red. "Me too."

I don't move, neither does she.

Is this a goodbye? Does she feel the same way I do?

After a long moment of silence, I sigh. How could she feel anything when we've only known each other for a few hours? I guess it was all in my head.

"Well," I say, turning away.

Suddenly, she grabs my hand. "Would you . . ." Her voice trails off but then she raises her chin and continues, "Would you like to come up for tea?"

I grin. "Yes, I would."

CHAPTER 37

LILLA

After descending a few minutes, we reach the bottom of the cave. Looking up, I can't help but marvel how deep the cave system goes. How full of life it is.

We swim toward a tunnel on my right and follow it until we reach the end. Then we climb up a dozen stairs leading us out of the water. At the top of the stairs, another cave awaits, dripping but otherwise dry. The cave walls, covered with a mix of luminescent sponge creatures and flower-like pink stars, create a welcoming ambiance.

Kerr turns to me and removes the orb device from my head. I inhale the damp and moldy scent of the cave as I wring water out of my dress and hair.

What a beautiful place this is, dear.

Let's hope that it's not only an illusion.

A slender older woman steps out from a tunnel on the left. Long, teal-colored hair frames a stunning face. She too wears the green pantsuit decorated with shells. The pinkish fins on her legs and arms lie flat on the fabric. Her three pair of gills stay closed on her light-gray-colored neck.

When her dark teal gaze lands on me, she blinks as if she recognizes me.

That would not be possible, dear, would it?

Correct. I've never been on Cathal before.

Kerr places the glass orb on a nearby rock and bows his head. "May you swim in clear water, Matriarch."

She bows her head and murmurs the same words back to him.

Kerr gestures for me to step forward. "Allow me to introduce you to Lilla."

I bow.

"Lilla, this is our clans' uniter, matriarch, and leader of all the Neath people, Larr-Na, from the clan of Narral."

"May you find calm waters, Lilla," she says in a cool voice.

I'm sensing a bit of resentment coming from the matriarch, dear. I find that interesting.

"Who are you?" Larr asks. She looks me up and down with a frown.

"I am Lilla, as Kerr told you, from the oceanic world of Uhna, located in Galaxy Five."

Kerr crosses his arms and positions himself next to me.

Larr glances at him. "You are quite a distance from your home world. What brought you here?"

"I came here with the Teryn praelor," I say, avoiding the full answer to her question.

Larr tilts her head. "What is a 'praelor'?"

"It is title that means emperor," I explain.

She watches me, her irises contracting into narrow slits. "Are you a Lumenian?"

Twice since we've come to this planet has someone inquired about it, dear. While the legends of Lumenians are widespread, this feels more than just a coincidence.

My gaze flickers to Kerr. He studies me, waiting for my answer as well.

I don't respond.

Technically, dear, silence is an answer on its own.

But not a full acknowledgement.

Kerr clears his throat. "We don't have a lot of time to waste. I brought Lilla here to talk to you and not to be interrogated. She needs our help."

Larr blinks and her irises return to their normal round shape. "Kerr, I wasn't interrogating her. I simply asked a question." She adds, "I see you've already bonded. I do hope you won't make the same mistake twice."

Kerr's expression shuts down, becoming unreadable.

I wonder what mistake his matriarch is referring to, dear.

"How are you doing, Kerr?" Larr asks.

Kerr stares at her in response.

Larr sighs. "Please wait here, Kerr."

Kerr inclines his chin.

Larr turns away from him, then gestures to a tunnel in the middle of a small cave. "Then let us talk."

CHAPTER 38

Larr and I enter a narrow barely illuminated tunnel. She goes in front of me, as it's only wide enough for one person.

My head and elbows scrape at the tight space. Suddenly, my chest tightens, and cold sweat breaks out on my body.

Remember to slow down your breathing, dear.

Focusing on inhaling the humid air, and blowing it out through my mouth, I convince myself that everything is going to be okay. That this tunnel cannot last forever.

Larr looks over her shoulder, watching me with an expression void of compassion, then turns back.

That's it, dear.

Finally we leave the tunnel and enter a roughly rectangular shaped cave with eight sections of walls covered in paintings—some faded and old while others are in a better condition.

Larr stops at the closest painting with most of the color gone. "Behold the history of the Neath people."

I wasn't expecting a history lesson.

The matriarch might be testing you, dear. My advice would be to pay attention.

I turn to the first illustration that shows Cathal covered in many lakes and connected by rivers with an ocean visible at the bottom.

"A long time ago we lived in harmony on this world, ruling the waters with no one threatening our safety," Larr says with a wistfulness in her voice. "But the planet changed and so did our lives."

The next section portrays the lakes and the ocean disappearing, retreating under the ground.

"We adapted as best as we could, forming clans, ruled by a matriarch or patriarch," Larr explains. "The role is an honorary one, not hereditary but earned. We still spent half our lives Above on the land—as there was no one else outside of us—the other half in the Neath."

The third illustration shows people arriving from space.

Larr's voice deepens with emotion. "Then the colonists arrived, claiming Above with their vast numbers. Building their cities. The Above people evolved, forgetting all about their origin. We did not interfered or fought them. Instead, we withdrew to the Neath and to our caves. We loved and still love our aquatic life."

The fourth mural depicts thriving Neath clan members playing, swimming, and frolicking with animals or with their youngsters.

The fifth illustration displays the same swimming Neath clans but there is blood saturating the top of the mural.

"Then war ravaged the planet, destroying cities. The Above decided to hide behind a force field, abandoning their surviving cities only to focus on building this society. Then not long after they hid, almost three hundred years ago, a sort of madness infected many driving them to a killing spree against their own. The Eldryan Elders fought them and exacted a price from all related to them."

The sixth section depicts the Neath people cradling babies and other young Eldryan children.

"On the Night of Blood, I made the decision to save the younglings who had nothing to do with their families' madness. We hid them until we found them new homes Above, one where no one would look."

The seventh mural shows Neath clan members dragged from puddles, or being beaten, or hanging from trees.

"I should have known better than to interfere," Larr says, her voice buckling. "I risked too much with my compassion. Above people and Neath people are not compatible. They discovered what we did, helping the Children of the Cursed, but couldn't find where those younglings disappeared. We told them we knew nothing of what happened, which was a partial truth. Once we found an Above person to take the children, we did not ask any questions for our own sake. But the Eldryans didn't believe us. They punished us, hunted us, and killed many of us. Years passed and the Above people still did not forget."

The eighth illustration is only half finished, displaying Larr talking to someone in a white robe.

"I made a pact with the Eldryan Elders to save my clans," Larr says bitterly. "I promised the Above people a hundred years of servitude—one sixth of our lives—as long as they don't kill any more of my people. They accepted. Now we shall see how the rest of our history will play out."

Oppressed and forced into servitude, all because of saving children.

History rarely makes sense, dear. It only cares about the victorious and ignores those who lost.

Larr steps to the first mural, acting as if she is not watching me, but when I focus on the painting, I feel the matriarch's eyes on me. Moira was right. This is important to the matriarch.

"Preserving your clan's history is a very important job," I say. "If we forget our history or ignore our mistakes, we can never learn from them." I look at her and add, "However, I do not consider saving children a mistake, for whatever it's worth."

Larr clasps her hands.

A sparkle catches my eye just above the first section where Larr is standing. I make my way toward it.

The words seem familiar, as if I should be able to read them, but I cannot. The letters are curling, beautiful, and the writing seems ancient, older than the paintings.

"What is that language above the mural?" I ask, gesturing above the mural.

Larr's gaze follows where I point. "I don't see anything there."

It must be a magical language that only I can see.

It seems so, dear.

"Thank you for sharing the history of your people. I am humbled. I can promise you that I will not take advantage of Kerr or you."

Larr inclines her head. "Time will tell who you really are. We best get back, lest Kerr will be worried."

I follow her into the tunnel. "I came to ask for your help. Will—"

"I know," Larr interrupts. We emerge from the tunnel into the cave much quicker than on the way to the murals. "However, there is no more time today to discuss the matter. You must come back tomorrow. I do not want to keep Kerr away from the elders' home for too long or he will get into trouble."

CHAPTER 39

CALLUM

Callum cuts a dark fiend in front of him into two with a powerful slash of his longsword. Hot oily blood spatters across his face.

He wipes the blood off, ignoring the putrid smell. Then he turns to face another corrupted monster standing on eight disjointed insect legs with a protruding stomach and a short neck. Almost-humanoid dark eyes shine blankly, giving away that there is no intelligence there, just hatred.

"How much longer?" Rhona asks from his left, slashing at two dark fiends, cutting one's arm off at the shoulder and slicing the other across its protruding stomach.

They've been coming back and fighting by the force field where his wife disappeared for three days now. Fearghas has joined them too, kicking and clawing the rock outcrop disguise, but no cracks have appeared so far. S'affi emerged too, fluttering at the rocks, revealing the disguised force field. Her transparent and glittering wings leave a sparkling magical trail, but do not affect the force field otherwise.

I should have been the one stuck there! Gods know what Lilla must be going through!

He ducks under a jab from the leg of another insectoid monster and cuts it off at the joint as he straightens up. Then he dances away before the clawed hands can tear into him.

If I must kill every one of these abominations to get to Lilla, then I will!

Callum pulls his longsword back, steps to the side, and slashes a monster across its hairy chest. The fiend stumbles and falls to the ground.

"Rhona has a point," Teague says, his left shoulder bandaged. "We can only keep at this for so long."

"I don't want to discuss it," Callum growls, and kicks a skittering dark fiend away from him. Then he hammers a punch at another and stabs back-ward at an insectoid monster lurking behind him.

Rage boils inside of him every time his mind replays the moment the force field closed in front of Lilla. He was too far away from her, lost in the battle fever.

Four ursine dark fiends with burly bodies and two heads rush at him. He jumps up and kicks the first one in the head, propelling it into the others. The bear-monsters turn on each other, snarling and biting, momentarily forgetting about him.

"The possibility for the force field opening in the same spot is exponen-tially low," Rhona says, as she cuts the head of a twig-like monster with a dozen arms.

A simian dark fiend claws Fearghas's hide. The battle horse bucks. The kicks land in the middle of the beast's chest, breaking through bones with a terrible crunch. The fiend crumbles to the ground. S'affi levitates the second fiend before it can reach Fearghas, then vanishes the monster. Both return their attention back to the fake rocks, clawing or battering them.

Teague sidesteps a porcine monster, then slams his longsword down into the middle of its back. It lets out a piercing shriek as it flails. "I second what Rhona said."

Callum slices ursine monsters with methodical swipes. "I'd rather die than move from this spot." He removes the dark blood from his blade by dragging it through the thick fur of the closest twitching dark fiend.

I will get back to Lilla, even if it's the last thing I do.

"You know it's only a matter time before these dark fiends regenerate," Rhona says, eyeing a large group of corpses in front of her. "These are at least half-corrupted." She wipes sweat off her face, smearing the black blood drops on her cheek.

Teague nods. "We have to go. The sun is already setting too."

Fearghas neighs, and S'affi chitters as if in protest.

Callum understands their reasoning, but that doesn't mean he agrees with them.

He lifts his head and roars his rage to the green-hued sky.

Teague puts a hand on Callum's shoulder. "It's what Lilla would want."

Fearghas snorts, stomping and swishing his tail. S'affi bats her transparent wings, the glitter turning dark red as if responding to the magical animal's temper.

Callum curses and whirls toward the force field, shaking off his friend's hand. Fearghas moves to the side to make room for him. S'affi hovers at his back as if protecting him. Then Callum swings his sword into the force field multiple times.

Sparks fly but nothing else happens.

"Let go, brother," Teague says. "Recover. Then we can come back with renewed energy."

Rhona strides to Callum, stepping over scattered monster parts. "We *will* come back."

Fearghas neighs and bobs his head while S'affi settles on the battle horse's back. Callum pats his muscled neck.

I hate that Rhona is right. I hate the setting sun's light. And I hate that I must wait the whole night.

A still-mobile dark fiend drags its severed upper body toward his sister.

Callum slams the sword into its spine, twisting it. "Fine. We will come back by dawn."

CHAPTER 40

With the help of Kerr, I climb out of the puddle. A cool breeze cuts through my wet dress, and I shiver. His green jumpsuit is already dry.

"How is that possible?" I ask and gesture at his clothing.

"Our jumpsuits are designed to dry quickly once out of water."

To my suprise, I wish that I could access my magic to dry my dress. Ragnald would be proud to know I paid attention to his lessons. I hope he's keeping Glenna safe among all the mages.

"We should go," Kerr says, leading me away from the puddle.

I give a last wring to the soaked fabric, then follow him, heading toward the mansion.

The traffic on the streets has lessened as the sun nears its horizon. My teeth chatter and my body shudders over and over again.

A swirl of fabric from around the corner grabs my attention.

A blond woman hurries by, looking like a ghost from my past.

Without thinking, I turn and follow her. When I get close, I grab her arm and turn her to face me.

"Let go of me," the stranger says.

I release her arm and murmur an apology. Kerr bows to the lady, then we cross the street, away from the upset woman.

What is it, dear?

I thought I saw Beathag.

Isn't she dead, dear?

She is. It was only my imagination playing a trick on me.

I sense that there is more to this, dear. Care to enlighten this old queen?

You are not old, but sure. I have been having recurring nightmares about the battle with DLD, back on Uhna. I always see my half-brother Nic die, then Irvine, followed by Beathag. I wish . . . I just wish I could have . . . I don't know.

Moira nods. *It's grief, dear, mixed with a big dose of guilt.*

I laugh bitterly. *How can I have any guilt over Irvine, who was a horrible ma'har? Or Beathag, who betrayed me, lied to me, and hurt me so many ways I lost count? How can I put them in the same group as Nic? Why should I feel culpability over those two deaths when I should feel grief only for Nic's?*

Grief and guilt often go hand in hand, dear. Our heart has other ideas than our mind. There is no logic in grief. While guilt is another manifestation of regret. We often regretting missing out on a chance or an opportunity.

Frowning, I come to a halt.

Are you saying that I have regrets?

Think about it, dear. Why else would you think about them in such order?

Kerr turns right only to retrace his steps when he realizes I am not following after him. He frowns in disappointment.

I increase my pace to catch up.

"We are almost at the house," he says. "Please don't wander off anymore."

"I won't."

You're right, Moira. I'm regretting how harsh I was to Beathag. She reached out to reconnect with me, but I refused to even hear her out. I pushed her away when she gave back my mom's diary and confessed what she did. I did not have it in my heart to forgive her or forget all that she did against me.

Forgiveness does not mean forgetting, dear. It means you let go of your regret, your guilt, and your anger toward that person.

It's not that easy, Moira. Beathag almost caused Belthair's death. She kept from me the secret of being my half-sister. For godssake, she married Father!

Full of disgust, I don't pay attention to where I step and I stumble, earning a questioning look from Kerr.

Now let's be reasonable here, dear. First of all, your father didn't know that Beathag was his daughter. Second of all, from what I've seen in your memories, it was obvious that she wanted to have power. Third of all, just because Beathag married your father doesn't mean she had a wedding night, now does it?

I think through Moira's suggestion as we sneak back into the mansion through a side entrance used by the servants. We nod at the Neath clansmen, then hurry up the stairs. I stop at Caderyn's room to check on him, but he is not in. Same with the twins and Ivy.

Kerr escorts me to my room, then leaves.

I did notice that Beathag used a minor form of magic to manipulate Father, though at the time I wasn't sure what she was doing.

I drop down in a chair, staring out the window at the last orange rays of the setting sun. There is another platter with fruits, nuts, and root vegetables waiting for me next to a pitcher of cold water and an empty glass.

Then it is highly possible, dear, that she had been manipulating him a lot longer than you might have been aware of. By the time she married him . . .

He would not have even noticed if she made him fall asleep alone after the wedding.

Exactly!

For a few seconds, I concentrate on eating my dinner. Then I pour myself a glass of water.

It is true that Beathag was interested in becoming a queen and nothing else, I know that much.

Your father, dear, was the easiest path for her to achieve her goal. Once becoming a queen, she probably would have killed the ma'ha to avoid sharing the throne with him. She might have killed Nic too, seeing how he was the direct heir to the throne. Which also explains why she convinced your father to arrange marriage contracts for you—so she could get rid of you before you could stop her machinations.

I pop a handful of nuts into my mouth. They taste slightly sweet.

That does not change the fact that she lied to me, and how far she was willing to go for power.

Dear, she cared for you, in her own strange way. Remember, love that turns to hate is still rooted in love.

I doubt Beathag loved anyone but herself.

Moira stifles a yawn. *She is gone now, and you have nothing to worry about. Try to forgive her, then live your life in peace. Besides, you have bigger problems to deal with—such as getting out of this place.*

CHAPTER 41

CADERYN

Under the weak light of the setting sun, Caderyn examines the hundred and fifty revolutionary men—all above the age of forty, some even as old as eighty—gathered in a wide alleyway behind a cloudscraper. The smell of garbage irritates him, but he refuses to acknowledge it. Instead, he clasps his hands behind his back and glowers at the men.

"Woeful," Caderyn says, as he marches in front of the first line. "Weak. Disappointing." None of these wimps even know how to stand strong or wield a weapon other than their makeshift bats and axes. *Useless.*

Caderyn exhales. It didn't take long for him to realize how little organization went into the Grandfather Revolution. They were almost relieved when he took over their leadership—all he had to do was to glare at their so-called leader and the leadership was his. And that wasn't the worst of it.

None of them have ever seen combat or know anything about fighting.

Corrigan crosses his arms. "Do not underestimate these men, many served as elders before. They're brave and courageous."

Caderyn glowers at Corrigan.

I should have never allowed him to join the revolution. He is the weakest of them all.

"Is that right, ex-elder?" Caderyn asks. "What do you know about fighting and revolution?"

Corrigan pushes away from the wall and kicks a piece of trash out of his way. "I know that you will train these men. We will oust the elders and establish a new rule."

He is a power hungry one, isn't he? It's good to have ambition, but too much of it will lead to disaster. Not that I care what happens to this pathetic ex-elder.

That's one thing Lilla doesn't have—a craving for power. On one hand, I find that admirable. I always know where I stand with her because she is honest and straightforward.

On the other hand, I worry Lilla will make the wrong decision, trying to avoid the responsibility that comes with leadership. It will only make others pay the price of such a mistake.

Caderyn pokes a man between the shoulder blades. "Straighten up."

The man jerks up, practically peeing in his pants.

By the age of twenty, Korhina knew what she wanted—to be the best general in the Teryn armada. She fought for that aspiration every single day.

Lilla does not know where her place is, even if she's claimed the sybil rank. She is disrespectful toward the archgods, calling them by silly nicknames. She is still searching for her true place in the Seven Galaxies.

If only she would listen to me when I try to help her. Everything would be better.

Caderyn stifles a growl and makes his way behind the last line of men. Then he returns to the front to address them.

"I do not care what kind of rule you will establish," Caderyn says. "I am here to lead this . . . revolution to success. Then I am leaving the Eldryan society with the others."

The men, including Corrigan, cheer.

Gods, they are contemptible! As long as they serve my purpose, I will not let my distaste for them affect me.

CHAPTER 42

My k'bug crackles behind my ear, waking me up from a restless sleep in the middle of the night.

"Lilla?" Callum's voice sounds. "Can you hear me? Is this thing working?"

I sit up in the bed, blinking in the dark as if I could conjure him in the room. "Callum? Is that you?"

Moira snuffles, then continues snoring in my head.

Teague's voice sounds muted in the background. "I told you she is fine."

"You owe me a favor for getting you a dozen k'bugs," Rhona says, her voice similarly muted. "You're lucky Dad is not here, or he would have grounded us."

"I am not doing anything that breaks the Ground Rules," Callum growls. "Now, can you two give me some privacy? I'd love to talk to my wife."

"Just remember," Teague says, "the tent's walls are thin, and we can hear *every* word."

A thud sounds.

"No need to throw your boot at me," Teague grumbles. "I was merely being helpful."

"Just go," Rhona says. Then receding footsteps sound.

"How are you, my love and life? Are you okay?"

I close my eyes and imagine him sitting next to me on the bed. "I'm doing well, considering."

"I miss you."

Tears spring into my eyes but I don't let them fall. "I miss you too."

"What happened? Where are you?"

"We ended up in a secret society called Eldryan. They live under a force field and are governed by elders who are in reality young men, ranging from late teen to forty. They gave us guest rooms and treat us well. They called your father an esteemed grandfather."

Callum snorts. "I bet he didn't like that."

I laugh, recalling Caderyn's offended expression. "Not one bit. How are you? How are Teague, Belthair, and Arrov doing? Were their injures serious? How are Fearghas and S'affi?"

"I don't care how they are doing." I hear Teague from the background, "Hey! I care! Tell her that we are fine. None of us had a critical injury. Fearghas and S'affi are missing you—"

Another thud sounds.

Teague yelps. "Callum, stop throwing your boot at me!"

"I will when you stop interrupting my conversation with my wife! Lilla, when are you coming back?"

"I am not sure. We' re a bit stuck here for now but trying to find our way back to you."

"If I could break down that force field I would. I won't stop until I see you again."

Rhona's voice sounds, "Oh my gods! Is that why I stole those k'bugs, so you can chitchat?! Ask her how the force field works! Or if she found out anything useful for us."

"Rhona, butt out of this conversation," Callum growls. "Lilla, are you safe at least?"

"Yes, as safe as possible. They've assigned guards to us, and we bonded—" The second the words are out of my mouth, I know I made a mistake.

"Bonded? Teague, what does 'bonded' mean?"

"Now you want me to be part of the conversation? How would I know?! I am sure it's nothing like being mated."

"It's not what you think—" I manage to say.

"I don't like the sound of it," Callum snarls.

"Why don't you ask Lilla if you're so worried about it?" Teague asks.

For the love of deepwater sharks! "It's not like being mated! Only a formality."

Callum inhales sharply. "Good. That's good."

"I smell blood," Teague says. "Callum, one of your wounds is bleeding again."

"Wounds?" I squeak.

"It's nothing to worry about," Callum responds, just as Teague says, "He's been fighting by the same spot you disappeared for days, wearing himself down and getting injured."

Oh no!

"Callum, you should have taken better care of yourself."

"I was," Callum mutters.

"He wasn't," Rhona says. "He keeps running into battle."

Buckets of fishguts!

"Try not to spend too long on the k'bugs," Teague says, "or they will implode from the strain."

"I hate being away from you," Callum says.

I wipe at my eyes. "Me too, light of my life. I will find a way back, I promise."

"Don't make promises you can't keep," Rhona says snidely.

"Remember, who we're talking about," Teague says. "She might be directionally-challenged but she found a way back from the Spirit Realm when no one else ever did."

Rhona scoffs. "That might be true; however, Lilla lacks common sense."

Do tell how you feel. "Thanks, Rhona."

"I believe in you," Callum says, his voice encouraging and full of emotions. My poor Callum!

"I will come back to you," I say. "I love you."

"I love you t—"

The call disconnects.

CHAPTER 43

Kerr climbs up the cave stairs in front of me, then helps me out of the water. I pull off the glass orb and place it on the ground.

Glancing around, I note that most of the sponge-like creatures that bring illumination to the cave are closed. It's too early for them too.

Kerr and I left the mansion before dawn, hurrying through the sleeping city in the dark to get here. The puddle water was much colder too than yesterday.

I quiver, then press the water out of my tunic and pants.

Larr steps out of a nearby tunnel and points a webbed finger at us. "You're late." She wears the same green jumpsuit as yesterday; the only difference is the addition of a thin black cloak over it.

"And may you swim in clear water as well," Kerr says. "How can we already be late? I don't remember you specifying a time for our meeting. Hence, we are here at the first light of dawn."

Larr squints at him, then turns to me. "Lilla, it's time for you to be honest with me."

Moira snarls in my mind.

"What are you implying?" Kerr asks while I remain silent.

Larr smiles, showing of tips of her fangs. "I revealed my clans' history. However, you hid much from me. I expect you to reciprocate my honesty."

I cross my arms. "Why should I trust you? You didn't even give me a chance to explain what I came here."

Larr pulls her cloak closer to her body. "Without transparency, we cannot decide the path we must embark on. There are many paths to choose from, not all favorable."

"You mean, *you* cannot decide," Kerr says.

Larr's gaze flickers to Kerr, then back to me. "What will you choose?"

We need her help, dear, that much is true. But I am not sure if we can fully trust her. You must decide if this risk is worth taking.

Moira is right. I need someone's help to get out of this place.

"As Kerr told you, I am Lilla. My rank is sybil to the Archgoddess of the Eternal Light and Order."

"I knew it," Larr says.

"This explains the tremendous power I sensed in you when we bonded," Kerr says, then drops down to one knee in front of me. "Sybil Lilla, I am yours to command."

Larr frowns at Kerr. "Get up this instance."

Kerr looks at me, waiting.

"Thank you, Kerr," I say, then gesture with my hand for him to stand up. With a stubborn expression, he does.

"Will you tell me know what that language is above the murals?"

Larr's considers me. "Were you able to read it?"

I shake my head.

"That's too bad. My ancestors met someone who could read it and told them that it was an ancient Lumenian language. It is rumored to have been there before the Neath people took to the caves. Some say that language is as old as the sculptures, which are truly ancient—they are from a time before the Seven Galaxies. I—"

I raise a hand to interrupt her. "Before the Seven Galaxies?"

Larr nods. "They are estimated to be sixty-thousand years old in galactic time."

That is well before The Lady, who came into existence around the galactic year 10,000.

I gulp. "How is this possible?"

Larr spreads her hands. "I'm not a historian, but even I can tell you that there are many mysterious artifacts scattered all over the Seven Galaxies. They were not left behind by our Omnipower. You can find an example here—the seven sculptures."

Moira, did you know about this?

No, dear. There were no ancient artifacts on Teryn when I was the queen.

"Are you saying that there were Lumenians *before* the era wars?" I ask. If

The Lady created the Lumenians, then how can any Lumenian exist before that time?

"It does look that way, doesn't it?" Larr says. "Shouldn't you know this already? Aren't you a Lumenian?"

"Yes, I am." The last one in fact, but that's not information I want to share.

Larr tilts her head. "You don't look like one though."

I've heard that a lot, though I wish I'd know why. There was nothing about this in my mom's diary.

"That was rude," Kerr says.

"Anyway," Larr says, "you have passed two tests."

I raise my eyebrows. "Tests?"

"The Test of Compassion," Larr explains, "and Test of Honesty. Now you must pass the third and hardest test of all. The Test of Truth."

"What are you doing?" Kerr asks. "Where did these tests come from?"

Larr's expression turns cold. "As your clan leader, I allowed you quite a leeway and tolerated much of your disrespect. But now I've reached the limit of my patience. Leave us."

Kerr presses his lips together into thin line, then bows his head.

As he passes me, he gives me a warning look, then wades into the water. He descends the stairs, and swims away.

"What is this test?" I ask. I never liked tests. Failed more than I care to remember in my time as a princess on Uhna.

Larr raises an eyebrow. "The more important question is, are you ready to partake in it or not?"

I am afraid, dear, that we don't have a choice. Yet again.

Stifling a sigh, I incline my head. "I am ready."

CHAPTER 44

"Please," begs the Youngest Elder Christen, who cannot be older than seventeen. Tears stream down his pale face as he kneels in front of me with his hands clasped together. His white robe, with dangling gold ropes, hangs open on his hunched shoulders, revealing a simple white shirt and pants underneath. His bare feet slide in the urine pooling on the marble floor of his opulent house. "Please spare my family!"

It took me days to find a crack wide enough for my smoke form to enter this cursed society. Then just as I started to slip in, the force field closed. I had to fight my way through, and it took a lot out of me. I'll have to replenish my lost energy soon.

Urges rise in my not-so-alive body to take his blood and silence his whining. How pathetic.

"You were not supposed to allow your guests to leave the elders' mansion," I say in a guttural voice. It's difficult to speak around the fangs.

After I met with the Sybil in the Cathal jungle and she escaped, I was frustrated. I was so close to getting her. Then she stumbled into an opening in a force field and slipped through my claws. I knew I needed help. It didn't take long for me to find the right person for the job.

I visited this young elder in his dreams—a new power I possess, thanks to the growing imbalance between the archgods. He was ripe for corruption thanks to his greed—he yearned for power akin to tyranny. I promised him what he wanted and instructed him to hold the newcomers, but he failed to follow through.

I allow Black Fla'mma threads to rise in my palms, shaping them into dark flames that dance on my hands.

"I tried," he stutters. "I made sure to assign guards to them."

Shaking my head, I throw one of the flames on his robe.

It catches on black fire, smoking.

Christen yelps, throwing off his robe. The skin of his arm already blackened and blistered. He would have been a useful dark servant.

It should have been easy for me to gain access to the Sybil now that she is stuck here, but twice I've come to the elders' mansion, and twice she was not in her room. Using my magic to disguise my presence—on top of entering the force field—depleted my reserve. I do not have unlimited power. Yet. Once I take the place of the archgod, then I'll have all the magic, all the power, and all the worship I deserve.

Focus!

I growl in frustration. This new Ankhar body doesn't operate as smoothly as my previous one. My temper ebbs and flows. My hunger never satiates. But I won't let this stop me from achieving my goals. Punishing the Sybil as an additional perk.

"I did everything you asked of me," Christen says, sobbing. He wipes snot off his face with a shaking hand. "I can be useful to you. Please!"

I watch the young man. On one hand, he is weak and pliable. On the other hand, I am hungry and in desperate need of replenishment.

I smile, revealing sharp fangs. "There is one thing you can do, Christen."

I gesture for him to rise up. He gets to his feet, trembling in fear.

I grab him by the shoulders and dive into the crook of his neck, my fangs piercing his arterial vein.

He tries to scream but only makes a gurgling sound.

Once I am done here, I'll be coming for the Sybil.

There is nowhere she can hide from me.

CHAPTER 45

LILLA

Larr gestures for me to follow her through the central tunnel. We exit into a smaller cave with few sponge-like creatures lighting the way.

Two Neath men wait at the corner of the cave. At other side of the sloping cave, a dark lake laps the rocky ground.

A foreboding feeling raises goosebumps on my body.

I don't like this, dear.

I take a few steps back, bumping into someone. I glance over my shoulder to find a Neath man blocking the exit out of this cave.

Buckets of fishguts!

The Neath man pushes at my back. I have no choice but to move.

Larr clasps her hands in front of her, patiently waiting.

"What happens if I change my mind?" I ask.

"Then you are no longer welcome among us."

I can't afford to alienate her until I know how she could help.

I'm afraid, dear, I concur. This test cannot be so bad. The other two were simple.

Fine. "I'll do it."

Larr points at the water. "Then take your third and final test in the Deep Dark."

I raise a hand. "In there?" I'm a good swimmer, but all my instincts scream at me to avoid that murky lake at all costs.

Larr gestures for me to come closer.

I shake my head, backing away once again. "There must be another—"

The two Neath men each grab one of my arms, then drag me backwards toward the lake. Before I can scream, they jump into the cold water, holding me between them.

The last thing I see is the matriarch's satisfied expression.

CHAPTER 46

Putting a hand above my eyes to block out the glare, I scrutinize the thirty-foot-tall sculpture from afar.

The sunlight emphasizes the smooth reddish surface of the female warrior with long braided hair. She wears a pointed helmet and armored dress that reaches above her knee. Her feet are enclosed in open scandals with their straps wrapping around the muscular calves. Her eyes are closed; her expression serene.

"Do you see what I see?" I ask Bella. We're four blocks away from the sculpture. A few passersby, older couples, stride past us, goggling as if they've never seen twins before.

Bella nods. "There are no seams or cracks visible anywhere on it."

"Which means it was built by magical means." I would have preferred technological means. Neither Bella nor I have any magic.

I point at the children playing around the sculpture's feet. "It seems safe to touch."

Bella rubs her hands. "Then what are we waiting for?" She gives me my bag we made out of the bedsheet, filled with wires and other pieces of tech that we took out of the mansion's wall.

We hurry down the street until we reach the sculpture. The children shriek and dart away when they see us.

We walk around the huge feet, taking in the exquisite details.

Bella squints upward. "What do you think is the purpose of these sculptures?"

"They all seem to be warriors. I would venture to guess that they are some kind of protectors."

"I agree. But why are their eyes closed?"

"Could it be that they are sleeping?"

Bella leans against the sculpture's foot. "But why?"

I can't even guess. "I have no idea."

Bella tilts her head at the sculpture. "Do you think it's hollow inside?"

I step around the giant right foot until I reach the heel. Bella follows me. I run my hands on the smooth and warm surface. Then I bang my fists on it as hard as I can.

"I heard it reverberate," Bella says, excitedly.

"Me too."

"Maybe there's an entrance somewhere."

We put our hands on the sculpture, then walk around examining every inch of the smooth surface again. After an hour we stop.

I wipe sweat off my face. "Nothing moved."

Bella sighs. "Nothing clicked."

We try the key we made for the guest rooms in the mansion, but no luck.

I fidget with the key. "I'll need to assemble a special glass that would allow me to see through the layers of the sculpture to find a way in. I have some pieces I can use, but I don't have a complex alternator that would serve as the filter. Without it, we are stuck."

Bella looks around. "Can't you build one?"

I shake my head. "I'm missing too many pieces to build one from scratch. Besides, it would take me too long anyway."

"Where are we going to find a complex alternator here?"

I shrug. "We should look around to see if there is any."

We spend the next hour combing through the streets and alleys.

"I am not a fan of walking," Bella whines, limping.

"Just a little bit more," I say. I hide my wince from her. My feet are on fire, and each step is an effort.

I almost run into a man with gray hair who bursts out of a cloudscraper's entrance pushing a strange wheelless and hovering barrow.

"Hold your compass," I say and jump out of the way.

The older man waves his hands. "My apologies. I wasn't paying attention."

Bella squeaks and points at the barrow.

I look where she's pointing. One of the pieces of equipment on the side of the barrow looks familiar. "Is that a complex alternator?"

The older man hesitates. "I wouldn't know."

I need that equipment. "I'd love to buy your barrow."

Bella raises an eyebrow and curls her fingers together in a quick motion. *What are you going to pay with?*

I can't just steal it outright. Lilla wouldn't like that.

I sign back. *Not sure.*

The older man rubs his chin, his stubble making a scraping noise. "I am not authorized to barter with you."

Barter? Interesting. "Then who is authorized?"

"That would be the Head of Building," he explains. "You must convince her."

CHAPTER 47

LILLA

The cold dark water envelops me as the two Neath men dive under the surface of the Deep Dark, holding me between them. No light penetrates the black water. I cannot see beyond a few inches. It gets colder and colder with each second. Nothing else moves through the water.

I struggle against the two Neath men, but they continue their relentless plummet.

Moira! Can you help me?

No answer comes from the spirit queen.

Pressure builds on my body. My skin feels frozen. My lungs strain for air.

Desperate, I kick and twist.

This is where I'll die.

I want to live!

Suddenly, my air runs out.

The two men let go of my arms and shoot upward, swim away and abandoning me.

I reach toward them, silently screaming, *don't leave me here to drown!*

But it's too late. They vanish from my view.

Then blackness overtakes my consciousness.

CHAPTER 48

We enter the building, following the older man. He places the hovering barrow in a nook. My gaze lingers on the complex alternator I desperately need. But first we have to convince the Head of Building to acquire the equipment.

"My name is Corban," our escort says, as we climb the stairs. "This way. The Head of Building, Corra, lives on the top floor."

Bella and I tire after the first ten floors, our breathing loud and ragged. Corban treks in front of us as if he is merely taking a stroll.

Bella signs. *Just don't think about the physical exertion.*

It's not that easy.

Finally we reach the thirtieth floor and exit the stairway. White double doors block our way. Corban knocks, then steps to the side, waiting.

Bella and I pretend to study the green vines that cover the wall while we catch our breath. The air smells sweet from the small yellow flowers that bloom on the vines underneath its thorny triangular leaves. Long cracks show around the doorframe. The paint is peeling on the door. The carpet under our feet looks worn but clean.

We wipe sweat off our foreheads at the same time with our right hands. Corban's eyes widen, and he looks away.

Right. Most people are freaked out by "twin stuff." Good thing that Bella and I never cared about what other people think.

One of the doors opens. An elderly woman, with her white hair in a neat braid, steps out. She wears a simple but elegant light blue dress—clearly homemade. Her jewelry consists of bracelets and a necklace made of plastic beads. Her feet are tucked into a leather sandal.

"Together, we are happy," she greets Corban, who repeats it back to her.

"Corban, what are you doing back already? Shouldn't you be getting compost from the neighbors, or are they giving you a hard time again?"

Corban gestures to us. "I was on my way when I ran into these nice ladies. Corra, this is Isa and Bella. They wanted to buy our barrow. I told them to talk to you."

"The barrow is not for sale," Corra says, as she turns her hazel gaze on us. "You must be those newcomers who fell through the force field and ended up in the elders' mansion."

There is no point lying. "Yes, we are. I really need a part that's in your barrow, called a complex alternator. Please tell us how much it costs, and we'll pay it."

Corra and Corban burst out laughing.

Bella frowns. "What's so funny?"

Corra gestures for us to come inside. "Let us talk comfortably."

We enter the spacious apartment.

Everywhere I look, plants, shrubs, and dwarf trees cover tables, shelves, and most of the hardwood floor. Some pots even hang from the tall ceiling. Other plants perch on the windowsill in white clay planters.

Among all the greenery nestles a white sofa, two armchairs, and a coffee table. Behind the sofa a door leads to a balcony with even more plants and vines—like a mini farm.

In the back, an open kitchen is visible. I notice a square device on one of the counters. I elbow Bella and nod toward it. She follows where I gesture and sees the device too. She quickly surveys it with her rectangular scanner.

What is it? I sign.

It's a cooking device. It operates on scrap food and other organic waste. Unfortunately, it doesn't have a complex alternator.

Corra and Corban take the chairs. We settle on the sofa.

I cross my legs. My foot barely avoids a tall plant with long leaves, full of round red fruits.

"Please explain why you found our request ridiculous," I say.

Bella reaches for one of the ripe fruits. "May I take one?"

Corra shakes her head. "No. We are observing a fast to honor my brother-in-law, who passed away unexpectedly yesterday."

Bella sits back. "Oh, sorry to hear that."

I'm not sure if my sister is referring to the tragedy or to the lack of hospitality.

Corra shrugs. "It's life. As for acquiring that piece of equipment, it is vital for the operation of the barrow, which we use to maintain our crops. Our livelihood depends on it. Thus, you won't be able to afford it."

I lean forward. "I understand that the Eldryans like to barter. There must be something you want."

Corra threads her fingers together in her lap as she considers me. "My building has suffered many setbacks in the past few weeks. We had a horrible harvest last month. My tradeswoman who negotiates with other buildings got sick and still hasn't recuperated. There is a fungal infection that affects my vegetables. We cannot find a cure for it, because my plant doctor married into another family and moved into their building, leaving us without a replacement."

"And your brother-in-law passed away," Bella adds.

Corra waves a hand. "Yes, that too. But the most important part is that our crops are in danger of wilting and that would spell disaster to everyone living in the building."

"How so?" I ask.

"We must have good crops to feed everyone in the building," Corban explains. "We also must have surplus to trade with our neighboring buildings or barter with them at the neighborhood market."

Bella clasps her hands. "What do you need us to do?"

"Find me a new plant doctor," Corra says. "Bring new seeds that can replenish the vegetable plants that stopped giving crops. Bring me the cure for the fungal infection. Solve these problems, and I will give you the equipment you want."

Bella and I stare at her.

I don't even know where to start.

Corra frowns. "Off you go. You have plenty to do."

CHAPTER 49

Pain bursts in my throat and head.

I wake up and open my eyes.

Immediately a coughing spasm racks my body.

I turn to my side and spit out water onto the pristine sandstones. Not a speck of dust mars their surface.

Did I die? Is this what the Lume looks like?

Somehow, I doubt that.

Moira? Are you with me?

Silence is my only answer. I try not to think too much about what could be blocking communication with my melded spirit. Instead, I sit up and look around.

I find myself alone in a square-shaped chamber with windowless walls covered in metallic gold writing that I can't quite make out. Fla'mma-infused torches, one on each of the four walls, light the small sand colored room. Geometric patterns crisscross on the floor around me, though I cannot depict their meaning.

Craning my neck, I look up.

Beyond the torchlight, darkness obscures the ceiling that could be ten feet away or maybe even farther.

"How is this a test?" I ask, but no one responds.

My gaze snags on the golden writing. Something about it beckons to me.

I get to my feet and lean forward a bit. It's the exact same writing that I saw above the cave murals.

What does this chamber have to do with ancient Lumenians and the Neath clans?

Taking a few steps, I reach out with a finger to touch the golden letters.

A loud click sounds.

Everything disappears and the floor gives out underneath me.

CHAPTER 50

Bella and I leave the cloudscraper after our talk with Corra, the Head of Building.

"Where will we even start?" Bella asks. "This is beyond our skillset."

I turn around on the corner of the street, lost. The pressure to do something, *anything*, is almost unbearable.

"We can't give up," I say. "Lilla is counting on us."

Bella nods.

I point across the street at a neighboring building. "We can start there."

Bella and I cross the street and enter the pyramid-shaped building with plants clinging to it.

The temperature feels much cooler inside. White tiles cover the floor. Dwarf trees in wooden planters pepper most of the small landing. To our left, a steep stairway leads upward. To our right is an apartment with its door open. Muffled cursing comes from inside of it.

Bella and I exchange a look.

I step to the doorway and knock. "Hello?"

Footsteps thud.

A burly man in his sixties marches to us. Salt and pepper hair covers his round face which shines with sweat. He frowns at us.

"Who are you two?"

I grin. "Together, we are happy!"

He mutters the greeting back.

"We are Isa and Bella, and we're here to barter. We're looking for a plant doctor; a salve for a fungal infection on plants; and some seeds to replenish wilted crops."

He points his thumb at his hairy chest visible through his gray shirt. "Bert is my name. Is that all you need?"

"I guess." I know it's a tall order, but if I keep acting like it's not, maybe I can convince him and myself. I do enjoy a challenge—especially one that seems impossible at first glance.

I gesture at the apparatus in his grease covered hand. "We can fix that in exchange."

Bert's gray eyebrows lift. "Now you're talking. Come with me. The building's water pump has been dying for some time now. Fix it, and I'll get you a plant doctor."

I rub my hands together. "Show me the water pump." I love nothing more than dismantling things, then repairing them to be better than new.

All told, it takes us three hours to fix the water pump—it's a technology we have not encountered before, but we figure it out. It's obvious that the high level of technology in these buildings is something no one knows how to use or repair beyond the superficial approach. They kept patching it up over the years but now it's on its last leg.

Once we prove that the pump is in working order, we are directed to the plant doctor, Juny, in the same building. She's a single young woman, the sixth apprentice of their current plant doctor. Juny has no prospects of becoming their lead plant doctor ever. One of the reasons is that Juny has no interest in marrying, which makes it even harder for her to advance, as married women have higher status. It doesn't take much convincing once Juny learns that she would be the *only* plant doctor, and thus revered, in the building where we came from.

However, for the fungal infection, Juny is too inexperienced to offer a cure, but she recommends going to another building only two blocks away from our original starting point.

This building, a tapering and twisting roughly rectangular shaped structure, had similar issues with their water pump. It takes less time to repair it, since we learned the technology before. The building's plant doctor, an older woman with large moles covering her face in various places, whips up the salve and sends us on our way. Unfortunately, they have no interest relinquishing any seeds.

It takes another three hours to find a building willing to barter their seeds in exchange for us fixing their water pump. We only succeed because their pump has not been working for days, and they are desperate. Seeds, as we learn, are of utmost importance and protected by all the building tenants like treasure. Each building has their own variety of plants, vegetables, and fruits that they've been cultivating for generations to their specific needs. If one building has little sun, they develop plants that can survive in the shade. If another building has insect problems, they improve the genetic makeup until the plants resist those insects. It is extremely rare that they barter with these seeds.

Restoring the pump takes longer than we hope. It is in bad shape and has to be completely disassembled. Then we realize that one of its components is broken. Bella improvises and makes a new one on the spot. Finished, we get the bag of seeds with the caveat that we will never return.

Sweating and tired, we knock on Corra's door. Next to us, Juny fidgets, holding her meager belongings in a bundled sheet. Bella smiles at the young woman encouragingly.

Corra appears, then frowns at us. "Don't tell me you did it."

I beam at her, enjoying her shock. "Let me introduce you to your new plant doctor, Juny. She is young, smart, and eager to start working." Bella gently pushes Juny forward, who stumbles in her feet, then blushes awkwardly.

"We have a salve for the fungal infection," I say and wait for Bella to hand the tube to Corra. "Lastly, here are the seeds of a new variety of vegetables that are stronger and more resistant to insects." Bella gives the small bag of seeds to Corra.

I cross my arms. "We're going to need that complex alternator." I plan to stay here as long as it takes to force her to follow through on her promise. Bella mimics my body language, glowering at the Head of Building.

Corra looks at Juny, then at the tube, and the bag of seeds. "I can't believe . . . I mean . . . How . . ." Her voice trails off. With a resigned expression, she says, "Alright. Go see Corban. After this do not come back to my building. Ever!"

CHAPTER 51

LILLA

From one blink to the other, I am floating in the middle of space, surrounded by colorful stars, nebulas, and columns of gases.

Buckets and buckets of fishguts!

I should be dead, yet I can breathe. The harsh cold of space does not affect me at all.

Is this a pocket realm? Could this be The Lady's doing?

I wait for Her to appear next to me, as She has done before, but I remain alone.

"This could all be yours," multiple divine and powerful but distorted voices say, though I cannot find their origin. "Claim it. Take it. Now!"

Magical pressure bears down on me, a mix of the six light elements—Fla'mma, A'ris, A'qua, T'erra, A'nima, and even Lume. They envelop my body, trapping me like amber traps insects, pliable and soft in the beginning, but I know without a doubt that once this pressure solidifies, I won't be alive.

"What do you want from me?" I shout, fighting the hold of the magical pressure to no avail.

"Take it! Claim the Seven Galaxies! Become its one and only ruler! Become its true queen as a Lumenian!"

Temptation takes hold as the voices echo louder and louder with each repetition. The magical pressure intensifies with each beat of my heart until it's constricting my whole body like a palm snake does to its prey.

I close my eyes to block out the divine voices.

Who are these powerful beings? How can they use all six light elements at the same time? Why do they want *me* to rule the Seven Galaxies? Did Lumenians rule it before? Where are the archgods?

The desire to take control of the Seven Galaxies grows too strong. It would solve the Era War. There would be no more corruption. No more dark servants and dark fiends.

Suddenly, I cannot form any more thoughts.

My heart beats in my throat. Cold sweat breaks out on my body. Claustrophobia rears its head under the magical pressure, robbing me of air.

Images of my possible future bombard my mind—the new benevolent ruler. One that everyone loves. One that is fair. One that brings justice to all. One that protects the innocents—like the promise I made to my mom.

Me.

No! No! NO!

I don't want power. I never did.

I don't want to rule the Seven Galaxies.

I don't want to be anyone's queen.

With each refusal, the pressure of temptation recedes.

All I want is to live my life with Callum, free of gods and war.

Suddenly, my mind becomes clear.

The magical pressure diminishes, freeing me.

A loud click sounds.

Then space vanishes.

CHAPTER 52

DAY 5—LILLA

Blinking against bright light, I groan from disorientation. My vision blurs. Nausea makes my mouth sour, and I close my eyes.

I turn my head to the side. A headache bursts behind my eyelids.

My fingers curl into my palms, my nails dragging on rough ground. I force myself to take slow breaths—in and out—until the headache lessens and the nausea subsides.

What happened?

Moira groans. *I am not sure, dear. I seem to have fallen asleep, though I do not feel refreshed, just drained.*

I couldn't talk to you, and I almost drowned. Then I was in a strange chamber. Then in space.

Are you sure, dear, that all this happened? Could you have imagined it?

Yes. I mean no. I don't know.

With a groan, I open my eyes.

"May you swim in clear water," Larr greets, looking down on me. "You survived the Deep Dark. Though it did take a whole day. I almost gave up on you."

Buckets of fishguts!

I can't afford to lose a day.

She reaches down with a hand.

I accept it, allowing her to pull me to my feet.

"It was the hardest thing I had to do," I mutter, recalling the temptation.

She lets go of my hand. "It couldn't have been that bad."

I sputter. "I almost drowned."

"You survived. I knew you'd be the one to accomplish the impossible."

"What do you mean by 'impossible'?"

Larr waves a webbed hand. "Never mind that. Now ask me."
"Can you assist me to leave this city?"
Larr smiles. "No, I cannot."

163

CHAPTER 53

FIONA

Gently I move a few strands of blond hair away from Ivy's closed eyes. She sighs a little in her sleep but doesn't move on my bed.

We spent the night talking in my small one-bedroom flat in the attic of the narrow brick building. I've never invited anyone in, but after the wondrous day I spent with Ivy, I couldn't say goodbye to her. I couldn't let the day end as if that's all there was for me—going back to the never-ending monotony of being alone. It took all my courage to ask her to stay; and thank the gods that's what she did.

I rise up on my elbow and study Ivy. She looks peaceful, so unlike when she is awake. Her long hair cascades over her right shoulder. I marvel how gorgeous she is in her minidress that leaves her slender legs bare. I could never wear anything like that; I am not brave like her.

I pull up the threadbare blanket from the end of the bed and tuck it around her. She murmurs in her sleep.

I smile at how cute she looks.

Cold air seeping through the cracks of the roof sends goosebumps down my arm. I shiver.

I don't mind being cold—I'm used to it by now. At least I can make Ivy warm while she is resting. Once she wakes up, she will see my flat in a whole new light—different from the candles' soft illumination that obscured the shabby surroundings. But for now, she sleeps unaware, without any judgment.

I look around my flat with a skeptical eye.

Peeling wallpaper that was once a cheery scene of flowers now faded to gray pulls away from the wall. Ants hurry on the white bricks behind the paper. The wobbly state of the narrow wooden bed—we barely fit on it together—is quite pitiful. The chair looks rickety next to the round metal table which has rust covering its bright green surface. Worn carpet with swirling patterns complete the look I jokingly call modest. My family calls it poor.

For now, Ivy sleeps unaware and without any judgement.

I smile remembering how excited she was when we talked. It was as if floodgates opened for us—we shared so many of our favorite childhood memories, our hopes, and our dreams for the future. Who knew we had so much in common.

The early morning light peeks through the dingy, ragged lace curtains.

I get out of bed and head to the narrow counter with a sink.

At least everything is clean, even if it's all tattered and outdated. My dishes and plates rest on the dust-free shelf above the chipped sink. The noise of the street drifts through the windowpane, the city's workforce heading out to maintain the Eldryan society. I don't have a job to attend to; I've been living here, hidden away with my life put on hold for the past five years, ever since I turned sixteen.

I grab a ceramic mug from the shelf, fill it with water from the sink, and sprinkle in a few dried tea leaves I've saved for days when I get a cold. I tend to get sick around this time. My family used to say it's because I am weak and fragile; that's why I always got the spring cold the others managed to avoid.

I place the mug into the cooking unit—a white cube that functions as oven, cooktop, toaster, and food printer all in one. It's the only luxury item I have, gifted to me by my family more out of pity than generosity. It's one thing for me to stay hidden and forgotten, another thing to die of malnutrition on their watch.

I feed it with scraps of leftover food and plastic wrappings from a side bin. I press a button. The tea heats up in mere seconds.

Carefully, I take the steaming mug and shuffle to the bed. Then I hesitate.

It seems rude to wake Ivy, but I also can't wait to hear her voice and see her smile. I decide to tantalize her with the sweet aroma of the tea and lower the mug close to her face.

Ivy's eyes snap open, and she swipes the mug out of my hand.

I see it happening as if time has slowed down.

The arc of the hot tea, above the falling white mug, still steaming.

Without thinking, I reach out with my mind and grab the mug, then guide the tea back into it.

Ivy stares at the mug, full of hot tea, hovering a few inches from her face. Then her green gaze locks on my face. She sits up and plucks the tea out of the air warily.

Heat of shame burns on my face. I cover it with my hands.

I can't believe I did that. Now Ivy knows the reason why I have to hide. Why my family doesn't want me around. Now she's going to hate me too, and I am going to be alone. Again.

The blanket rustles on the bed.

Gentle fingers pry my hands off my face, but I avoid looking at Ivy.

She places a finger under my chin and turns my face to her.

"What's the matter?"

Tears well in my eyes. "I'm so sorry."

Ivy puts her mug on the floor, then pulls me down to sit next to her. She wipes a tear away from my cheek. "Why are you sorry? It was amazing."

I study Ivy. Her expression is open and curious, without any sign of judgement.

"You're not angry with me? Or afraid of me?"

"No," Ivy says and cups my cheek. "I am not angry. I doubt there is anything you can do to make me afraid of you. How did you do it?"

I look into Ivy's earnest green eyes and get lost in their warmth. No one has ever looked at me with so much kindness, and with something more . . . with desire.

I touch her hand.

Ivy blushes.

I clear my throat. "To answer your question, I am not exactly sure how I stopped the mug, but I know it's not magic. It has to do with my mind."

"Is it like telekinesis?"

"I guess. I've had this skill since I was very young, but I try not to use it."

"Do you practice it at least?"

"No, never! My Aunt Corina saw me using my skill when I was six. I lifted a toy off a high shelf. She was furious with me. She berated me and told me to never reveal it to anyone, including my family. I obeyed her, but somehow my family still found out about it."

"You make it sound like having telekinesis is bad."

I nod. "It's the worst."

Ivy frowns. "Why?"

"No one in my family has telekinesis. It's a forbidden skill. That's all I know."

Ivy points at the silver band on my right hand. "Is that a wedding ring?"

I twirl it between my fingers. "It is. I got married at the expected age of sixteen."

"Are you still married?" Ivy asks in a cool voice.

"No, I am not. When we discovered I could not bear a child, my husband annulled our marriage. Producing two children was the whole point—to contribute to society. I couldn't do my part. I understand why he did it. I may have done the same in his place."

"I doubt it. Then what happened?"

"He married someone else and had exactly two children. I ended up as a spinster living with my family again. I blamed myself. I was nothing but a burden. Soon after that I realized that I was casting a bad light on my sister by staying at home, ruining her chances to marry and be useful as intended. I decided to leave them."

Ivy curses under her breath. "You are not a burden. It's terrible how your family treated you."

"They had no choice."

"There's always a choice," Ivy says with a dark expression. "Trust me."

I stay silent. It hurts to think about my family. I miss them, but I'm also sad that they let me go so easily.

"We must know more about your skill."

I shake my head. "I told you; it's forbidden."

"Exactly why you should learn more about it. I want to leave this place with my friends, and you said you want to leave too. This might be the key that helps all of us."

"I don't know . . ."

Ivy grabs my hands. "Don't you want to leave with me?"

"I do." She understands me like no one else does.

Ivy grins. "Then this is our start. This is our first thread in a jumble, and we must pull on it until it unravels."

"Are you sure that's a good idea?" I can imagine my family's expression. But instead of stopping me as it should, it only makes me want to do it even more. I've lived here alone wondering long enough about my wrongness. It's time I got some answers.

Ivy laughs. "It always worked for me before. Plus, this way, I get to help my friends and you at the same time. One meteor, two spaceships."

I smile. "Alright."

Ivy leans forward and kisses me. "Let's go meet your family and asks some annoying questions."

CHAPTER 54

LILLA

I stare at Larr. "Could you please repeat that?" I could have sworn I heard her say no to my request for help.

"I said, I cannot help you."

I pinch the bridge of my nose. "That's what I thought."

I went through such a horrible experience for nothing?

What is wrong with her, dear?

"Then what can you do?" I ask, forcing patience on me.

"I can teach you how to glimpse the past," Larr says.

I exhale. I really don't want to snap at the matriarch of the Neath clans, but it's getting harder to restrain myself. "I don't understand why I'd need to read the past when it's already happened, and there is nothing I can do to change it."

Larr shakes her head. "Knowing the past is not about changing it. It's about having information that can be of use in the present. Also, by learning to discern the magical threads of the past, you might be able to discern the future ones as well."

That would be useful, dear.

"Would you like to learn this skill?" Larr asks.

"Sure." Why not?

"One thing to keep in mind—only major events will leave enough trace on the surrounding elements that they can be viewed in such a way. Trivial events will leave behind nothing."

"Got it," I say. "How does one look into the past and into the future?"

Larr gestures with her hand. "The magical elements are all around us. Asking the right question is vital to find the answer you seek. It doesn't always work. Some answers we are not meant to have. To start the process all you have to do is use a small amount of your Lume magic, ask the question, and wait for the answer. That's it."

"Sounds easy," I say. "Did you say Lume magic? Does this mean you have it too?"

Larr shakes her head. "As I told you before, I don't have Lume or other magic. I have a different way to seek answers of the past regarding my clans, but it is not powerful enough to be of any help for you."

"I see. Wait. How do you know so much about this?"

"I have this knowledge because I received it during my Journey of Soul. But I couldn't remember it until you came back from the Deep Dark. Then I knew what to tell you."

Hmm. "How do I know this is not another one of your tests?"

Larr spreads her hands. "You already know the answer to that question."

So it seems.

Then I remember that I can't access my magical orb. "How can I learn this skill if I cannot use my magic here?"

"Don't worry about that. It's the force field that blocks your magic. It's an ancient technology the Eldryans appropriated for their selfish use. But there is one place you might be able to use your magic and learn the skill."

"Let me guess." I point toward the dark lake. "In there?"

Larr nods.

"Aren't you going to come with me?"

"There is no point. I won't be able to help you beyond what I already told you."

Buckets of fishguts!

Resigned, I take a deep breath, then jump into the Deep Dark.

CHAPTER 55

FIONA

I hesitate in front of an ornate wooden door of an apartment in one of the highest cloudscrapers shaped like an oval.

All the way here, I tried to rehearse what I would say to my family—whom I have not seen for years, not since they gave me that expensive cooking unit—but I came up with nothing.

"Are you going to knock or should I?" Ivy asks and pops a hexagonal piece of pink gum.

I shrink back from the door. "I'm not sure if this is a good idea . . ."

Ivy bangs her fist on the wood. "All the more reason to do it."

Aunt Corina opens the door. "Who makes such noise . . . Oh, it's you," she says with an expression of disdain. "Leave before you bring any more misfortune to your family." She moves to shut the door.

"Together, we are happy," I mutter.

Ivy shoves her foot in the doorway before my aunt can lock us out. "Not so fast."

"Corina?" my mom asks from somewhere inside the apartment. Then she opens the door wide. "What is going on?" Her gaze flickers to Ivy, then she notices me. Her face pales. "We should not be having a conversation like this in the hallway."

Ivy grins. "I can talk anywhere, but if you insist." She puts a hand on my back, letting me enter in front of her.

Not much has changed in the luxurious apartment that could hold mine ten times. The white floor still shines clean, the white furniture remains in the same position. Only the green dwarf trees and evergreen shrubs have grown.

My mom gestures to the closest sofa while she and my aunt take a seat in chairs to the left of it.

Ivy and I sit next to each other.

"Why are you here?" Aunt Corina asks.

"Straight to the point," Ivy says, and crosses her legs. She gazes at my aunt with a nonchalant expression, though her green eyes flash irate.

I wring my hands in my lap. "I . . . I would like to—"

"Be careful, niece, your insecurities are showing."

"Don't listen to her, Fiona," Ivy says. She pulls a knife from her boot. Then using its tip, she cleans under her nails. "It's you who should be careful, Auntie Cor. Your ugliness is definitely showing."

My aunt gasps in outrage.

My mom exhales with a forced calm. "What happened?"

I clasp my fingers tight to stop their shaking. "I have accidentally used my—"

Aunt Corina jumps to her feet. "Do not say another word. You will ruin this family."

Ivy touches my forearm. I put my hand over hers, taking comfort in her support.

I raise my chin. "I used my mind."

Aunt Corina paces in front of us. "I told you this would happen, sister. You should have never married him. He was tainted, but you didn't believe me."

"What is she talking about?" I ask.

My mom stands up and slaps Aunt Corina. "That man was my beloved husband. Don't talk like that about him." She closes her eyes and wipes at their corners, then adds, "Is that what you think of our family? That we are all tainted?"

Ivy grins, observing the clash with interest.

Aunt Corina holds her reddened cheek. "Of course you are tainted. Thanks to me, no one knows about your daughter's failings. I was the one who lent you support when your husband died. I was the one who ensured Fiona's bad behavior wouldn't come to light and paid off her husband to leave her quietly. I was the one who found her that flat far away from us when she almost ruined us. I did nothing but protect you and your family. How can you be so ungrateful?"

My mom shakes her head. "I have tolerated your interference because I love you and you are older than me. However, you didn't help us out of the goodness of your heart. You protected your own interests to ensure you always fit into society. I let you get away with it for too long. Now leave us."

Aunt Corina recoils. "But . . . Will I have a place to come back to?"

Mom raises her chin. "It depends on how fast you leave."

Aunt Corina presses her thin lips together, then marches to the door and exits the apartment.

My mom puts a hand over her mouth, her shoulders shaking.

"Mom, what did she mean by Dad being tainted?"

She turns to me, and says, "It's time you meet your father's family—or what's left of it."

CHAPTER 56

LILLA

I stumble on the sandstones, back in the empty square chamber. The Deep Dark must be a conduit that transports me here. I wonder how Larr was able to set up a test so complicated, elaborate, and so full of magic.

Then my gaze catches the Lumenian writing on the wall.

It must have been *them*. It wasn't a test. It was probably a magical trap. But who set this up in the first place and why? And how did Larr know about it?

What do you think, Moira?

She doesn't answer.

Right. She's cut off again.

I examine the geometric patterns on the floor. Last time, all it took was taking a few steps forward to trigger the magical trap. I recall that there was even a loud click as if I activated it, then I found myself in space. When I refused the temptation of power, there was another loud click as if I deactivated it.

The only way to see whether there are any more traps is to walk around.

With a deep sigh, I take a step forward.

Drawing my shoulders to my ear, I brace myself.

Nothing happens.

No click sounds.

Hopefully this means there are no more magical traps.

I stride to the closest wall with writing on it.

As I try to read the letters, I notice magical threads floating in front of the writing.

This is what Larr was talking about.

I reach for my magical orb. It's barely there, but a thin thread of Lume comes to me.

I frown at my glowing hand. Something here allows me to use a little bit of magic.

Just as Larr taught me, I thread my magic into the amalgam of magical threads in front of me, then I let it go. Now, to ask the crucial question.

"What happens if I fail my mission?"

I wait for an answer.

None comes.

"Well, I know the answer to that—everyone dies and there won't be much left of the Seven Galaxies."

Larr did say that it has to be the right question.

Let's try something else. "Where does the ancient technology used by the Eldryans originate from?"

The magical threads light up, and the walls fall away.

An explosion of colors bursts in front of me. Then parts of a space nebula come into view with purple, blue, and orange gases that look like uneven columns. Something stirs in their depths.

Fear raises the hair on the back of my neck as if I am being watched by something powerful. Then the vision cuts off, and I am back to the sandstone chamber.

Not helpful.

When it comes to my past, I have one burning question. It's personal, but I really want to know the answer to it.

I thread more Lume ribbon into the elements floating around me. "Why do I look so different from other Lumenians?"

The magical threads pulse golden white. Then the walls fade away again.

Gray mountainside, covered in snow, comes into view. My mom walks around a barren tree until she finds a dark opening on the side of the mountain. Her long blond hair reaches to her waist, her skin beautiful golden brown. She peers around, then enters the cave. After a while, she leaves with dark violet hair and pale olive hue to her skin. Then everything goes black.

"What happened in that cave?"

I thread more Lume into the floating elements, but they do not react to my questions, no matter how I rephrase them. It's as if something or someone is blocking me from discovering the answer.

I fight the urge to hit the wall and take a deep calming breath.

I have wasted enough time on personal matters. It's best I hurry up and concentrate on more important issues.

"Why are these portals vital for the Archgoddess of the Eternal Light and Order?"

The magical threads light up bright white, and the sandstone walls dissolve.

A miniature version of the seven sculptures, facing outward, appear in a vision. Their eyes open, their arms pointing into the depths of the Cathal Jungle. Shimmering air emerges in seven places on Cathal, oval and ten feet tall.

The portals!

Armies of the archgod march through them only to appear in another world the next instant. That world stands without a chance against the flood of dark servants and dark fiends. One after the other, planets fall into DLD's control. All living things either join His army or perish. No one escapes.

I cannot let this future come to pass. I cannot let the portals fall into the possession of the archgod.

I take a step back.

The chamber disappears.

Blackness envelops me yet again.

CHAPTER 57

KERR

Kerr enters the cave where he, his family, and his clan used to live.

How many happy years I spent here. Yet foolishly I wished to be out of these caves as a youngling. How I wish that I could be back when everything was full of life and laughter. Before the Night of Blood.

Kerr was too young to recall what happened to his family. Only he survived.

He strides through the main cave full of mementos going back many generations—all the weapons, decorations, woven fabrics, children's toys, everything that tells the rich history of his family. It was his job to carry on the Norrek Clan's traditions. But he failed them all.

He stops in the middle of the cave on the straw covered floor. To his right, tunnels branch off to chambers, where his grandparents, uncles, and cousins used to live. The middle tunnel leads to his parents' and siblings' living place. None of them are occupied.

Kerr heads toward the left tunnel leading to his own chamber.

He enters the small space and halts.

Physical pain in his chest makes him double over, falling on his knees on the soft woven carpet his wife made for him. His Above wife.

Moisture wells in his eyes but he blinks it away.

Tears won't bring back those who have left me.

Kerr gets to his feet and strides toward the shelf, carved into the gray and dripping cave wall. He touches a bunch of dried flowers in a metal mug—he gave them to Linni on their first date. Then his finger runs over a pocket watch with a rusted chain—the first gift Linni gave him as his wife. He cleans mold off the books she brought with her when she first moved in.

Linni was courageous to abandon her Above family. She knew she could never go back. She knew that her family would disown her for marrying a *puddle dweller. But she didn't care. She faced the hostile clan members of her new home with strength. She didn't back down when Larr tried to make her feel unwelcome. She fought hard for us. Yet I failed her too.*

With heart throbbing in his throat, Kerr walks around their chamber where they spent many nights during their two-year relationship. He still hears Linni's soft laughter every time he surprised her with a hug. He still feels her soft arms around him when she nestled into his embrace.

Gods, how I miss my wife!

Kerr sits down on their bed, a flat rocky area covered in thick carpet and piled with furs of seals.

He picks up her nightshirt. It used to be his, but Linni "borrowed" it until it became hers. He buries his face into the soft fabric and takes a deep inhale. He can barely detect her flowery scent.

He hugs the shirt to him.

I should have never brought her to the Neath. I should have never married her. It's my fault she's dead.

Kerr lies down on top of the furs.

Everything was fine until Linni got pregnant. Larr warned us that we might not be well-matched—there was no Above and Neath marriage before. But I didn't listen—and Linni paid the price.

Kerr still hears her agonized screams as she struggled to give birth to their child. He asked for help from the Eldryan Elders, but they laughed in his face. He asked for Larr's help, but she didn't come.

After more than three days of struggle, Linni died in his arms along with their unborn baby.

When Kerr delivered the news of Linni's death to her family, they regretted abandoning her. They took her body, cremated her as is tradition, and placed her ashes in their family's resting lot. But they did not create a resting place for her unborn child, pretending her pregnancy never happened. He burned his baby son's body as clan tradition dictates. Then he scooped a small pile of ashes into a vial he still wears on a necklace tucked in his suit.

Kerr exhales deeply, his eyes closing.

Without Linni and my child, I do not care anymore. I have no purpose left. I have no home left.

CHAPTER 58

I find myself lying on my back in the cavern again with Larr on my right, and the dark lake on my left.

This time, there is no disorientation. When I sit up, there is no nausea to stop me.

"How did it go?" Larr asks.

I'd love to know that too, dear.

"It worked. Do you think it's possible that someone else can read the magical threads?"

Larr considers me. "It's quite possible. This skill I taught you wasn't ours. I do not know who gave us the knowledge."

I get to my feet and wring out water from my hair and clothing. "It felt as if someone was blocking answers from me."

She spreads her arms. "I'm afraid that's possible as well."

"May I ask why Kerr is upset with you?"

Larr stares at the cave ground. "I tried to help Linni—"

Kerr marches into the cave, his hands in fists. "Do not mention my wife's name."

Larr's eyes widen. "I didn't mean to—"

Kerr slices out with the edge of his hand. "You never do, don't you? You didn't mean to let her die, yet that is exactly what happened."

"I have apologized many times. What more do you want me to do?"

"I want you to turn back time," Kerr growls, "and help my wife give birth. I want Linni and our babe to be alive. I want to be happy with my family."

Poor Kerr, Moira says in my mind.

Larr looks away. "You know I can't do that."

Kerr clenches his teeth together until a muscle jumps on his jawline.

Larr puts a hand on his forearm. "I never meant to hurt you—"

Kerr shakes her hand off his arm. "Yet that's all you do. Because of your actions, my family and clan are dead."

Larr recoils. "You know it's not that simple! I—"

Kerr points to me. "Why is she dripping wet?" Then his gaze lands on the black water, and adds, "Did you send Lilla into the Deep Dark? Were you planning to make her go away?"

I turn to stare at the dark water where I jumped in not once but twice. "What is wrong with the lake?"

Kerr inclines his head. "Tell her."

Larr takes a deep breath and says, "That's where we send traitors to die."

Efficient execution via the magical trap, dear, if a bit unusual.

Kerr laughs and it's a bitter sound. "You risked Lilla's life without telling her the whole truth."

"She did teach me a useful skill that I can't use now, because of the force field."

Kerr shakes his head. "You taught her some useless trick. It's always like this with you—games and maneuverings. You almost killed Lilla when you know I bonded with her to keep her safe. I am done with your trickery. This is the last time you'll see me." Then he grabs my hand, leading the way out.

I try to pull against his hold. "I survived. No harm done, see?"

Larr screams.

"You must hear me," she says in a terrible grating voice, sounding as if each word is torn out of her by some invisible force.

Kerr releases my hand, and we turn back.

Larr stares at us with eyes gone white in a pale face. She points at me. "Heed my words, Sybil Lilla. You are cursed. Your sybil form lies dormant. Find the source of the curse and rid yourself of it, or you will fail against the dark god."

What is this sybil form, dear?

I have no idea.

Larr continues in a monotone voice, "Heed the prophecy, Sybil Lilla:

There will be a time when the War

Will be more devastating than ever.

Rules will be broken by both sides.

Life in the Seven Galaxies will be in jeopardy."

A cold shiver runs up and down my spine. The power of the prophecy saturates every part of my body, resonating inside like an unavoidable truth.

"The one who is nothing like others,

With heart full of doubt,

Will be the Conduit of End."

Aren't those the words, dear, that the Saage women cited during your Purification Process?

They sound familiar. Although Saage women never told me the full extent of the prophecy.

Larr blinks, her dark eyes returning to normal. "What was I saying? I can't remember."

"Nothing important," Kerr says. He gestures toward a tunnel. "We are leaving now."

CHAPTER 59

We enter the tallest twisting-ribbon-shaped building in the middle of the City of Enigma where my father's family apparently lives. We head toward the vine-covered stairway. Squirrels dash among the round leaves. Bumblebees buzz on the blue flowers, collecting nectar. Dwarf trees pepper every landing, bursting with orange-colored fruits. There is abundance everywhere I look.

"How far is it?" Ivy asks after we pass the tenth floor, her breathing loud.

Mom points up. "To the fiftieth floor."

Ivy curses. "How can these technologically advanced buildings not have an elevator or two?"

"There used to be lifts," Mom explains, "but they were the first to break down in the buildings hundreds of years ago. Nobody knew how to fix them. We're using the empty shafts to store compost."

"That's just great," Ivy says, panting. "I loathe stairs."

After a long time, we reach the top. We come to a stop in front of frosted glass double doors.

Mom taps on the glass pane.

A thin elderly woman opens the door. "Flora! To what do I owe your visit?"

"Together, we are happy," Mom says pointedly.

The other woman mutters it back.

"Dorina, we are here to talk about your husband, Fiona's grandfather. Would you like us to have this conversation out in the open or . . .?"

Dorina pales. "No! I mean, do come in."

We enter the attic apartment.

Clean and fresh air scented with sweet flowers and citrus smell greets us. Plants in brown clay pots and wooden planters cover most of the main living area. A dark brown sofa with three black chairs cluster around a white coffee table covered in tall plants with pink flowers.

We take a seat on the spacious sofa while Dorina sits in the farthest chair from us.

My mom glances around. "I see you acquired a few decorative shrubs."

I cover my mouth at the insult. To own a plant that does not have edible flowers or something to harvest is a luxury most people cannot afford. The elders have been talking about banning it altogether.

Dorina's papery cheeks turn red. "As Head of Building, I judged it safe. Why are you here? Surely, not to criticize my taste in plants."

Mom sighs. "We're here to talk about your husband as I said earlier—Fiona's grandfather, who was a child of the Night of Blood."

I gasp.

"Do you want to tell her or should I?" Mom asks.

Dorina fidgets with the hem of her blouse. "My dear husband was a child of one of the fourteen original elders. He was running an errand when his family went mad and massacred each other. He was only seven at the time. When he married into my family, into this building, he told me everything."

"I don't understand what this has to do with me," I say, looking from my estranged grandmother to my mom.

Mom clasps her hands. "Telekinesis was a skill only the original elders and their families had. On the Night of Blood many of these families were killed as they went mad. Those who survived their families' madness had to face the Protectors of Peace. The Protectors slaughtered the survivors to ensure the madness would stay contained. However, some children, like your grandfather, managed to run away and hide in the Neath. The new elders did everything in their power to hunt down these children. Fortunately, the Neath matriarch rescued them and informed the elders that they died."

Ivy snorts. "Except they didn't die, did they?"

"That's correct," Dorina says, then looks at me. "Your grandfather was hidden by the Neath matriarch and a new family adopted him in secret."

Mom continues, "When your father was a child he didn't exhibit any telekinesis. Then your older sister was born. She also didn't show this skill. Then you were born a few years later. You were such a happy and calm baby. We thought that we were safe, and that none of our children inherited the cursed skill. But when you were six. . ."

"I used my telekinesis skill," I finish my mom's sentence.

Dorina wrinkles her nose. "We cannot let the elders learn about this or both our families are doomed."

We fall in silence.

Ivy pulls out her knife from her right boot. It flashes and a purple apple falls into her hand from a nearby dwarf tree. "Let me guess, you all decided that the best course of action was to abandon Fiona." She peels the fruit, puts her gum in the peel, and takes a bite, chewing loudly. "I'm surprised you didn't murder her outright."

Mom jumps to her feet. "I would never do hurt my child!"

Dorina looks away.

Mom turns to me. "Fiona, darling, you have to understand. What your Aunt Corina did was harsh. But we thought it was the best option. We wanted you to live. We did it to save you from the elders who would have had you killed."

Ivy spits a few seeds to the side. "What's so important about this skill anyway?" She notices my fallen expression and adds, "It's great, don't misunderstand me. I'm just curious to know why the elders are afraid of telekinesis that they willing to kill anyone possessing it?"

Dorina frowns at the growing pile of trash around Ivy. "As I said before, it is a skill only the original elders and their families had, and also because our elders worry that the madness is contagious, as it did affect their close friends as well. There had been small outbreaks of the madness after the Night of Blood. A few of the surviving children had manifested the madness, killing many before they were stopped. The elders eliminated them and their family, keeping it all a secret, but I had connections—that's how I know about these incidents."

"Why keep it a secret?" I ask. "Wouldn't the elders want to assure the public that they are constantly banishing the madness?"

Mom shakes her head. "After the Night of Blood, the elders announced that they had taken care of the madness. We needed the reassurance to live peacefully. Even though much time has passed, the elders will never admit to their failure to contain all the madness years later."

Ivy puts her knife away. "But not all the surviving children went mad."

Mom and Dorina nod.

Ivy wipes her hands on the armrest of the sofa. "That's what I thought. Telekinesis is the connection to the original elders who had the madness. But the elders' assumption that all children who survived will go mad was also incorrect."

Mom smooths the front of her dress with nervous hands. "That's right. We couldn't risk the family's safety in case . . . Fiona would go . . ." She falls silent, then adds, "Or that the elders would find out and purge us just in case."

Dorina picks up the discarded peels from the floor. "We didn't want to risk another Night of Blood affecting many innocent families."

"Is that why you sent me away?" I ask, despising myself for the way my voice trembles.

"We knew we had to hide you," Mom says. "Your failed marriage was the perfect excuse to 'banish' you from the family to the workforce sector. No self-respecting Eldryan would enter that neighborhood, let alone look for you there."

"I can imagine it was not easy for you," I say. "You had to protect the family and had my sister's future to take care of as well."

Ivy scoffs. "Yet they did it anyway."

Logically, I understand why my family did what they did. But it doesn't make those miserable nights better. When I was wondering what was wrong with me. When I feared my own mind—of what I might do. I thought I was broken.

"Can you forgive us?" Mom asks with tears glinting in her eyes.

Dorina narrows her eyes. "I do not need anyone's forgiveness."

I ignore my grandmother. I don't know what to say. Worried that this moment could shatter with a wrong word. Worried that I'll be back in my apartment, living alone again.

Ivy puts a hand on my shoulder. "Forgiveness takes time. No one can rush it."

Exhaling, I push my warring emotions down. "I need to learn more about my skill. I need to know how to use it. I've suppressed it long enough."

Mom sighs. "It's probably for the best. I know where you can find more survivors of the Night of Blood. I'm sure they can teach you."

CHAPTER 60

"How much further?" I ask Kerr as we cross yet another street between two cloudscrapers. The early rising sun paints the windowpanes in pinkish-orange hue. But I don't have time to enjoy it. After what I saw in that sandstone chamber, I know that I must get to the sculptures and examine them.

Yesterday, Kerr and I returned to the mansion to regroup once we left the Neath caves. I couldn't find Ivy, the twins, or Caderyn in their rooms. It was too late to head back out anyway. The yellow uniformed P.O.P. patrolled the streets with increased numbers, enforcing a curfew for all. We had no choice but to wait till dawn, losing another day locked in the Eldryan society.

"As I told you before," Kerr says, "we must reach the outskirts of the city, near the force field, to find the closest sculpture. We are almost there."

At least there are few passersby to note our presence or ask questions. I don't have a face for lying. Besides, I prefer to tell the truth anyway.

Moira politely coughs in my mind. *Except when you lied to Callum about not being a spy. Or when you lied to Glenna about not being a rebel. Or when you—*

I remember, thank you very much. No need to remind me. I've learned my lesson.

Moira chuckles.

A sharp scream sounds up ahead.

Kerr bursts into a run a second before I do.

An older woman with torn clothing sprints past us followed by a group of horrendous eight-foot-tall dark fiends. The tentacled monsters with black viscous liquid oozing from their patchy fur stumble to a stop on their four muscled legs. Their three pairs of black eyes focus on us. They snarl, making a threatening rasping sound. The stench of rotting meat drifts to us.

Kerr's eyes turn black like a deepwater shark's. He extends his arms, revealing long webbed skin on his side. Six-inch claws descend from his fingers. His body thickens, turning dark gray with bulging muscles, while on his back, a series of fins rise up full of bone spikes. He bares elongated fangs at the dark fiends. Then he lets out an eardrum-bursting shriek.

The monsters stagger backward, thrown off balance.

Kerr tears into them, cutting them up before they could shake off their confusion. His claws part rotting skin like it's thin paper.

I try to reach for my magic but it's still inaccessible. Cursing, I kick out at the closest nightmarish beast, aiming at its knee. Its front leg buckles.

The creature snaps one of its tentacles. I duck underneath it, then pivot away.

Then Kerr is there, slashing its throat. The dark fiend falls to the ground next to the six other corpses.

I watch them closely but they do not regenerate.

Thank the ocean for that!

Kerr points to our left at five groups of roving dark fiends. "There is no time to rest, I'm afraid."

CHAPTER 61

BELLA

My older sister by fifteen minutes, Isa grins widely as she looks around at the cloudscrapers. "Night is when the ugly truth of every society reveals itself."

She is right. Once the sun sets, nothing seems as perfect and shiny anymore.

I squint at the horizon. "Then we best make the most out of these last hours of darkness, before the sun rises."

We stop next to the female warrior sculpture with closed eyes.

Isa nods. "Now that we have the complex alternator, I can build a device that would allow me to see the layers of the sculpture. Then I will know what kind of key is needed to open it. I hope there is a way in."

"There must be. Otherwise why would it be hollow?"

But Isa doesn't pay any attention to me. She riffles through component parts, busying herself building the device.

The rising sun chases the darkness away from the sky in increments. For a second, I soak in its beauty, then my mind starts whirling with questions, distracting me.

I pull out the calculator I built back in the guest room at the mansion. Ever since I saw those plants on the sides of the buildings like vertical farming, I was curious to find out how efficient they were.

I scan the surrounding buildings with the round calculator, then press the red button to compute its findings.

"I was right," I say, staring at the numbers.

"What are you muttering about?" Isa asks without looking up. She pushes the tip of her tongue out as she threads a green wire into the complex alternator.

"Based on my calculations, the Eldryan society will run out of food in five years."

Isa glances up. "How is that possible?"

I point at the nearby buildings. "The plants are young and from a limited variety in many cases. Also, they are not practicing soil rotation. Already, the resources they harvest are barely enough to support their society. I also noticed many plants are dying from lack of sunlight or overzealous insect activity. There aren't bird or other wildlife to fight the insects and the Eldryans are losing the battle against them."

"What about the cooking device we saw in Corra's kitchen? Others must have it, too."

I shake my head. "It's not very efficient. It requires scrap food and trash to fuel it."

Isa sits back on her heels. "What can we do to help them?"

"Nothing. They have to leave the force field to replenish their food sources."

Isa finishes building her device and gets to her feet. "Let's see what we can find."

She walks around the humongous foot of the sculpture. She mumbles to herself, sounding frustrated.

I guess it's not going to be as easy as she hoped.

A group of ten older men dashes down the street in panic.

Isa ignores them.

I glance over my shoulder, following them with my gaze. "Aren't you curious what made them run?"

"I have a feeling we'll find out soon enough. Now stop distracting me."

Isa takes another few steps to the right.

I follow her. "How much longer?"

"I don't know. I'm still looking."

A pained scream sounds close by.

I turn.

Thirty feet away horrendous dark fiends with eagle-like beaks at the end of their three heads chase an older man. Withing seconds, the five monsters surround the man, cutting off his escape. Then they tear into him with their sharp beaks, shredding his clothing.

The elderly man screams in pain.

I gulp. "Isa?"

"What is it now?"

The man's scream cuts off.

Oh, gods!

The dark fiends, finished with the man, look around for their next victim.

"Did you find a way in yet?" I ask, stepping closer to her.

As if attracted by my movement, the dark fiends turn their heads toward the sculpture, their black gaze locked on me.

"Almost."

"You have to hurry."

Isa looks up. "Why?"

I point at the stalking menace of dark fiends.

Isa blinks. "Good news is that I found the lock . . ."

"Bad news?"

"I must build a key for it."

"Do it!"

With daft fingers, Isa takes apart one of our room keys and rearranges pieces of it while adding more yellow wires to the mix.

The dark fiends increase their pace.

Isa blindly searches the ground for a piece of metal.

I pick it up and shove it at her. "Please hurry!"

The dark fiends burst into a jagged lope. Their muscular eagle-like legs pound the ground, swallowing up the distance between us.

"Gods, they are almost here!" I yell. Isa frantically slides wires and pieces in place. Then she trains her newly built key on the big toe of the sculpture.

A click sounds.

A round stone sinks in, at the ankle level. Then the four-foot radius stone rolls to the side, revealing a dark, circular entrance.

Isa glances behind me and her eyes widen. She grabs my hand and pulls me inside the sculpture after her.

I turn as the round stone slides closed, staring right in the snarling maws of the dark fiends.

CHAPTER 62

I bend over my knees after the last monster falls at our feet.

We spent most of the day cleaning up groups of dark fiends who managed to find a way inside the force field, threatening and killing innocent Eldryan bystanders. The P.O.P. didn't know how to deal with the monsters, often getting overwhelmed, but they had no problem dumping the dark fiends' bodies in a crematory afterward. They were lucky that none of these dark fiends were fully corrupted.

Kerr retracts his claws and fins, then reaches out and wipes black blood spatter off my neck. "You are covered in scratches and bruises."

I shrug, then flinch from pain. All that fighting without my magic took a lot out of me. "You as well," I say and point at the torn green jumpsuit.

Kerr smiles, his teeth back to normal. "It was a good battle. Though your hand-to-hand fighting skill could use a bit of improvement."

Moira frowns. *I think you did well, dear.*

"What are you doing here?" Caderyn asks, traipsing to us, followed by a ragtag group of older men, all covered in dirt and bleeding wounds. He looks around and adds, "I see your guide took care of the dark fiends and protected you."

Kerr blinks. "It wasn't just—"

"His name is Kerr, and yes he did," I cut in. "How many dark fiends did you encounter?"

Kerr frowns at me as Caderyn recaps his experience with the monsters.

Why did you let Caderyn make such an incorrect assumption, dear? You did your part too.

Because the praelor believes in what he sees, not in what he hears. It would have been pointless to argue with him. Besides, the truth is that Kerr did most of the fighting. I wasn't much help without my magic.

You held your own, dear. I wish it wouldn't matter to you what Caderyn thinks of you. I'd advise you to stop trying to get his validation. He will never give it to you.

Is that what you think I'm doing? I don't care whether he supports me or not. I just need him to respect me enough to cooperate when I deliver The Lady's commands.

He may not be capable of that, dear.

"Fortunately, none of them were fully corrupted," Caderyn finishes. "We were able to take care of them easily. Right, men?"

The men behind him mutter in agreement.

Interesting friends your father-in-law keeps, dear. They look like a badly organized militia of the retired.

"Who are these people?" I ask.

The praelor crosses his arms. "The better question is, why did you disobey me and leave the mansion?"

"Getting some fresh air?"

Kerr laughs but covers it up with a cough.

Caderyn raises an eyebrow. "Are you asking me or telling me?"

I cross my arms too. "I'm telling you." He has no right to order me around anyway.

"I hope you haven't been meddling in affairs that are none of your business," Caderyn says.

"I wouldn't know what that means," I respond sweetly.

Caderyn raises an eyebrow.

I force a smile, and say, "It's getting dark." I grab Kerr's arm, pulling him back toward the mansion, and add, "I'll see you later."

Caderyn grunts as we retreat, following us with his gaze.

The second we are out of his sight, I release Kerr's arm.

I glance up at the darkening sky. "We've lost another day."

Frustration builds, fueling my fear that I won't get out of the Eldryan society in time.

"After what happened today," I declare, "we must inform the elders about the dark fiends. The Era War does not spare anyone, including the Eldryan society. This should make them see reason." And maybe then they'll finally let us leave.

CHAPTER 63

BELLA

I let go of Isa's hand. "That was too close, don't you think?"

"We made it just in time; that's what matters."

I strain my eyes in the darkness inside of the statue but I cannot see anything.

"Don't move," Isa says. "I need to look for traps magical and otherwise."

"Do you need anything?"

Isa curses. "I left the bag with the extra pieces outside."

"I have some in my pockets I was saving for later. Here." I take out a bunch and hold it in my fist.

Isa's fingers land on my fist and I transfer the contents to her.

It takes a few minutes for her to build a trap detecting device.

"Done," Isa says. A faint green glow comes from her direction, then I hear two beeps. "It's safe to go. Now we just need to find something we can use for light."

Moving slowly with my hands extended in front of me, I search the smooth walls. It is strange to walk around in pitch dark, straining my eyes. I try not to worry about what could be lurking in the blackness.

I inhale a calming breath like I've seen Lilla do a myriad of times. The air smells stale as if this area has not been visited for a long time.

After a few minutes, light bursts from my right.

Isa stands under a torch. She holds a makeshift flint she must have made from the buttons of her dress, judging by the deeper cleavage she's now having.

There is nothing much in this chamber, only yellow sandstone that covers the floor and the wall. Unlit torches perches on each section. A dark corridor on the right branches off into darkness.

"Now what are we going to do?" I ask.

Isa chews on her lower lip. "We can't go outside, not until those dark fiends leave. We might as well see what's in there."

"Are you sure that's wise?"

Isa waves an elegant hand. "We'll be fine. I will keep using my trap detector just in case."

She wrestles the torch from its holder until it comes free.

Isa was always the more courageous one. I pretended that I liked adventure just so I could follow her.

Isa grins, holding the torch high. "Let's go."

I fall in step behind her.

She carefully treks ahead, guided by her device that emits a green light and beeps from time to time.

The corridor becomes steeper, then it widens into another room.

Isa stops and lifts her device, scanning the room.

It beeps twice.

"We are safe to enter," she states.

We stride around the square room. Two of its walls have golden writing on it in runic letters. At the far end of the room, the corridor continues.

Isa looks at me. "Can you build a translator? You're better making them than I am. I'd love to know what that writing means. Might be important."

I nod.

The next few minutes I spend taking apart the complex key Isa made only to assemble the translator device.

"Finished, I raise it toward the letters. It scans them, seeking out patterns to translate it to basic Galactic language. It's rudimentary at best, but better than nothing.

"It needs more," I say.

Isa gestures toward the corridor. "Let's keep going to see what we can find."

We follow the increasingly steeper corridor into two more rooms, fortunately without any traps. My device scans the writing on their walls, adding it to the others.

Then I wait for the translator to compile the results.

Isa leans close too, peering at the device.

Words pop up on its small screen.

"Lumenians . . . sculptures . . . portals . . . guarding . . ." I read it out loud.
"They repeat over and over."
We look at each other.
"It's time to bring Lilla here," we say in a unison.

CHAPTER 64

"What was so important that it couldn't wait until after I talked to the elders?" I ask the twins. I hope this detour is worth it, when I'm already running out of time and the portals could be opening any minute.

In front of us, a thirty-foot-tall sculpture towers, depicting a warrior woman with braided hair. I remember seeing this very sculpture when we first entered through the force field.

When Kerr and I returned to the mansion, the twins excitedly grabbed me. By the time we made it to the warrior woman sculpture, it was already past midnight.

A familiar pull tempts. This time, I catch myself before moving closer.

Isa takes out a small rectangular device with wires sticking out of it and aims it at the foot of the sculpture. "You'll see in a moment."

A loud click sounds, and a section of the ankle slides to the side.

I point at the dark entrance. "I guess you want us to go in there."

The twins nod.

We enter. The round section of the sculpture slides closed, shutting us into darkness.

"Don't panic," Isa says, and Bella adds, "There are torches on the wall. We used them when we were here earlier."

To my surprise, a faint pulse comes from my magical orb as it did when I was in that sandstone chamber.

"No need for the torches, I've got it," I say, then lift a Fla'mma thread and guide it toward the wall. A swoosh sounds, and fire lights on a torch to my right.

The familiar sandstone walls greet me.

I must have been inside a sculpture when Larr tested me.

Moira, what do you think?

She doesn't answer, just like before.

"Strange," I mutter.

"What do you mean?" the twins ask in unison.

I catch them up on the past few days' events.

"You must have disabled all the magical traps of the sculptures," Isa says. Bella adds, "Well done! Ragnald would be so proud to see you using your magic instinctually now."

I grimace. "It doesn't take much to make Ragnald proud of me." Everything I do somehow fits into his "legendary" Lumenian idea. I just hope I can live up to his expectations.

I look around the rectangular room. A golden sparkle catches my interest—lines of beautiful writing.

"There are three more rooms like this one," Isa says. Bella adds, "Can you read it?"

Stepping close to the wall, I study the first line. Again, I have the feeling that I should be able to read it and understand it.

"Nothing jumps out," I say, frustrated. "I recognize the writing style. I've seen similar to this in the Neath's cave. They were above the historical drawings. Though it was only me who could see them."

I glance around the room again, this time focusing on magical threads. Everywhere I look, the air is saturated with magical elements, with Lume the most dominant one. No wonder the twins were able to see the writing as well. The letters glow full of power, visible to all.

I touch the smooth sandstone wall. "Also, the room I visited during my final test looked like this one. But I didn't have time to explore more or to go outside of it."

Kerr crosses his arms. "They must be connected somehow."

Isa and Bella tilt their heads and say, "We agree."

Reaching up, I trace the golden letters. Their sheen and color reminding me of the Lume element. Maybe they need more than just physical touch.

"I wonder . . ." My voice trails off as I reach for my bright white magical orb. Hot-and-cold-and-hot-again feeling envelops. I lift up a thin Lume thread.

Isa frowns. "You're glowing, Lilla. Is everything okay?"

Focusing on the task at hand, I let the Lume thread spread through the first line of letters.

Suddenly, the writing on both walls light up bright white. Then the words shift, not physically but magically, and meaning bursts into my mind.

Isa and Bella grab each other's hands. "Is it working?"

I nod, then follow the magic into the other three rooms, absorbing the meaning of the writing. Processing it as fast as I can.

Kerr and the twins look at me.

"What is it?" Isa asks, and Bella adds, "What did you learn?"

I take a moment to collect myself, and say, "These sculptures have been here before the Eldryans. Before the Neath clans. They were left behind from the war between the Omnipower and the Ancient Powers."

"What war?" Isa asks, and Bella adds, "What are these Ancient Powers?"

Kerr shrugs. "Never heard of it."

"There is not a lot of information regarding them or their war," I say. "These rooms focus on the true purpose of the seven sculptures, the Guardians." I take a breath and add, "The enormity of what I am about to reveal will change the Eldryan society forever."

Kerr and the twins lean closer.

I continue, "These seven Guardians are meant to protect the seven portals that open every seven hundred years of Galactic time. Not the Eldryan society."

"Protect them from what?" Kerr asks.

I shrug. "From any power trying to abuse it."

Isa asks, "What are these portals anyway?" Bella nods.

I point at the closest wall. "According to this, these portals provide instantaneous travel throughout the whole Seven Galaxies. Any planet in any galaxy. All you have to do is to think about your destination and it will take you there. Now imagine moving a whole army in an instant to an unsuspecting world."

The twins gasp. Kerr's expression darkens.

"Evidently, once you hold a portal, you control the rest. They don't stay long, about a year or so, then they retreat into a pocket realm where they reside. They only appear when seventy planets line up in a perfect circle at the edge of Galaxy One—which is today. Their location on Cathal is random due to the position of the planet itself when the event occurs."

"Can the portals appear inside the force field?" Isa asks, and Bella adds, "That would make our job easier."

I shake my head. "Sadly, no. The sculptures act as a repellent to the unformed portal. Once the portals solidify, then the Guardian's job is to protect them. The writing is vague about what it means 'protecting' these portals."

"What do the portals look like?" Kerr asks.

"They are shimmering oval circles that accommodate the size of the person or people entering it."

"I wonder how they actually work," Isa says, and Bella adds, "They must operate similar to a wormhole."

I shrug. "There was not a lot of explanation about the technical specifics. What I do know is that they are one way—once you enter, you cannot go back the same way. But that's not the worst of it."

Kerr gestures for me to continue.

"The force field that covers this society is only meant to cover each individual sculpture so they can protect the portals from anyone who wants to take advantage of them."

Kerr lifts an eyebrow. "If that's true, then how did the Eldryan society come to live under the force field in the first place?"

I recall what I learned in the caves with Larr, pulling together the strands of the Eldryan history. "There was some kind of war that demolished their cities, scaring them so much that they chose to create the force field and seclude themselves."

"It was probably the sixth Era War," Isa says, and Bella adds, "The Archgoddess of the Eternal Light and Order almost lost that war. Many worlds disappeared while those who survived bear tremendous scars."

"Right," I say. "Then soon after they hid under the force field, there was a madness infecting their ruling class, causing a killing spree to which the elders responded by murdering anyone who got in their way."

Kerr nods. "The Night of Blood."

"Did you find out anything about the force field?" Kerr asks. "About how to control it?"

"No," I say. "Most of the information was about the portals and a little about the Lumenians that came, before my people. Though, sometimes they called themselves Lumerrian, meaning Taker of Light while Lumenian means Bringer of Light."

Isa and Bella exchange a look. "We know the answer."

I gesture for the twins to keep talking.

"The controls for the force field must be in that cave we spied the elders in, behind the mansion," Isa says, and Bella adds, "We followed them on the first night and overheard them talking about some kind of ritual that they must perform, probably to maintain the force field over the society. Today is the day for their ritual."

"Then we must prevent them from following through with their ritual," I say, heading toward the exit.

The others fall in line.

"But how?" Isa asks, and Bella adds, "Not to mention, we have to convince them to lower their force field."

Kerr crosses his arms. "If they agree to lower their force field, which I doubt, but if they do then it will mean they can't hide from the Era War any longer. They couldn't even deal with the few groups of dark fiends that found their way in. They won't be able to defend themselves. The Eldryans have no army, just the Protectors of Peace."

"It's not going to be easy," I say and push the ankle door open. "A problem I have to solve later. First things first, I must talk to the elders."

We step outside, letting the round door slide shut.

Moira yawns, then shakes her mane in irritation. *I really despise the feeling of being cut off from you, dear. It already takes tremendous effort to stay awake thanks to the force field, but those chambers knock me out in an instant. It's exhausting.*

Footsteps approach.

We turn to find six yellow uniformed P.O.P. marching our way.

"Lilla and company," the closest P.O.P. says, "you are to be contained for causing unnatural disturbances to the Eldryan society. Effective immediately."

CHAPTER 65

The P.O.P. shove us through the door into a smaller building behind the elders' mansion.

We stumble inside. The P.O.P. leader gestures to keep going toward the tunnel straight ahead.

With my luck, we're probably heading to a basement or to a dungeon.

Don't be pessimistic, dear.

I wasn't; I was speaking from personal experience.

My head brushes against the low ceiling when I enter the downward-slanted tunnel. Next to me, the P.O.P. leader crowds the narrow space barely wide enough for two people, pressing me close to the gray bricks.

I break out in cold sweats, gasping for air.

Squeezing my hands into fists, I take deep inhales. Then slow exhales.

That's it, dear. You're doing great.

The tunnel twists and turns for a while. Finally, we reach an archway with elaborate symbols carved into it. We march through it into an oval cavern.

We come to a stop on the slippery floor in the middle of the rocky chamber. Our escort, the six P.O.P., line up to the left near the abandoned workstations.

Kerr's expression turns furious as he stares at one of the older elders.

My gaze runs over metal workstations with levers, buttons, and small screens, covered in cobwebs. More levers stick out of the stone walls, along with other high-tech gadgets.

I glance at the twins for confirmation, and they incline their heads. This is the place where the Eldryan Elders met discussing the maintenance of the force field.

In front of the workstation, seven elders stand in their white robes with gold, silver, or bronze ropes across their chests. I don't recognize two young elders—they must be new additions.

Esteemed Elder Carther glares at the blond man. "Youngest Elder Dhon, why did you bring them into our sacred hall?" He swipes short black strands out of his eyes.

"I thought it fitting to see these troublemakers here," Elder Dhon says. "The sacred hall will humble them and make them realize how unimportant they are to us. Nothing else matters but the happiness of the Eldryan society."

"Together, we are happy!" the other elders say.

I raise a hand. "I would like to speak."

Youngest Elder Dhon smiles. "You are not here to address us but to witness our magnificence and benevolence."

"They lie," Kerr snarls. "They've never shown benevolence to anyone."

"Where are Ivy and Caderyn?" Isa asks, and Bella nods.

Youngest Elder Dhon ignores the twins and turns to the black-haired man. "Esteemed Elder Carther, care to enlighten us as to why we are missing two of our guests?"

Esteemed Elder Carther's expression sours. "I can't find them, Youngest Elder Dhon."

"We don't have time to wait for them," Youngest Elder Dhon says. "Old Elder Copper, please proceed revealing the charges to our guests."

Old Elder Copper takes out a white plastic tablet from his pocket. "You are charged with leaving the premises without permission; attracting dangerous elements into our society—"

"We didn't attract the dark fiends," I say. "I have no idea how they got inside."

Probably the same way we did, dear.

That's beside the point.

A muscle jumps under Old Elder Copper's left eye as he continues, "Causing unnatural disturbances—"

"What does that even mean?" Isa asks, and Bella giggles.

Kerr growls. "It probably means that we exist against their wishes."

"Showing no respect to the Eldryan society and its elders—"

"It sounds like they're making up charges as they go," Isa says and Bella laughs louder.

"For murdering Youngest Elder Christen and his family in his home—"

What? "We didn't murder anyone."

"Finally, for being ungrateful for our Eldryan hospitality," Old Elder Copper finishes.

I cross my arms. "These are false charges. I refute them."

Disregarding my comment, Old Elder Copper turns to a red-haired man. "Honorable Elder Colter, it is your turn to conduct our vote."

Honorable Elder Colter steps forward. "All in favor of guilty, raise both of your hands."

All seven elders raise their hands.

How predictable, dear. They're really had enough of us, it seems.

Youngest Elder Dhon smirks. "It seems our guests have been found guilty unanimously. I propose that their sentences for these serious crimes to be death by—"

Kerr plunges at Old Elder Copper. "You are the reason my wife is dead!"

CHAPTER 66

Kerr pummels Old Elder Copper with his fists while baring his white fangs. The elder hunches over with his arms wrapped around his head but does not fight back.

The six P.O.P. jump on Kerr with their batons raised. Kerr kicks one in the head, another in the chest. Then he punches a third P.O.P. in the nose and sends a hook at a fourth. He flows into an uppercut for the fifth and hits the last one with an elbow in the face. Within seconds, the six P.O.P. fall to the ground, writhing in pain or fully knocked out. Kerr spares them a glance, then goes back to striking the whimpering Old Elder Copper.

The other elders back away from Kerr, shouting for help.

Two dozen P.O.P. burst into the chamber, surrounding Kerr. Within seconds they restrain him, holding onto each of his arms.

Old Elder Copper straightens up and smooths down his white robe with shaking hands. Blood trickles from his mouth, and a purple bruise blooms on his jawline. "Took you long enough to come to my aid," he grumbles. Then he looks at Kerr and adds, "Your accusation is absurd. I did not kill your wife, nor did I kill anyone in my whole life."

Youngest Elder Dhon raises a finger. "Old Elder Copper do not engage these unworthy elements. They do not deserve your benevolence."

I don't think, dear, that they understand the meaning of benevolence.

"I appreciate your wise advice, Worthy Elder," Old Elder Copper says. "However, I wish to know why this Neath guide blames me. I've never met him before. I do not lower myself to get to know them in the mansion. There is no point when they all look the same in their green jumpsuits and weird shell jewelry."

Kerr struggles against the two P.O.P. men restraining him. "It's your fault she is dead! You forbade Linni's family to help her when she couldn't give birth. She and our babe died days later."

Old Elder Copper taps his chin. "I remember now. It was such a scandalous request in the first place. However, I stand by my decision. There should have never been a union between an Eldryan woman and a puddle man. It's not only outrageous, but unnatural too."

Kerr bellows, breaking free for a second. He punches Old Elder Copper in the nose. Cartilage breaks with a loud crack, and blood splatters on the elder's pristine white robe.

"Hold that puddle man," Elder Copper yells, cradling his bleeding nose in one hand. He glares from his left eye as his right eye's swollen shut.

Two more P.O.P. rush to Kerr. One of them hits Kerr on the back of his head with a baton while the other kicks the side of his knee.

Kerr's leg buckles. He drops to his knees on the ground. When he tries to stand up, the two P.O.P. hold him down by his shoulders.

Youngest Elder Dhon clears his throat. "Now that we are done with this daftness, it is time to act on the sentence." He gestures to four P.O.P. waiting nearby. They raise their batons. Electricity crackles on the wires wrapped around the batons like miniature lightning bolts.

Youngest Elder Dhon flicks his wrist toward us. "By all means, proceed."

The P.O.P. advance on us just as shouts sound from the tunnel, heading our way.

CHAPTER 67

CADERYN

Caderyn, Corrigan, and fifty revolutionaries burst into the cavern.

"Grandfather Revolution, surround the P.O.P.!" Caderyn barks and kicks the yellow uniformed officers away from Lilla. Then he punches the two P.O.P. who hold Kerr, freeing the guide.

Kerr jumps to his feet, striking the P.O.P. men, but the officers manage to detain him.

Caderyn turns back to glare at the esteemed grandfathers.

None of the revolutionaries obey Caderyn or lift a finger to help him.

For the love of sand!

Caderyn points at the men. "What are you waiting for? Do as I say!"

Corrigan laughs. "This is not your revolution, interloper." Then he gestures at two of the closest revolutionaries.

The two gray haired men push Caderyn to stand next to Lilla. In his surprise, he lets them manhandle him.

"Let me guess, you're here to save us?" Isa asks, and Bella adds, "When will you learn that none of us are princesses in need of saving?"

Caderyn mutters a curse.

Lilla glances at him. "How did you manage to lose a revolution without even noticing?"

"He underestimated them," Isa says, and Bella adds, "The way he does it to everyone."

My wife, Sorcha, likes to say that too. I never understood why until now.

A muscle jumps on Caderyn's jawline as he thinks through the past few days' events.

I didn't pay any attention to the warning signs: how Corrigan insisted on joining the revolution; how he always stayed behind—turning the men against me.

Caderyn growls. "I should have recognized the three 'I' marks of weakness in Corrigan: impetuous, impatient, and immature—none of these qualities are of a true warrior."

But these words describe these elderly revolutionaries, who are also spoiled, physically feeble, and mentally frail. No wonder they took to Corrigan who enabled their passivity.

Lilla sighs, her disappointment obvious.

Caderyn slants a look at her. "You probably didn't need saving, did you?"

Lilla shakes her head.

A P.O.P. shoves Lilla a step back from him. Another one kicks Caderyn at the back of his leg multiple times. Caderyn pushes the pain away and refuses to kneel.

"That's enough," Youngest Elder Dhon says. "We are not barbarians. Besides, they will be dead soon."

The P.O.P. steps away from Caderyn. He deliberately takes his place next to Lilla again.

"Your benevolence is wasted on these outsiders," Old Elder Copper says, with his head tilted back. The bleeding still hasn't stopped from his broken nose.

Caderyn scoffs. "You have no idea what 'benevolence,' means, do you?"

Youngest Elder Dhon points at him. "The Esteemed Grandfather will remain silent. He should be happy that he can be in the worthy presence of the elders."

Caderyn shakes his head. Then he looks around, taking in his defeat.

I don't understand how this happened. I've never lost like this. But ever since Lilla came to my family, bad luck follows me around.

He mutters a curse under his breath.

That's not true. I never believed in luck, good or bad. Everyone makes their own fortune with their actions.

He studies Lilla, noticing how hard she tries not to show her fear. She has grown so much since they first met.

He exhales his frustration.

I ignored the signs of Lilla growing into her role as a leader. I didn't give her room to learn. I didn't allow her to make mistakes. Instead, I dictated her actions, ordering her around, because I saw so much of my beloved Korhina in her. I thought I could shape Lilla into a great empress who one day would take over leadership of the Teryn Praelium, but I never asked her if that was what she wanted.

I made the decisions for her, just like I made the decisions for Korhina.

Looking back, now I know that I asked too much of my late wife, forcing her to take on more and more responsibilities. I pushed her to prove that she wasn't fragile; that she could become strong like me. Chasing my ideal killed her—she picked the wrong general to argue with. One who took advantage of the Ground Rules.

At that time, I didn't understand why she did such a foolish act. I was so angry losing her. But now I know she did it out of desperation, hoping to earn my praise. Hoping to earn my respect.

After her death, I blamed Korhina for what happened. For leaving me behind with two younglings. I never admitted any accountability for the role I played in the tragedy.

Lilla glances at him, and Caderyn notes her cold expression.

I failed Korhina, and now I failed Lilla too. If I don't back down, I'll lose her too.

Caderyn puts a hand on Lilla's shoulder, earning an astonished look from her. "It's time I let you make some decisions, daughter-in-law."

I will be there to support her when she needs me. The way I should have been there for Korhina.

CHAPTER 68

I gawk at Caderyn, wondering if I misheard him.

Moira chuckles. *No, dear. You heard him right—he just gave you his acceptance, and admitted his wrongdoing, albeit his own way.*

Then the situation is much worse than I thought.

Corrigan and the fifty revolutionaries line up on our left, near the elders.

Youngest Elder Dohn says, "You were right, Almost Worthy Corrigan, about the Esteemed Grandfather Caderyn. I applaud you for ensnaring him and taking your rightful place in the Eldryan society, supporting your worthy elders."

Corrigan bows his head. "Always."

Youngest Elder Dohn continues, "It's time we deal with our guests. We have wasted too much time on them already. We still have the ritual to complete later."

Commotion sounds from the back.

"Not so fast," Larr says as she bursts into the cavern, followed by thirty Neath clansmen and women, holding spears.

Bodies press against me. Spots dance in my vision, my skin turning cold and clammy. I gasp for air, but there is not enough.

Caderyn's voice breaks through the panic. "Focus on your breathing, daughter. Slowly."

I control my breathing until the claustrophobic panic retreats.

Then Ivy marches in with a young woman with chestnut brown hair. After them, twenty more men and women of various ages follow.

Ivy puts an arm around the young woman's shoulder. "I hope we are not late for the party." She turns to me and points at her companion, adding, "This is Fiona, isn't she great?"

I manage a nod, gaping at her and the crowd.

Who are these people, dear?

I have no idea.

Youngest Elder Dohn turns toward the closest P.O.P. "How many more idiots will just waltz in here? When are you going to do your job and keep us safe?"

Esteemed Elder Carther narrows his eyes at the newcomers. "I recognize you, Children of the Cursed. How is it that you are alive? We purged the madness-infected families a long time ago."

Ivy grins. "You missed a few. They were rescued—"

"By me," Larr says. "These are the surviving children of the fourteen original elders."

The ones Larr saved at the Night of Blood.

Youngest Elder Dohn points at them. "Leave now, before you spread your madness."

Fiona raises her chin. "We do not have the madness, only our skill—telekinesis. But you were so afraid of us using it to control the sculptures that you hunted us to near extinction."

"They must be the key to moving the sculptures," Isa and Bella say in unison.

Youngest Elder Dohn snarls in disgust. "Your 'skill' is an abomination. It is a sign that you are infected with the madness. Besides, we have the means to control the sculptures, not you." He gestures to the panels, behind the lines of P.O.P. and revolutionaries. "After the execution, we will reinforce the force field that will protect our society for another seventy years."

Larr bares her fangs. "There will be no execution." She raises her arms and shrieks. More Neath clansmen and clanswomen enter the already overcrowded cavern.

The Children of the Cursed turn toward the current elders, straining.

The seven elders rise up in the air, struggling as if held by a mysterious force.

Youngest Elder Dhon slashes out with his hand in front of him. A hint of black smoke trails after his hand, too faint to stay in the air for long.

The hair on my body stands up in a familiar repulsion.

The invisible telekinetic power that held the elders vanishes. They drop back to the ground.

The Children of the Cursed gasp in pain and stumble back.

Moira growls. *They stink rotten!*

I frown at the Eldryan Elders. "If I didn't know better, I'd say you're all infected with the 'madness.'"

Larr chuckles. "Oh, the irony! They have adopted a new ruling system to avoid the madness—by erasing any remnants of the original seven men and seven women elders. They did this to ensure that nobody over forty can participate in decision making—forty being the age most dangerous and susceptible to madness. They killed countless families and children, slaying them on the street. Now look at these infected elders."

I shake my head. "It's not madness that afflicts them. It's the Archgod of Chaos and Destruction's corruption."

CHAPTER 69

The seven elders laugh in unison. "We are not infected but evolved. We are powerful." They tear their white robes open as if shedding old skin.

Black veins bulge on their necks and on their chests visible through their white shirts. Their fingers curl in, their nails turn black and elongate into claws. Black smoke pours from their eyes, full of menace and hatred.

We gag on the rotting smell emitting from them.

Moira snarls in my head, baring her fangs. *Abominations!*

"We have caught you, Sybil," they intone it together. "We will deliver you to our master, the Archgod of Chaos and Destruction."

The Grandfather Revolution men and the P.O.P. position themselves to surround us.

"I won't go easily!" I shout, keeping them in my peripheral vision. Caderyn steps closer to me, doing the same.

Youngest Elder Dohn cackles, the black veins crawling up onto his cheeks, turning his skin a sickly gray. "You cannot resist us. You are outnumbered and trapped. There is nowhere for you to go. Our master has already placed His army near the portals, and their opening is imminent. You and your archgoddess have lost. Give into the omniscience of the Archgod of Chaos and Destruction."

"Never!" I shout.

Caderyn, the twins, Ivy, and Larr nod in agreement.

Get ready, dear.

Youngest Elder Dhon roars, "Capture the Sybil and kill the others!"

"For Eldryan!" Corrigan bellows along with the men in the Grandfather Revolution.

Like wildfire igniting in the depths of a forest, violence explodes around me.

Larr, Kerr, and the Neath warriors fight P.O.P. and the revolutionaries on my right. On my left, Caderyn, Ivy, the twins, and the Children of the Cursed battle against the corrupted elders and dozens of P.O.P. men.

The seven elders release black smoke of Acerbus from their hands. The acrid smoke turns into a black whip of magic.

How is that possible? None of the Eldryans had magic before.

I'm afraid, dear, that DLD is gaining new powers. He must have given them just enough Acerbus to use it like a weapon, instead of turning them into a fully corrupted servant.

How am I going to fight them without my magic?

Youngest Elder Dhon cracks his Acerbus whip my way.

I jump to the right. The putrid whip misses me by a mere inch.

Two P.O.P. men charge at me.

I kick one in the chest and grab his electrified baton. Then switch my footing quickly and send a hook kick at the knee of the other officer.

The first P.O.P. flies backward, landing on the ground with the air knocked out of him. A Neath clansman stabs him in the chest with his spear.

The second one's leg buckles but manages to stay upright. I hit him with the baton on the head. Electricity runs on the surface of the baton, shocking him. His eyes roll back, and he faints.

Grab the other baton, dear.

I pick up the second weapon, then leap to the side to avoid the black magic whip of Old Elder Copper.

Pivoting, I hit the corrupted elder on the back with the right baton. Then shove the left baton in his face. Electricity zaps him. His body locks up as he writhes in pain.

I dance back.

Old Elder Copper falls on his face on the ground, unconscious.

One down, six to go!

"Well done," Caderyn says to me, then knocks out a P.O.P. with a powerful punch. Three revolutionary men rush at us.

Caderyn grabs two of their heads and slams them together. They drop at his feet. A third P.O.P. raises his fists, punching at me with a jab-cross-jab combo.

I lean back, avoiding the strikes. The momentum carries the man forward, and I shove my knee in his face. His nose crunches, and he crumbles to the ground.

"We need to get to the remaining elders," I say to Caderyn. "The baton's electricity can disable them."

Caderyn inclines his head, then grabs a P.O.P. man by the back of his uniform, twists the baton out of the officer's hand, headbutts him, and drops him to the ground. "I'll lead the way."

We make a few steps of headway when four P.O.P. men block our way.

Two of the P.O.P. men lurch as if being hit. Then t-heir eyes roll back, and they collapse to the ground unconscious. Kerr grins behind them. Then he grabs the third P.O.P. by the throat and punches him in the face multiple times. When Kerr releases him, the P.O.P. plunges like a sack of crabs. Caderyn snaps a powerful kick out at the fourth man's head. The P.O.P. falls backward, and the praelor twists the baton out of his the yellow-uniformed man's hand.

Kerr picks up two batons from the fallen officers.

"There they are," I say, pointing at three corrupted Eldryans terrorizing the Children of the Cursed.

Six P.O.P. men rush us.

Kerr takes in a deep breath and shrieks at them.

The officers clamp their hands on their ears, blood dripping through their fingers.

Caderyn punches the first P.O.P. with a jab, and the second with a right hook. Kerr elbows the third, and double punches the fourth. I trip the fifth and Caderyn kicks him in the head while Kerr sends a shovel hook into the sixth officer's stomach.

Corrupted Dhon and the two newer elders sneer at us. "Surrender now!" They lift their black whips, snapping them at our heads.

I bend under the magical whip, the Acerbus singeing a few strands of my hair. Then spring forward and shove the batons in Corrupted Dhon's stomach. Caderyn and Kerr shock the other two elders.

The three corrupted Eldryans crumble to the ground.

Four down, three to go!

Larr and Ivy corner the remaining three elders. The women dodge the black whip, then attack two of them with the batons. The corrupted elders faint to the ground. Kerr lunges at the last elder, knocking him out in one hit of his electrified baton.

"You ruined everything!" Corrigan shouts and dives at Caderyn.

Caderyn grabs the other man's arm, twists it out of the socket, then hits the ex-elder with the edge of his hand on the back of the neck.

Corrigan crumples with his eyes rolled back.

Caderyn looks around and the battle scene. "Stop fighting!"

Larr repeats it to the clansmen and clanswomen.

The remaining P.O.P. men and revolutionaries hesitate.

Caderyn points at them. "Your elders are down. It's over!"

The Neath clansmen surround the still-standing P.O.P. and Esteemed Grandfathers.

Ivy grins. "Let's kill them all!"

"No!" I snap. "We won't kill them. They lost. Tie them up and lock them in the mansion."

Larr nods. "I'll have some of my clansmen stand guard over them."

"Thank you," I say and wait until the Neath men and women clear out the P.O.P., the revolutionaries, and the unconscious corrupted elders.

Larr wipes blood off her forehead. "What do you want to do next?"

I glance around the blood-stained cavern.

Ivy holds Fiona's hand. Two Children of the Cursed—a man and a woman covered in bruises and blood—help Isa and Bella to their feet. The twins limp toward me, smiling encouragingly.

You know what to do, dear.

I clear my throat. "We have to make a decision about the force field."

CHAPTER 70

Commotion sounds at the entrance.

"Let us in," two older women say wearing elegant green dresses. Behind them, more men and women wait, looking like they're heading for a party in their fashionable outfits, gloves, and hats. "If you are about to make a decision regarding the force field, then we have the right to be here."

Four Neath women bar the way with spears raised high.

Larr bares her fangs. "We can lock them up in the mansion, too."

Fiona steps forward. "Mom? Grandmother?"

Ivy chuckles. "Strange time to pick for a family reunion."

The two women clasp their hands in front of them, waiting.

"They have the right to be here," I say. "Let them in."

The Neath women lower their spears and step aside.

After Fiona's mom and grandmother, twenty women and seventeen men enter the cavern. They range in age from forty to ninety. Many women snap lace fans open in front of their faces as they step over puddles of blood in their leather slippers. The men frown at the Neath clansmen and women but do not make comments.

Fiona's mom looks at me. "My name is Flora. I have been a Head of Building for over two decades now. This is my mother-in-law, Dorina, who is also a Head of Building, just like these women. These men are Esteemed Grandfathers, some of them had been ruling elders."

"Head of Building is an important rank," Isa explains, and Bella adds, "They practically rule over their neighbors like mayors."

Good to know.

Flora continues, "We stayed silent long enough, letting the young men who called themselves our elders run our lives, making mistakes. It was us who have been managing our buildings, running the infrastructure of society for generations. These Esteemed Grandfathers did not show any sign of madness, yet their wisdom was ignored. We are here to represent the Eldryan society that the young elders ignored. We are the majority. We want to be involved in the decision-making."

The other men and women nod in agreement.

Perfect timing, Moira says in my head.

Larr smiles. "We, the Neath clans, want to have a say in this matter too. After the Night of Blood, we had even less a part in shaping our future. We refuse to be indentured servants any longer. We are Eldryans too."

A young woman raises a hand from among the Children of the Cursed. "We want to partake too. We had to hide and keep our skills in secret. We realized early on that the more skills we had, the less likely it was for us to come down with the madness. But the young elders would have killed us if we tried to integrate back into society. We had no voice for far too long. We have the right to be involved."

This is the real Eldryan society, dear.

I look at each faction's representative. "Some of you don't know who I am. Allow me to introduce myself: I am Sybil Lilla, right hand and general to the Archgoddess of the Eternal Light and Order in the seventh Era War. We are in the midst of another war between the two ruling archgods. A war that affects trillions of innocents, including you. It is my duty to protect you."

I fall silent. I made a promise to my mom to always protect the innocent who cannot protect themselves. Yet what I am about to ask will bring them tremendous danger.

You're doing what's right, dear.

"You did not ask to be part of this war," I continue. "None of us did. However, your world, Cathal, is unique—there are seven portals that appear here every seven hundred years. These portals can change the fate of the Era War, depending on who owns them. They provide instantaneous one-way travel throughout the Seven Galaxies, transporting armies to unsuspecting worlds. We cannot allow these portals to fall into the hands of the Archgod of Chaos and Destruction."

Everyone watches me with solemn expressions.

Isa says, "The force field that protects Eldryan society—originating from the sculptures known as the Guardians—is being misused." Bella adds, "The Guardians' duty, and your duty, initially was to protect the portals from abuse."

I continue, "However, probably after the sixth Era War, the Archgod of Chaos and Destruction began a long game—He infected your original elders with corruption but made sure to disguise it as 'madness.' His goal was to erase the duty of the past, reset the ruling order of your society, forcing you into hiding under the force field that should have never been activated this way. If it was not for the Neath clans who chronicled the past atrocities, no one would have known what happened."

Dorina clucks her tongue. "That explains a lot."

Larr laughs while the rest of the Eldryans in the cavern mutter agreement.

"They tried to erase your past," Ivy says. "They overlooked you in a misguided attempt to safeguard the society."

I continue, "This oppression created a society that is ruled by inexperienced young men who left out two-thirds of the population—you. This in turn resulted in an unjust culture that only looked inward. Only caring about their so-called happiness and nothing else. You have forgotten where you came from, how your cloudscrapers were built, or what the true purpose of the sculptures was. The Eldryan society stagnated."

"That's not all," Isa says, and Bella adds, "No matter how many surfaces you turn into vertical farming, by our calculation you will run out of food in five years. Change is unavoidable. You must keep this in mind and vote accordingly."

Larr crosses her arms. "I agree. We cannot stay in the past, hiding. We must join the Sybil in this Era War. As a representative of the Neath clansmen, I vote yes—to get rid of the force field."

Flora and Dorina put their heads together with the others. After a muffled discussion, Flora says, "We vote yes as well."

Fiona and the other Children of the Cursed argue in whispers, then Fiona says, "We vote yes as well."

CHAPTER 71

"Are you sure this will work?" I ask the twins, watching the closest group of people that consist of three Children of the Cursed and twenty Neath clansmen and clanswomen as their protection. The Head of Buildings and the Esteemed Grandfathers gather near me. Everyone is armed with the P.O.P.'s batons or with spears. We managed to gather a couple thousand fighters from the Eldryan society and from the Neath.

After the unanimous vote for removing the force field, all that was left is to figure out how to get rid of it. Larr pried it out of Corrigan which levers and controls they used to keep the force field in place, and the twins deducted which levers are left to use to remove it. At least, they claimed that it should work with a small margin of error.

Now we are here, at the closest sculpture of a warrior woman, ready to implement the final steps.

"Of course it will work," Isa says, and Bella adds, "Once the two Children of the Cursed use their telekinesis on the switches hidden inside each sculptures' head, the force field will be sucked back into the sculpture. At least, we hope."

Then there will be nothing between us and DLD's army.

Ivy twirls her black baton as she studies the thirty-foot-tall Guardian sculpture. "I don't understand. Why can't we cut a hole into the sculpture's face and climb in to do it manually?"

Fiona breaks away from the group and comes to a stop by Ivy. "Outside of the fact that it would take too long, these Guardians were built by magic," she explains. "They are probably close to unbreakable."

Ivy lowers her hand, looking skeptical. "I think a few well-placed explosives could do the trick. But I allow it."

"Your generosity never ceases to amaze me," Fiona says, hiding a smile.

Ivy pats her shoulder. "Thank you for noticing. Now, back to work with you." She playfully pushes Fiona, who giggles, then heads back to the group near the foot of the sculpture.

Isa glances at a makeshift communication device she made, a round plastic the size of her palm with a small display screen—she gave one to each Eldryan faction and kept one for herself. "Everyone is ready."

I glower at the force field, knowing what lies behind it.

Don't hesitate, dear, for long. The portals will be opening any second. There is no going back now.

I sigh.

Moira is right. There is only going forward.

"Proceed," I say to the twins.

CHAPTER 72

The warrior Guardian sculpture makes a loud ding. Her eyes open and she points toward the jungle.

Ivy hides behind me. "Is this normal?"

"So far yes," I say.

Isa taps away at her communication device. "All the other sculptures are behaving the same," she reports.

"Now what?" Ivy asks.

We all look up at the yellowish sky.

As if something melts the force field, it dissipates from above until parts of it end up on the sculpture, covering it like a yellowish layer of paint.

So far everything works as I saw it in that vision.

My sybil talisman comes to life, sending a painful zap down my spine. My chest bows from the agony.

Ow!

Grinding my teeth, I bear the pain until the talisman calms down and stops acting like a petulant child. Then I check for my magical orb. It waits for me, deep inside, with all six light elements in it.

Roars and growls sound from thousands of throats and maws, just beyond where the force field once was.

Caderyn pulls his sword out of its sheath. "Get ready to fight!"

Ivy frowns at him. "Where did you get that sword?"

Caderyn gives her a measured look. "I took it back before I had the revolution storm the elders' secret chamber."

Isa turns to me. "There is nothing more Fiona and the others can do." Bella adds, "What Isa means is that we activated the sculptures, but we don't know how to move the sculptures."

If the sculptures were made with magic, dear, then it stands to reason some controls would be also magical.

Good point.

I reach for a thin thread of Lume.

Caderyn growls. "Hurry up! The dark fiends are coming!"

With a glowing hand, I let a thread of Lume seep into the sculpture like a questing ribbon. I close my eyes and follow its the path, shutting out any distraction.

The Lume ribbon hurries past chambers going all the way up to the head of the sculpture. A round room with Fla'mma torches burning on the walls comes into my mind's view. Under the eyes, on the lower wall, golden symbols shine, and a lever waits.

This lever must have been what the telekinetics used to activate the sculptures. But how to make the Guardians to move?

I let the Lume thread touch the writing, seeking answers.

Three stone cubes with different symbols on their surface rise up from the floor, hovering four feet above it.

Then the meaning of the symbols blooms into my mind, as if an instruction.

I open my eyes. "I know what to do."

Gathering six more threads of Lume, I send them into the other sculptures as well.

When the magic touches the golden writing under the sculpture's eyes, three cube stones with symbols rise up in each sculpture, hovering. Then I let the Lume magic press the first two hovering cubes in all the sculptures at the same time, commanding the sculpture to move toward the portal and guard it once there.

The warrior woman Guardian sculpture creaks as she lowers her arm, then lifts her foot. She takes a step and another step, heading toward the orange-green jungle.

Isa pumps her fist. "The other sculptures are on the move as well." Bella whoops.

We cheer.

Ivy tilts her head. "How do these Guardian sculptures know who is allowed to enter the portals and who isn't?"

"We'll deal with that question later," Isa says, and Bella adds, "We have a more pressing issue right now." She points ahead at a charging horde of fiends.

CHAPTER 73

Caderyn takes up a fighting position in front of me. "Protect the Sybil and the sculptures!"

Larr raises her spear in the air. "Protect the Sybil and the sculptures!"

A cross of spider and a long-necked animal, a dozen dark fiends spot us. They let out guttural screams and gallop toward us on eight thin legs.

The Neath warriors bellow and follow the Guardian sculptures, battling any dark fiend getting too close.

Caderyn charges into the fray, cutting a path through the dark fiends.

Kerr shrieks and stabs the dark fiends while Ivy and the twins zap those who manage to go around him.

I reach for my Lume magic.

Don't waste it on these half-corrupted monsters, dear. We still don't know what happens if you overuse your magic. Best to use the other elements as they take less effort until we get closer to the portals.

Nodding, I release the Lume thread. Instead, I gather Fla'mma, A'qua, T'erra, and A'ris.

Hundreds more dark fiends dart toward us.

Caderyn lifts out his arms, transfiguring. Standing seven feet tall with a bulky battle form similar to Callum's, he lunges at the closest dark fiends, clawing them in half.

Fiona throws four dark fiends away from us with her telekinesis while Ivy electrifies them with her baton.

Isa and Bella zap dark fiends with their upgraded Eldryan batons—the electricity arcing out of the wires into multiple monsters' bodies, knocking them unconscious.

Using my Fla'mma magic, I burn two dark fiends, who fall to the ground, thrashing.

With each step of the sculpture, the ground shakes under our feet.

Chaos and cacophony reign around us.

I send an A'ris tornado at six skittering fiends, a cross between a millipede and an island kraab. Then I stumble from the effort.

Caderyn leaps at the dark fiend, clawing it in half. Dark blood splatters me.

Gagging at the rotting smell, I wipe the oily blood off with my glowing forearm, then kick at an ursine monster. Before it can counterattack, I sink it into the ground with my T'erra magic.

Something hits the back of my head.

Blackness swallows me whole.

CHAPTER 74

BACK TO NOW—LILLA

Groaning, I struggle to wake. The ground shakes under my body. Lukewarm healing spreads into my spine from my sybil talisman. I open my eyes.

Orange-green tree crowns cover most of the sky.

Explosions mix with shouts of agony and sorrow, creating a chaotic disharmony.

I scramble to my hands and knees. My vision contracts into a pinpoint. A concussion hammers my head with unbearable pain. Nausea and dizziness threaten to overwhelm me.

Blood flows to my neck from the various cuts on my face, then to my back under my black shirt, stinging all the wounds. My vision blurs.

Get on your feet, now! Moira yells in my mind. *We are in the midst of a battle!*

With effort, I straighten up. Swaying, I take in the battlefield.

Everywhere I look, dark servants and dark fiends of the Archgod of Chaos and Destruction pour out of the jungle.

To my right, the twins electrocute a scorpion-like dark fiend. Then Kerr stabs it with his spear.

To my left, Ivy zaps a feline monster. Fiona uses her telekinesis skill to push the rest of fiends away, then breaks their legs.

Caderyn lunges at a huge ursine dark fiend, tackling it to the ground behind Ivy.

Fights rage around me like a churning maelstrom.

How are we going to win? I ask Moira. *We are outnumbered a hundred to one even with our makeshift army.*

Don't give up! Moira snarls, her voice strained and tired. *We never give up!*

With a sigh, I gather multiple threads of Fla'mma, T'erra and A'qua magic from my pulsing bright magical orb. A hot-and-cold-and-hot-again feeling envelops me, as I layer them on my glowing right arm.

Can we transfigure?

Not yet, dear. I need time to reengage the meld after being cut off by the force field for so long. It took a lot out of me to combat the effects of it.

The ground shakes again under my feet.

A thirty-foot-tall shadow passes over me, blocking out the light for a few seconds.

The twins fight back-to-back, like a whirlwind of an electrical zapping machine, taking out ten feline corrupt creatures in a quick succession.

Caderyn roars and claws a simian monster across the chest, then cuts it in half with his sword.

We are running out of time! Moira yells.

Lifting a thick thread of Fla'mma from my arm, I shape it into an infernal spray and burn the pressing dark fiends. They shriek and draw back, their injuries already healing.

I curse under my breath, wishing I could use my Lume magic, but I have to preserve it.

A rustling sound comes from a nearby thicket.

I whirl toward another group of canine monsters and wrap them in A'qua threads, freezing them the second the ribbons touch their rotting furs. They drop to the muddy ground among the twisted roots and vines, growling but staying put.

Black dots dance in my vision.

Do something! Moira yells.

Like what? Maybe instead of complaining, you could offer some solutions?

Moira lets out a frustrated roar.

Not helping!

A group of nightmarish creatures approaches from the left, stepping over their injured brethren. One of them, an insectoid, lunges at me.

I kick out. My foot hits in its chitinous chest, propelling it backward. Then I grab the last magical ribbon of T'erra from my arm and shove it into the ground—a technique Ragnald enjoys deploying.

The ground opens up under the insectoid fiend's feet, swallowing it up to its waist. It scrambles with four of its jointed arms, gouging deep gashes into the ground, but stays stuck.

Ivy shoves the black baton into the face of the insectoid creature. It shrieks and collapses.

Suddenly, dozens of dark servants and dark fiends swarm out from among the trees, surrounding us in seconds.

They part for an Acerbus-disguised black figure, its face hidden under a hood.

My heart jumps into my throat. I recognize the repulsive and powerful magic ripples emitting from the figure—the new Ankhar.

"We meet again," it says in a distorted voice. "How fortuitous."

CHAPTER 75

"There is nothing fortuitous about this meeting," I growl. "You can't stop us."

Caderyn, Kerr, the twins, Fiona, and Ivy move closer, flanking me.

The Ankhar laughs in a distorted yet ethereal voice. "You never know when to stop, do you?"

Caderyn grunts. "Sybil Lilla is not a weakling to give in so easily like you."

The Acerbus cloud thickens around the Ankhar, lifting it off the ground, four feet into the air. It spreads its arms with palms facing down.

"Silence!" it says in a different voice, one that is much deeper and more powerful. "Behold Me, the Archgod of Chaos and Destruction, Annihilator of Worlds, and the Dark Lord of Destruction. Bow before Me!"

None of us obeys.

"Let me demonstrate my powers," the Ankhar/DLD says, and claps its hands.

Fear and all-encompassing dread choke me. I gasp for air, clawing at my throat.

Moira snarls.

Caderyn roars, holding his furry head in his clawed hands.

The twins fall to their knees, whimpering.

Kerr grunts, his face contorted in pain, struggling to stay upright.

Another round of fear and horror washes over us like a crushing tidal wave.

Dread locks my muscles tightly until tremors shake my body. A powerful push pressures me to kneel and beg for mercy.

We will not cower, dear, in front of Him!

Clenching my teeth, I fight off the trepidation and fright.

Caderyn and Kerr lean forward as if swimming against the torrent of terror.

"What do you want?" I ask, struggling to keep my voice steady. I refuse to let Him see my fear.

"Peace, of course," Ankhar/DLD says. "Ever since The Lady came into existence, my children and I have not had peace. She disturbed the Balance. But I will set it right when I control the portals. There will be no more era wars. There will be no more power struggles in the Seven Galaxies. I will rule them as I did before. As it is prophesied."

"You lie!" I shout.

The Ankhar/DLD tilts its head. "Everything I told you is the truth. However, it seems The Lady has been lying to you again."

Cold washes over my body, as if I've been dunked into a barrel of frozen shrimp.

"Have you not experienced terrible headaches when trying to recall a memory?" Ankhar/DLD asks. "A memory about what happened when you were on Teryn in front of their senatus?"

Frowning, I try to remember that moment but sharp pain jabs into my temples. I hiss out a breath.

"That's the one," Ankhar/DLD says. "But that is not the only thing She has been hiding from you."

I stare at the Ankhar/DLD.

Can it be true what it says—that The Lady has been lying to me? What kind of secret could She be hiding from me anyway?

A few pages appear in the hands of Ankhar/DLD. "These are missing pages from your mother's journal." The Ankhar/DLD releases the pages, then floats them close to me until I can make out the writing. It asks, "Do they look familiar to you?"

I squint at the letters. They look like my mom's handwriting.

But how is this possible? I doubt that my mom would have freely given the pages to Him.

I cross my arms. "How do I know they are not fake?"

"You don't," Ankhar/DLD says, and takes the pages back. "Ask yourself, what benefit do I gain by faking pages from your mother's journal? Pages that explain why she and you look so different from the other Lumenians. I already know the answer. Don't you want to know it too?"

"What if I say yes?" I ask.

Kerr turns to me. "Do not give into its manipulation!"

Caderyn yells, "Stay strong, daughter!"

"Then all you have to do is walk away," Ankhar/DLD says. "Give up the portals. I will even allow all of you to go back to Teryn."

"But then The Lady will lose this Era War," I say. "With the portals, you can go anywhere in the Seven Galaxies and take over those worlds, including the Teryn planet."

Ankhar/DLD shrugs. "That is the nature of losing a war. The winners have the right to shape the future of the losers."

"You mean kill them all?"

"I can promise you a few weeks of freedom and a quick death when we meet again if that makes you happier," Ankhar/DLD says, spreading its arms.

It does not.

"The Seven Galaxies were never meant for you," Ankhar/DLD says. "It was meant for my children and me. I have the true right to decide the fate of everyone, because I was first. I nurtured the Seven Galaxies until The Lady intruded, upending the Balance. She killed my children and my only son, causing me pain. It's Her fault that we have to fight in the Era Wars."

"Are you always blaming others for your mistakes?" I ask.

The twins and Ivy chortle.

The Ankhar/DLD points at me. "You and the Lumenians should have never existed in the first place. I simply corrected the course of the Seven Galaxies as it should have been a long time ago."

How big-hearted. "Your children do not have more right to peace than anyone else."

"That is where you're wrong," Ankhar/DLD says, and waves an arm in circle. "Things are about to change. Let me show you where we stand right now."

The air shimmers, becoming a screen. On the screen, Callum, Rhona, Teague, Belthair with his three arms in a cast, Arrov, and Fearghas with S'affi fight, looking exhausted, against a horde of dark fiends that keep regenerating.

"No!" I shout.

My heart aches, knowing that Callum and my friends are outnumbered. I love my husband more than anything. I fought side by side with my friends. We've been through hardship together. They are my family now. I want to abandon everything and run to them. To protect them. To use my Lume magic until I cleanse every one of the horrid dark fiends. Until my magic runs out.

Ankhar/DLD snaps its fingers. The air screen with Callum and the others on it vanishes.

"You have a choice to make," Ankhar/DLD says. "What will it be?"

CHAPTER 76

I stare at the Ankhar/DLD.

What I wouldn't give to read those pages from my mom's journal. To know what happened to her that made us so different from the rest of the Lumenians. To know what The Lady is hiding from me.

I stifle a groan of frustration.

I understand how difficult this must be for you, dear. On one hand this could help us. Maybe even give us a hint as to how to defeat the archgod. I would be lying if I didn't tell you how tempting that is.

I glance away.

But I do not have the right to sacrifice other's lives for that knowledge, I say to Moira. *I do not have the right to give up the portals and allow DLD to win the Era War. No matter how much this knowledge might give us an upper hand. It might not be enough to compensate for the loss of the portals and to turn the tide.*

"Before I make a decision, tell me how you got those pages," I demand.

"I received them from Loch Ramor. He found the diary in a fireplace in the Crystal Palace. He tried to bargain with it, but the only item of interest were those pages. I tore them out and gave him the diary back. I do not know what he did with it afterwards."

He probably gave it to Beathag, who in turn tried to elicit my sympathy by giving it to me years later. It did not work out well for her.

I laugh bitterly, remembering.

Beathag made it sound as if she was the one who saved the journal from the fire after she threw it in there in the first place. As if she had a change of heart. I should have known she lied.

The Ankhar/DLD scoffs. "This is not a laughing matter! But I should not be surprised at your immature behavior. You are the worst Sybil I have encountered in all seven Era Wars. You are untested and fumbling. The Lady has, indeed, lowered Herself this time to find you—an inept princess as Her right hand. Now She is stuck with you."

Don't let Him make you feel inadequate, dear. He is playing games.

I grind my teeth. *It's hard not to feel that way. I knew that The Lady only picked me because She had no one else for the Sybil task. I did my best to grow into the role, but I have so much more to learn.*

And you will learn everything you need, dear. In time. No one ever becomes perfect at what they do overnight or without practice. You are doing your best. Remember that with mistakes come knowledge. But they are, too, part of the lesson.

Moira is right.

"There is nothing wrong with being inexperienced," I say. "Because every mistake I make, I learn from. I will become a better Sybil through these experiences. I won't stay untested for long."

That's the spirit, dear!

"Unlike you," I continue, "who is set in your ways and will never change. You are a tyrant and an oppressor. You wouldn't know what peace looks like because all you care is chaos."

"You are wrong," the Ankhar/DLD growls.

"How is your shoulder by the way?" I ask, sweetly.

The Ankhar/DLD touches its right shoulder briefly, then snaps its arm down. "Because of your recklessness the Eldryan society will suffer. I wager you never enlightened them what it means to fight in the Era War. You are just like me—you lie and manipulate to get what you want."

"I am nothing like you, but I was reckless."

I shouldn't have run out with Fearghas on a late-night ride that ended up meeting with the Ankhar. I shouldn't have taken Callum and my friends to attack the dark fiends, causing Arrov, Belthair and Teague to get injured. I shouldn't have jumped through the crack in the force field, getting separated from my husband and my friends. I shouldn't have interfered with the Eldryan society.

I look at Caderyn and say, "I let my emotions to get the best of me and didn't listen. Then I glance at Kerr and Fiona and add, "I should have warned you about the perils of the Era War."

"We still would have come," Kerr insists, and Fiona nods.

"We both had to learn our lesson," Caderyn grumbles.

I direct my words at the Ankhar/DLD. "I have made my decision."

CHAPTER 77

Taking a deep breath, I look at Caderyn in his battle form, then at Kerr with his hands in fists, at the twins, and finally at Ivy and Fiona.

They nod in encouragement.

I exhale and say, "I reject your offer."

"You made the wrong choice," the Ankhar/DLD snarls. It gathers Acerbus smoke to itself.

"Attack!" Caderyn bellows and swings at the closest dark fiends.

The beasts advance on us, blocking the view of the Ankhar/DLD.

Fiona shoves eight dark fiends away with her telekinesis skill, breaking their arms and backs while Ivy knocks them out with the baton. Isa and Bella zap five dark fiends with a chain of electricity, then Kerr shrieks at the other monsters who step over their brethren thrashing on the ground.

The Ankhar/DLD releases Acerbus snakes and wraps it around Caderyn. Then it sends one at Fiona, Ivy, the twins, and Kerr.

I gather Lume from my bright magical orb. Then I slice the Acerbus snakes off my friends.

The Ankhar/DLD recoils. "You shouldn't have been able to do that!"

I bare my teeth at it. "Care to test me?"

"Capture the Sybil and kill them!" the Ankhar/DLD shouts. Then a column of Acerbus shoots upward, leaving the Ankhar behind.

I guess the archgod got scared of you, dear. Again.

Caderyn and the others shake themselves, then jump back into the fray.

Isa checks on her plastic communication device. "The groups are reporting casualties, but the sculptures are progressing toward the various portal locations. There are visible shimmers now in seven areas."

Reaching for my elemental magic, I bombard the vicious dark fiends with Fla'mma balls, A'ris icicles, A'qua daggers, then bury them with T'erra quakes.

Each step is a torturous battle.

A new wave of dark servants and dark fiends floods the battlefield.

Then dozens of mercenaries step around the dark army, holding laser rifles aimed at us. A burly man says, "Surrender yourself to the Archgod of Chaos and Destruction!"

CHAPTER 78

Ivy scoffs. "What are you doing siding with the Archgod of Chaos and Destruction? You're Marauders, for poison's sake!"

"Crown Princess Intonia Varia Yane," the burly man says, "your mother, the Dowager Queen, sends her regards." He lifts his rifle and shoots at Ivy.

"No!" the twins and I shout.

The laser bullets stop inches from Ivy.

Fiona strains, holding the laser shots in place with her telekinesis.

Ivy grins at Fiona. "You do care!"

Fiona eviscerates the laser bullets. "That's not a thank you."

Ivy beams, then turns her attention to the Marauders. "I should have known that the Dowager Queen would side with DLD." She glances at me and adds, "This explains how the archgod got so many dark fiends onto Cathal—dear Mum must have provided Him with transportation."

Fiona grasps Ivy's arm. "I'm sorry."

The mercenary guy shrugs a shoulder. "We get paid all the same." He flicks his hand.

All the thugs cock their laser rifles, aiming at us.

An upheaval sounds from the back row of the dark fiends.

CHAPTER 79

Shouts of anger mix with whimpers of pain and agony.

The Marauder goons turn their backs on us to fire at something only they see.

Caderyn and Kerr lunge at the unsuspecting mercenaries while Ivy, Fiona, and the twins zap the dark fiends and dark servants. I burn any stragglers with my Fla'mma magic.

Well done, dear!

Suddenly, there is a circle of bodies around us.

"Lilla?" I hear a familiar male voice.

I look over my shoulder.

Callum breaks into a run with open arms.

I sprint to him. We crash into each other halfway through. Then I jump into his arms, locking my legs around his waist.

Callum grasps my head in his two hands. He kisses me as if he hasn't seen me for years. As if he cannot get enough of me.

I return his kiss, my fingers clasping his shoulders, conveying my happiness and relief to see him. Getting lost in his embrace. Everything else ceases to exist.

"Gods, I missed you," Callum says, panting. Then he puts his forehead against mine, gazing into my eyes.

"I missed you more," I say, gulping air. My heart is so full of love that I'm afraid it will burst.

He kisses my lips one last time. Then makes his way to my jawline and to my neck. I slide my fingers into his short hair, holding him to me.

"We can see you," Ivy, Rhona, and Teague say in unison.

Reluctantly Callum and I break apart.

Belthair, with his three right arms in cast, inclines his chin toward us in greeting. Arrov grins, and Fearghas neighs indignantly, S'affi flutters up and down on his back.

"Fearghas, my boy," I exclaim. He makes his way to me, bobbing his head. I reach out and pat his thick neck. S'affi chirps excitedly.

"S'affi, I can't believe you followed me here," I say and rub her head. She presses against my palm.

Then a huge explosion rings out in the sky.

CHAPTER 80

We look up to see a Teryn ship, broken in half, falling out of the sky. It crash-lands in the jungle hundreds of feet from us.

An ear-shattering rumble reverberates. Then the ground trembles under our feet.

A fiery explosion erupts into the sky, followed by dark gray billowing smoke.

High above, a terrible battle with laser cannons and plasma weapons rages.

Then dozens of blue spaceships dive toward the jungle.

"Those are Marauder carriers," Ivy says, "capable of holding a thousand soldiers each."

"Just what we need," I say, "more reinforcement for the archgod."

Isa's communication device beeps. She checks it, and says, "Oh, no! DLD is breaking through the force fields on the Guardian sculptures."

"Protect the sculptures!" Caderyn bellows.

We charge into the jungle, jumping over twisting roots and ducking under dangling vines and gnarled branches.

As we near the warrior woman Guardian sculpture, its force field splotchy in places, hundreds of dark fiends with large predatory heads of a wolf and ursine bodies block our way.

"Retreat!" Caderyn roars.

We backtrack to the right when we run into a hundred insectoid monsters led by Marauder thugs with laser rifles.

We turn around but there is nowhere to go.

We are surrounded.

Caderyn glances at Callum. "Where is your battle form, son?"

Callum curses. "Some of the dark servants had extraction wands that interrupted my battle form. I can't transfigure so soon. I need more time to recuperate."

"Same here," Teague says, looking pale.

Fearghas kicks out with his back legs, sending two dark fiends flying over the others. S'affi vanishes in and out of existence as she grabs onto the corrupted creatures, transporting them far away.

But too many dark fiends are left, growling. They keep advancing on us.

Forcing calm on myself, I gather Lume in thick ribbons to me. My hair flies around me on invisible wind. My arms glow. The hot-and-cold-and-hot-again feeling encases my body, raising goosebumps. Small rocks and branches lift up into the air all around us, hovering at eye level.

What are you doing, dear?

A last-ditch effort. I finish building an orb of Lume six feet in radius. Then I let it explode out of me in an arch.

Hundreds of dark fiends and dark servants screech as the Lume magic blasts them. Their Acerbus melts. Their empty shells drop to the ground.

The light all around us becomes blinding for a moment.

Black spots dance in my vision. I cover my eyes with my forearm.

Then the brightness recedes.

The dark fiends and dark servants have dissolved into an oily black puddle at our feet. The Marauder mercenaries lay on the ground, knocked out.

"To the sculptures!" Caderyn roars and breaks into a run.

We follow after him. Callum holds on to my left elbow, guiding me when I stumble.

"I have good news," Isa says, and Bella adds, "And bad news."

"What's the good news?" Ivy asks.

"The portals are beginning to take shape not too far from us," Isa says.

"And the bad news?" I ask.

"The force field is almost completely gone from the sculptures," Bella says, "Now the dark fiends can damage them."

Ivy frowns. "I thought you said that the sculptures were built by magic and cannot be destroyed."

"It's true that they cannot be destroyed by simple means," Isa says, and Bella adds, "These dark fiends have just enough Acerbus clinging to their claws and fangs to cause harm."

Barrels of fishguts!

"Stop chatting," Caderyn snaps, "and keep running!"

We burst into a clearing, cutting through long grass with red tufts on their ends. We barely make it halfway across when colossal monsters, simian in shape, leaning on their fists flatten the trees around them as they traipse closer to us.

CHAPTER 81

We stumble to a stop in the middle of the field, pressing our backs to each other as we face the new advancing threat.

The trees creak as they break under the weight of the fifteen-foot-tall simian monsters who crush them like they are sticks. They clear out the forest in a ring, a horde of fiends shuffling toward us from all directions.

"Ugh! They stink the worst," Rhona says and waves a hand in front of her face.

"There must be a thousand," Arrov says, then pauses to count. "No, make that two thousand."

Isa clucks her tongue. "You forgot to count the ones behind you." Bella adds, "It's closer to five thousand."

"We are doomed," Belthair growls.

It was an honor to meld with you, dear.

My gaze tracks the movement of the nightmarish creatures.

I reach for my magical orb. It does not pulse brightly anymore, acting as if it's depleted.

"I'm out of magic," I say.

"You shouldn't have shown off," Rhona snaps.

"Stop your complaining," Ivy says. "Lilla is a power wrapped in kindness, while you are a sauntering disapproval personified, poking at everyone with your unnecessarily complex words."

A muscle jumps on Rhona's jawline. "At least I am not a treacherous Marauder."

"That's enough of that," Caderyn says.

Callum reaches for my hand. I wrap my fingers around his.

"My love, I will buy you time to escape," he says.

I shake my head. "I won't leave you."

Caderyn looks at every one of us. "We will make our stand here. If we die, we'll die with honor."

CHAPTER 82

The humongous simian dark fiends near our clearing, barely ten feet separating them from us.

"I don't want to die," Ivy whines. "Caderyn, can't you use your k'bug and call for reinforcements?"

"The archgod has continuously been jamming the communication lines," Caderyn growls.

Ivy's expression falls as she mutters, "I'm too young . . ."

Fiona hugs Ivy's shoulders.

Kerr raises his spear. "We will fight as long as we can."

Callum clasps my hand. "I love you, my love and life."

"I love you too," I say, blinking tears away before they could fall.

Teague sighs. "I would have loved to say goodbye to Steaphan."

Belthair bares his teeth. "I will take down as many as I can."

Arrov nods. "My crossbow bolts will find many targets."

Fearghas rears up on his hind legs, neighing, then stomps his front foot and shakes his mane.

"I agree, boy." I pet his black mane in comfort.

S'affi appears, then perches on my battle horse's back. Her ear twitches, and she reaches out with a paw. "S'affi, leave before it's too late." I pet her belly, and she hugs my hand to her for a second before letting it go, but does not leave.

The rotting smell grows in intensity, inundating the air. We switch to mouth breathing.

Suddenly, the ground trembles as if shaken by T'erra quakes.

The dark fiends stumble to a standstill, unsure.

"Is this your doing?" Rhona asks me.

"No," I say, searching for the source of the new danger.

Mounds of dirt rise up from around us in random locations as far as we can see. Then skeletal arms burst through the dirt, some completely bone, others with sinew hanging off like gray meat ribbons. Then heads emerge, followed by torsos, until they climb out of the soil as if Mother Planet has given birth to her dead.

"What on A'ice is going on?" Arrov says and hops out of the way of a dead corpse with half its skin still sticking to its skeletal frame.

We adjust our position as more dead creep out of the ground, many in advanced state of decay, while others are nothing but porous bones.

The simian monsters growl at the dead army but don't attack.

Callum and Teague raise their swords to cut them down.

"Help us!" the dead plead. Though they do not speak, yet I can hear them.

"Stop!" I shout at the men. "Wait!"

How are we supposed to help them, dear?

I have no idea.

Suddenly, all the dead turn to look right as if waiting for a command.

"This is your chance to right the wrong that was committed against you by the Archgod of Chaos and Destruction and His minions! Now is your chance to heal your soul and move on to Lume! Avenge yourself!" a strong female voice says, full of strange magic.

The army of dead bursts into a jagged-limping run, swarming the fifteen-foot-tall simian dark fiends.

The monsters bat at the skeletal soldiers to no avail.

The dead take the monsters down to the ground, viciously clawing and slashing.

The fiends roar and desperately fight back, tearing into the dead. But for every fallen skeleton, three take its place like a never-ending flood of deceased.

The onslaught of the dead overtakes the nightmarish creatures until they stop moving. Then the skeletons march into the jungle with a single purpose.

We gape at the bodies of the dark fiends and bones scattered all around us.

"What just happened?" Ivy asks with Fiona holding onto her arm.

CHAPTER 83

Isa shakes her head. "This was not technology." Bella adds, "It was magic."

Belthair asks, "But who is capable of doing something like this?"

"Me, of course." I hear the strong female voice.

We all turn.

Glenna strides toward us, stepping over fallen monsters. Next to her Ragnald marches. Behind the mage, a troll ambles covered in green roots, wearing only a pair of ragged brown pants. Lastly, six-foot-tall Fla'mma, A'qua, and T'erra elementals tread.

Without waiting, I rush to Glenna.

Glenna squeals and hugs me.

"I was so worried about you," I say, hugging her back.

"I am sorry I couldn't come sooner," Glenna says at the same time.

We break apart, grinning.

The twins dart over. "Glennie, we missed you!"

Ragnald nods at the men, who solemnly return the mage's nod. "I see we arrived at the right time."

Caderyn opens his mouth to talk, but Ivy shrieks, "I'm so happy I didn't die! I have too much to live for."

"I'm glad to see you too Ivy," Glenna says. "I've missed your jokes about the Marauder's ways."

Ivy frowns. "They were not jokes."

Isa asks, "Are you okay?" Bella adds, "Did you get rid of your problem?"

"I am as well as can be," Glenna responds. She notices Kerr and Fiona. I quickly introduce them.

"How… I mean, what did you do?" I ask my healer friend.

Glenna smirks. "Do you like my new talent?"

Ivy slaps Glenna's shoulder. "I didn't know you were a necromancer."

Glenna grimaces. "Yes, I mean, technically no. I am the Weaver of Light and Healer of All, including the dead whose souls cannot move on, thanks to the murder DLD and His henchmen committed against them."

Rhona crosses her arms. "I don't say this often, but I am impressed."

Caderyn eyes the troll. "And who might you be, son?"

The green troll bows his head. "I am Angus Wanderer, Swamp Troll from Raghild."

Belthair walks around the three elementals who do not have any facial expression, yet it's clear that they are smiling. "Did you make them, too, Glenna?"

Glenna shakes her head. "It was Ragnald. Aren't they the cutest? They protect me. The Fla'mma elemental is Flame, the T'erra elemental is Pebble, and the A'qua elemental is River."

Ivy squints. "Is that a flower rooted on the rock elemental?"

Glenna smiles. "Oh, yes. That's Mia, a vegetarian carnivorous flower I rescued. Isn't she adorable?" The flower waves at us with one of its twirling green vines.

"Yes, adorable," Caderyn says, wryly. "Now that we've wasted enough time with chitchat, can we turn our attention back to this pesky problem of the portals?"

Our expressions sober up.

Isa clears her throat. "Let me check on the status . . ." She falls silent, busying herself with the communication device. Bella peeks over her sister's shoulder, and adds, "Uh oh."

Caderyn glowers. "What's the problem?"

Isa looks up with a pale face. "The communication device stopped working. I have no idea what's happening."

CHAPTER 84

"What do you mean you have no idea of what's happening?" Caderyn growls.

Isa shakes the plastic device at the praelor. "Exactly what I said." Bella adds, "Or do you have so much brawn that it affects your—"

"Then we need to find another way to find out more," I say, cutting in, already an idea forming in my mind.

Can we transfigure now?

Moira nods.

The transfiguration lifts me a few feet off the ground. I hover in the air, suspended in a cocoon of energy for a moment, then I drift down in the next, in my cymmerion battle form.

Fiona and Kerr stare at us.

Angus's jaw drops.

We open our twenty-foot-long leathery wings.

"That's . . ." Fiona's voice trails off as she swallows, her throat clicking dry.

"Impressive," Kerr says, studying us. We grin back at him from an eagle-like head, a dra'agon-like head, and a wolf-like head.

Angus snaps his mouth closed. "I've never seen anything like . . . her."

We wrap our tail, ending in a scorpion stinger, around our legs, basking in their surprise.

Can we fly? I ask Moira.

Why don't you give it a try, dear.

We beat our wings once, twice, three times, then we are off the ground, gaining height. We rise high above the jungle tree crowns, surveying the area.

We find the seven guardian sculptures with little force field around them marching toward the shimmering portals a few miles away. A horde of dark fiends trails them, attacking and causing substantial damage.

Loud engine noise buzzes.

We turn to see fifty space vessels dive toward the ground in a sharp angle near the sculptures.

The eagle head screeches.

Ivy glances up. "Oh, don't worry. Those are smaller Marauder transport ships. They can only carry two hundred and fifty solders."

Belthair grunts. "That's still bad news for us."

The space vessels hover ten feet above the ground. Then they open their back hatch.

Tall and wiry dark fiends standing on two feet pour out of the ships. Their small wings flap open, allowing them to glide to the ground.

"We are never going to catch up to them!" we shout from three heads.

That's not all, dear. Look behind you.

Hundreds of flying monsters hurtle toward us.

Fly, dear! Fly!

We beat our wings, picking up speed.

Shrieks and high-pitched screams follow us, getting closer.

Faster, dear!

The jungle blurs under us as we soar toward the sculptures.

The shimmering oval portal looks almost solid by now.

There are too many dark fiends barreling toward the portals, dear!

There is one thing left to do—the third symbol in the sculptures.

We reach for our pulsing bright orb and select a thin thread of Lume. It takes tremendous effort to drag up the thread from the dimmed magical orb. We separate the Lume thread into seven thinner ribbons. Then we thread a ribbon into each sculpture, reaching for that third hovering square with a symbol on its top.

Suddenly, the meaning of the third symbol bursts into our mind—the failsafe.

We touch the Lume ribbon to the symbol.

Are you sure, dear?

Yes. It's not an option that I would have picked initially, but we are out of time. It's the best I can do under the circumstances.

Loud chimes sound from the sculptures.

Then something tackles us from the back.

We plummet out of the sky, claws digging into our side.

We slam our stinger into the fiend holding onto us.

It yowls but won't release us.

The ground rushes toward us. But we still see the sculptures burst into a run. Then they jump on the freshly formed portals before the dark fiends and dark servants can reach them, closing them irreversibly. Thus completing the failsafe.

Moira chuckles. *Brilliant! Now brace yourself.*

Then we hit the ground and darkness swallows us.

CHAPTER 85

"Lilla, can you hear me?" a voice asks—Callum's.

I force my eyes open. I find myself in one of the medic rooms on the Teryn spaceship, lying on a hovering metal bed with Callum sitting by me. Lukewarm and unenthusiastic heat trickles down my spine from my sybil talisman.

"See? She is fine," Teague says, leaning on the wall by the entrance.

I groan. My body feels as if every inch of it was beaten by a plank. The pain more dull than sharp.

Falling from great heights tends to do that, dear.

I check my limbs. Nothing feels broken.

Isa giggles from my left, sitting in a chair. "You should have seen Callum. He picked you up and ran all the way to the med bay." Bella, standing by her sister, adds, "He carried you in his arms."

Ivy, Fiona, and Glenna sigh together, sitting on the bed next to mine.

"So romantic," Fiona says.

Ragnald frowns behind Glenna, uncomprehending.

A knock comes from the metal door.

Teague opens it to reveal Kerr.

"I would like to fight alongside Lilla in this Era War," the Neath guide says, "if she'll have me."

Fiona nods. "Me too."

"It would be an honor to have you both," I say.

Fiona smiles. Kerr bows his head, then strides to stand near my bed. Callum eyes the Neath man coolly, preventing him from getting too close.

"The Lady is not going to be happy with you closing the portals," Belthair says, breaking the tense silence. He leans on the wall by the other side of the entrance, fiddling with his three casts.

I sit up, and Callum takes a seat behind me, propping me up.

"I didn't have a choice," I explain. "We were too far away, while the dark fiends and dark servants were closer the portals. I had to use the failsafe command the sculptures to shut down the portals before they could reach it."

Ragnald puts his hands on Glenna's shoulders. "You did it just in time. The sculptures were in a bad shape."

"What about DLD?" I ask.

Ragnald shakes his head. "He fled, taking His spaceships with him, though He left behind many of His army."

Ivy adds, "The Marauders vanished too, along with the Ankhar."

I sigh in disappointment.

"Technically, you completed your mission," Isa says, and Bella adds, "It's not your fault that neither archgod will be able to use the portals any time soon."

I'm not sure The Lady will see it that way.

But She is not here today, dear. Let's worry about Her later.

"How long was I out?" I ask.

"Only a few hours," Arrov says from the foot of the bed. "Caderyn ordered everyone to take down the wandering dark fiends and dark servants. He's also searching for any survivors."

I get to my feet. "Then let us join them," I say, swaying a little, but Callum is there to hold me up.

"It's too soon," Callum says, his expression concerned.

"I want to help," I say and implore him with my eyes.

Callum nods. "Then that's what will do."

EPILOGUE

My friends and I spent most of the day looking for survivors among the corpses of dark fiends, dark servants, and Marauder mercenaries.

Callum tried to keep an eye on me, but I separated from him. Now that the archgod stopped jamming our signals, all the k'bugs started to work again. I told Callum I would call him if I needed his help. I waved off Kerr too when he tried to follow me. I had to walk the battlefield on my own.

The jungle bore much damage. Many trees were burned down, others were stomped on.

We suffered heavy casualties too. A hundred spaceships were destroyed. Ten percent of Caderyn's warriors died. More than twenty percent of the Eldryans, including the Neath clansmen, perished. The horde of the dead dissipated the second the dark army was defeated.

I wipe away tears for all the fallen, sending a quick prayer to The Lady.

We are made of Lume. When we die, we return to Lume.

It's a miracle we won with how badly we were outnumbered.

Well, we won *this* battle, but we are far from winning the Era War.

I hug my elbows.

Don't tell me you feel regret closing the portals, dear.

No, I don't. I hope I did the right thing for the whole Seven Galaxies.

I notice a crawling dark servant to my right. I gather a thin Lume ribbon and touch the corrupted minion.

Acerbus escapes from it.

At least most of the dark fiends and dark servants weren't fully corrupted.

That worries me, dear.

Why?

He didn't deploy any fully corrupted—His strongest soldiers—to get the portals. Which means the archgod must be saving them for a time when it is most advantageous for Him.

I trip over a root and wince in pain.

We'll deal with that new threat when the time comes, I say to Moira.

Something ahead catches my attention.

I look up to see the ghost of Beathag flitting barefoot between trees wearing a flowing pink dress with her long blond hair down, her back to me.

I push a branch out of my face, wanting to see her better.

I wish life would have turned out better for her.

Everyone must pay the price of their actions, dear. No one can hide from their past.

When I look again, the ghost is gone.

"Lilla," Rhona shouts, sprinting toward me. "Wait!"

I stop and turn. "What is it?"

Rhona frowns into the jungle, then says, "You have been ignoring your k'bug. Callum sent me to tell you that there are no more dark fiends or dark servants left to take care of."

That's good, because I can barely stand on my feet. But I would never admit that to her out loud.

"Any news about reinforcements?" I ask.

Rhona shakes her head. "We were never able to send a signal for them."

"I see. Is that all?"

"No, there is one more thing—"

Loud snaps of twigs and branches approach us, interrupting her.

We turn.

Fiona bursts out of the long green leaves, swiping insects off her face. "Have you seen Ivy? Please tell me you know where she is!"

Rhona curses. "That was the other thing—Ivy was kidnapped by the retreating Marauder mercenaries. We tried to shoot their spaceship down, but they successfully eluded us. We gave chase, but they have . . ." Rhona's voice trails off.

"They have the fastest ships in the Seven Galaxies," I say, finishing Rhona's sentence.

"Ivy must be terrified to know that they are taking her back to the Dowager Queen," I say, imagining the worst.

"Oh, gods!" Fiona cries out. Then she faints.

Rhona catches her and lifts her slender body up. "Don't worry, Lilla. I'll bring Ivy back to us."

I nod. "Go."

ACKNOWLEDGEMENT

I'm so happy to present you, dear readers, the fifth installment in the Last Lumenian book series.

A lot of teamwork goes into creating a book. I would like to thank these wonderful individuals who helped bring this book to life:

Thank you, Matt, Leslye, Mimi, and JD, for balancing out my "bad" author habits (i.e.: sitting a lot).

Thank you, Julie and Andy, for the skilled editing you both provided. You help make this series amazing. I appreciate you both very much.

Thank you, Dan and Natasha, from NY Book Editors. I know I can always count on you.

Thank you, Jenny, Mandy, Clare, and Kelly, for the great support and enthusiasm you show for this series. So happy to have you on board.

Thank you, Tony and Liliana, for your amazing support and help throughout my writing journey.

Thank you, Mario, for your continued support for this book series. It means a lot.

Thank you, Ed and Don, the best PR guys in the whole Galaxy One.

Thank you, Melissa, the best operation director, and friend in the whole Galaxy Two.

Thank you, Clif, the best map illustrator in the whole Galaxy Three.

Thank you, Tim, the best cover artist extraordinaire in the whole Galaxy Four.

Thank you, Lukas, the best illustrator in the whole Galaxy Five.

Thank you, Ray and Abigail, the best web design wizards in the whole Galaxy Six.

Thank You, dear readers, for being the BEST READERS in the whole Seven Galaxies. It was a pleasure to see you this year during events. Your support means the world to me!

Last but not least, thank you God, for this amazing writing journey. I can't wait to see what else is in store.

Family—see dedication page. (I love you but no need to be attention hogs.)

257

GLOSSARY

A

Academia of Mages
Where the mages reside. It's quite spacious.

Acerbus, Element
One of the six chaos elements. Corruption magic.

Aisla, Acolyte
She is an acolyte goddess to the archgoddess. She often scowls at Lilla. She had a career change recently. To find out more, read Book 3: Proud Pada.

Ancient Powers
They ruled the Seven Galaxies before the Omnipower took over.

A'nima, Element
Nature magic.

Ankhar
Right hand, avatar, and general to the Archgod of Chaos and Destruction.

Archgod of Chaos and Destruction
The other ruling archgod. He is ageless. He possesses the dark elements and corrupts others into dark servants or Turned, if they have magic.

Archgoddess of the Eternal Light and Order
One of the ruling archgods. She is ageless and fights on the side of Light and Order in the Era War. Lilla is her sybil. She is the mother of all Lumenians. Her acolyte is Aisla.

A'ris, Element
Air magic.

Arrov, Prince
Seventh son of Queen Amra. He is from A'ice. A great pilot. Very handsome. He can turn into an A'ice giant.

A'qua, Element
Water magic.

B

Battle form
This form originates from melding with a spirit warrior, and provides superior skills, strength, and a high level of magic immunity.

Beathag, Ma'hara
Ex-best friend of Lilla.

Belthair, Captain
Six-armed ex-rebel who once was Lilla's boyfriend. Now he is an opinionated, I mean valuable ally.

Benevolence
A word the Eldryan Elders favor but tend to misuse.

Bride's Choice
An ancient Teryn tradition where a woman can claim a man as her intended, which Lilla did. On Callum.

C

Callum, a'ruun
Second war general in the Teryn army. His clear blue eyes tend to glint with intellect in his tanned face. He always looks sharp and confident in his black, military-style uniform that emphasizes his muscular body. Lilla loves him.

Caderyn, a'ruun

An imposing and large but fit older warrior who is the emperor of the Teryn empire. Callum's and Rhona's father. He has a well-established beard.

Carther, Elder

A black-haired Esteemed Elder, who is thirty-eight years old. He has bronze rope to indicate his rank and age over his pristine white robe.

Cathal, Galaxy Seven

Orange-green jungle planet with a peaceful atmosphere. It is the location of Lilla's second mission as a sybil.

Christen, Elder

He is a Youngest Elder at the age of seventeen. He is not a fan of Corrigan.

Colter, Elder

He is a red-haired twenty-six-year-old Honorable Elder.

Compound, Teryn

It consists of the black spaceship and many camouflaged orange-green tents that function as barracks, mess halls, medical centers, etc.

Copper, Elder

He is a thirty-two-year-old, ranking as Old Elder.

Cosmic-Web Propulsion, aka CWP

A Teryn technology that uses the cosmic-web-like space highways for faster space travel. With the help of the beaked salamanders, the Teryns collect space particles, then they filter them down to hydrogen atoms to slingshot to their destination, cutting down travel time to a few weeks as opposed to a few lifetimes. One side effect: it tends to push space debris ahead of them.

Consuasor, Teryn

A Teryn title, meaning senator.

Corrigan

He is thirty-nine-year-old Esteemed Elder who really didn't want to give up his seat among the ruling elders.

Crystal Palace

Home of Lilla and Glenna, who also worked there as a healer. It was destroyed by the Archgod of Chaos and Destruction.

D

Dark Fiends

They are the creations of the Archgod of Chaos and Destruction. They tend to be monstrous.

Dark Servants

They are the creations of the Archgod of Chaos and Destruction. They don't like Lumenians or anything alive, to be honest.

DLD

Shortened version of the Dark Lord of Destruction, a nickname the Archgod of Chaos and Destruction prefers to use. It does drive the point home, if I may say so.

E

Eilish, Lumenian

Lilla's mom. She made Lilla to promise that Lilla will always take care of the innocents who cannot protect themselves.

Elder Ranks, Eldryan

There are seven elders. They have different ranks based on age. Youngest Elder: from age seventeen to twenty, wearing gold rope; Young Elder: from age twenty-one to twenty-five, wearing gold and silver rope; Honorable Elder: from twenty-six to thirty, wearing silver rope; Old Elder: from age thirty-one to thirty-five, wearing silver and bronze rope; Esteemed Elder: from thirty-six to thirty-nine. They refer to themselves as Worthy Elders, and call the previous elders Acclaimed Elders.

Eldryan

It is the name of the society and people who hide under a forcefield on the planet called Cathal.

Elements, Chaos

There are six Chaos Elements that are the domain of the Archgod of Chaos and Destruction—Murky A'qua, Black T'erra, Shadowy Fla'mma, Dusky A'ris, Rabid A'nima, and Acerbus.

Elements, Light

There are six Light Elements that are the domain of the Archgoddess of the Eternal Light and Order—A'ris, T'erra, A'qua, Fla'mma, A'nima, and Lume.

Era War, The

A devastating and recurring galactic war between the two ruling archgods that happens when the imbalance of power between them becomes too great. Like now.

F

Fearghas, Battle Horse

Lilla's powerful battle horse. He tends to bite or charge at you, or escape barns. Sometimes he is called Nasty Beast for this very reason.

Flame

Fla'mma elemental golem.

Fla'mma, Element

Fire magic, one of six Light Elements. Fun fact: can be formed into fireballs!

Fye Island, Uhna

A snow-covered island where once the Crystal Palace stood, half carved into the Piercing Mountains. Then DLD happened… To learn more, check out Book 1: The Last Lumenian.

G

Glenna, Healer
Petite best friend of Lilla. Talented healer. Has beautiful dark crimson hair with white strands and dark crimson eyes.

Grandfather Revolution
It is a revolution consisting of men above the age of forty.

Ground Rules, Teryn
Ten rules with fifty sub-rules and hundreds of addendums that are very important to the Teryn warriors.

H

Heart
Many people, including the author, put their hearts and souls into this story. Enjoy!

I

Intonia Varia Yane, aka Ivy
A blond crown princess from the Marauders' Syndicate. She is a friend and ally to Lilla. She has a certain preoccupation with poisoning.

Irvine, Ma'har
The overseer of refugee affairs. Not a nice person.

J

Jokes, Plenty
There are some good jokes in this book as well.

K

K'beast, War Tank
A huge brown animal with four legs. It has six long horns curving around its triangular head.

K'bug, Communicator
Teryn technology. It is a white, button-sized insect that attaches to the back of the ear. The thin, long hairs on its leg resonate when pressed on its back, creating sound waves that can reach another bug "device" to far distances.

K'hogs, Teryn artillery
A six-foot-tall gray boar that pulls armored guns on two wheels.

K'iguana, Teryn Flamethrower
A dark green lizard that's five-foot-tall at the shoulder. It can spit fire.

Kerr-no, Neath
Kerr-no, from the Clan of Norrek, is a Neath man. He was assigned as a guide (it really is a guard position) to Lilla. He is a great swimmer thanks to the gills on his neck.

L

Lady, The
It is the favored nickname of the Archgoddess of the Eternal Light and Order.

Larr-na, Neath
She is the matriarch, leader, and uniter of the Neath clans. She is also a great swimmer.

Lilla, Sybil
A nineteen-year-old ex-princess-turned-rebel-turned-sybil. She is also the best friend of Glenna.

Loch, Ramor
Mysterious person. Learn more about him in Book 1: The Last Lumenian.

Lume, Element
Powerful magic of light and energy.

Lumenian, Legendary
A legendary race that the Archgoddess of the Eternal Light and Order created. There is only one left now—Lilla.

M

Mages
They rule Raghild and horde magical knowledge.

Mia
Glenna's rescued vegetarian carnivorous hybrid flower babe.

Moira
Queen of the original Teryns and melded spirit to Lilla.

N

Niall, Ma'ha
Ex-king or ma'ha of Uhna, father to Lilla.

Nic
Lilla's stepbrother and Glenna's love. Learn more about him in Book 1: The Last Lumenian.

O

Omnipower
An unknown power that governs the Seven Galaxies with balance in focus.

P

Pebble
T'erra elemental golem.

Praelor, Teryn
Title, meaning emperor.

Praelium, Teryn
Name of the Teryn empire.

Protector of Peace, or P.O.P.
They are the Eldryan version of police. They are men who are above forty. They wear yellow uniforms.

Q

Queen, Dowager
Her name is Sheela. She is the ruler of the Marauders' Syndicate from the House of Two Guns and a Dagger. She is also Ivy's mother.

R

Ragnald, Elementalist Mage
A loyal friend and ally to Lila. He is a two-hundred-year-old and handsome mage who is expert in magic. He has triple elemental affinity in T'erra, Fla'mma, and A'qua elements. On occasion, he is known to build stairs for himself out of rubble by using his T'erra magic.

River
A'qua elemental golem.

Rhona, a'ruun
She is a Teryn warrior woman who wants to be a general. She is also Callum's sister.

S

Sa'ffi
A mysterious bunny-squirrel-with-antlers who follows Lilla. She can appear and disappear at will. She is also really cute.

Sculptures
There are seven warrior-like sculptures under the forcefield. They are quite mysterious.

Senatus, Teryn

Teryn senators as a group. They have their own building, rules, and guards.

Seven Galaxies

Where this story plays out. It has (you guessed it!) seven galaxies in it.

Spirit Realm

Lilla and friends visited this realm in Book 2: True Teryn.

Steaphan, Consuasor

A young, handsome Teryn man who is a senator. He is also Teague's partner.

Swamp troll

Angus Wanderer is a Swamp Troll. He lives in the Swamp of Misery, on Raghild.

Sybil

Right Hand, Avatar, and General to the Archgoddess of Eternal Light and Order. Lilla holds the honor of being the current one.

T

Talisman, Sybil

A talisman that is finger-long, oval, and transparent. It is lodged into Lilla's spine with intricate gold filaments that are coming from a pair of crab-like claws at each end of the talisman.

Tier One Factions

Seven worlds that the Teryns conquered first. These are: Pada, Marauders Syndicate, Industrial Conglomerate; Farmers' Partnership; Miners' Coalition; Merchants' Verde; Free Traders.

Teague, Colonel

A Teryn colonel who has streaks of scarlet, white, and blond in his black hair that frames his tanned face. He constantly munches on something while mischief glints in his dark brown eyes.

T'erra, Element
Ground magic.

Teryn, Galaxy Six
Name of the planet and its people.

Turned, Mages
A corrupted magic user who is bent on destroying everyone and everything in their way. Blood-thirsty and ruthless.

Twins, Isa and Bella
Isa and Bella are twin princesses from Barabal. They are great hackers and friends of Lilla.

U

Uhna, Galaxy Five
The oceanic home world of Lilla. It is also the name of the planet and its people.

Umbrea Gauntlets
These worn leather gauntlets, four of them, were snuggled in by Xor. They are for short-distance travel with a maximum capacity of two people. They open a gateway that seems to consist of swirling shadows.

V

Very nice!

W

Warship, Teryn
A tremendous, black, rectangular ship. Its size is so massive it could easily double for a small city. Its jagged surface is covered with world-erasing cannons, space missiles, and energy-shield-piercing arrays. In other words, very dangerous.

Weaver of Life
Glenna acquires this name that means healer on Raghild in Book 4: Meddling Mages.

X

Xor
The ex-leader of the rebellion from Uhna. He has three eyes but keeps the third closed most of the time.

Y

A letter in the ABC. Also, short for why.

Z

Zillion Dark Servants
A lot of dark servants. Really.

.

AWARDS

2020 Annual Best Book Awards
Winner: Best Cover for Fiction

2020 New England Book Festival
Winner: Science Fiction
Honorable Mention: General Fiction

2020 New York Book Festival
Winner: Romance
Honorable Mention: Science Fiction

2020 San Francisco Book Festival
Winner: Science Fiction

2021 Cygnus Book Awards
Finalist: Science Fiction

2021 eLit Awards
Winner: Science Fiction/Fantasy
Winner: Romance
Winner: Book website for fiction

2021 Eric Hoffer Award - First Horizon Award
Finalist

2021 Eric Hoffer Award - Da Vinci Eye Award
Finalist

2021 Eric Hoffer Award - Grand Prize
Short List

2021 Eric Hoffer Award
Honorable mention: Science Fiction/Fantasy

2021 Firebird Book Award
Winner: Sci-Fi Fiction

2021 Independent Author Network
Finalist: First Novel, Fiction: Science Fiction

2021 IAN Book of the Year Awards
Finalist in First Novel over 80,000 words
Finalist in Science Fiction

2021 Independent Press Award
Distinguished Favorite: Fantasy

2021 Los Angeles Book Festival
Runner-Up: Romance and
Honorable Mention: Science Fiction

2021 Readers Favorite Book Award
Romance - Fantasy/Sci-fi

2021 Speak Up Radio Firebird Award
Winner: Cover Design for fiction

2022 Beach Book Festival
Runner-Up: Science Fiction

2022 Best Book Awards
Finalist: Best Cover Design: Fiction
Finalist: Fiction: Fantasy
Finalist: Fiction: Science Fiction

2022 Bookfest Book Awards
Winner: Fiction > Romance - Science Fiction | Fiction > Sci-Fi - Action & Adventure | Fiction > Women's - Fantasy

2022 Cygnus Book Awards
Grand Prize: Science Fiction
Finalist: Science Fiction

2022 Chatelaine CIBAs
Finalist: Romantic Fiction

2022 eLit Book Awards
Silver: Best Book Website: True Teryn

2022 IAN Book of the Year Awards
Finalist: Action/Adventure and Science Fiction

2022 Independent Press Award
Winner: Best Cover for Sci-fi Fiction
Distinguished Favorite: Fantasy

2022 Independent Publisher Book Awards
Silver: Book/Author/Publisher Website

2022 Indie Ink Awards
Finalist: This Book Made Me Hungry/Thirsty

2022 International Book Awards
Finalist: Fiction: Fantasy
Finalist: Fiction: Science Fiction

2022 London Book Festival
Runner Up: Science Fiction

2022 Los Angeles Book Festival
Honorable Mention: Science Fiction

2022 National Indie Excellence Awards
Finalist: Book Cover Design: Fiction
Finalist: Science Fiction

2022 New England Book Festival
Honorable Mention: General Fiction

2022 NYC Big Book Award
Distinguished Favorite: Fantasy

2022 New York Book Festival
Honorable Mention: Science Fiction/Horror

2022 Ozma CIBAs
Finalist: Fantasy Fiction

2022 Readers Favorite Book Awards
Finalist: Fiction - Adventure

2022 San Francisco Book Festival
Honorable Mention: Science Fiction

2022 The Wishing Shelf Book Awards
Finalist: Books for Adults

2023 San Francisco Book Festival
Runner Up: Science Fiction

2023 Wishing Shelf Book Awards
Honorable Mention: General Fiction

2023 Southern California Book Festival
Gold: Books for Adults
Finalist: Science Fiction

2023 Firebird Book Awards
Winner: Book Cover Design/Fiction
Winner: Coming of Age
Winner: Science Fiction

2023 Independent Press Awards
Winner: Fantasy

2023 Los Angeles Book Festival
Honorable Mention: Science Fiction

2023 Eric Hoffer Award
Finalist

2023 National Indie Excellence Awards
Finalist: Science Fiction

2023 International Book Awards
Finalist: Science Fiction
Finalist: Fantasy

2023 New York Book Festival
Runner-Up: Science Fiction/Horror

2023 Chatelaine CIBAs
1st Place: Romantic Fiction

2023 Cygnus Book Awards
Finalist: Science Fiction

2024 The BookFest Awards
First Place: Fiction - Romance - Science Fiction
Second Place: Fiction - SciFi - Action & Adventure

2024 Best Book Awards
Finalist: Fiction: Fantasy

2024 IAN Book of the Year Awards
Finalist: Action/Adventure and Science Fiction

2024 eLit Awards
Gold: Best Book Trailer

@SGBlaiseAuthor
/thelastlumenian
sgblaiseofficial

www.sgblaise.com

To receive exclusive content sign up for the S.G. Blaise newsletter at
sgblaisenews.com